PRAISE FOR AJ WHITTIER'S WORK
ALWAYS NEVER MEANT TO BE

"Whittier deftly creates moral ambiguity in the characters' actions... This engrossing, plot-driven novel will keep readers glued to the pages. Similarly, as the duo scouts movie locations, traveling from popular tourist haunts like Pike's Place Market to lesser-known scenic parks, the author creates a love letter to Seattle, such that readers might find themselves planning a trip... The ultimate outcome is neither predictable nor trite. An engaging, thought-provoking love story."

— Kirkus Reviews

Also by AJ Whittier

Standalone Titles in the Magical Seattle Series

Book 1: *Always Never Meant To Be: A Love Story*

Book 2: *The God in 3B*

More to come!

Sign up for my newsletter for news, updates, and a special, same-universe bonus story at AJWhittier.com

MAGICAL SEATTLE SERIES

UNCROSSING THE STARS

AJ WHITTIER

To my mama, who was a writer, too

Content Notes

This is a book I couldn't get out of my mind. But this story started long before this book. It began, of course, with its predecessor, *Always Never Meant To Be: A Love Story.*

Almost from the moment I conceived *Always Never Meant To Be,* I knew how it had to end. It was very clear from the beginning that book was going to be a bittersweet love story, not a traditional romance. Perhaps it was in its DNA, since it was inspired by such a bittersweet song (*Right on Time* by Brandi Carlile, for anyone keeping track), but I knew that the leads of that book were not going to end up together. I wanted them to be happy, and grateful for the love they shared, but not together.

I stayed true to that vision to the end and I wrote exactly the book I wanted to write the first time. But it took me a long time to write my first book, and over the years, Sarah and Joe got under my skin. I fell in love with them, and just like many of you, I was so sad they couldn't be together. I still loved my original story. I would never change it, but I loved Sarah and Joe, too. And I just kept thinking about them.

Could they meet again? What might another meeting look like? These two tethered souls have woven in and out of each other's lives since birth. Why couldn't they have another shot? Would Fate really stop them from ever meeting again after twisting them through each other's timelines so many times before? Now that they finally know each other and know what they share, how might things be different if they met again?

Uncrossing the Stars is the answer to those questions. It's the second chance Romance that I believe Sarah and Joe deserve. And speaking not just as the author, but also as a reader, I believe it's the second chance we all deserve. Because life is indisputably full of bittersweet moments that stick with us forever, but when we're open to it, life can also be so full of joy.

I should note that this book does contain some topics that may be triggering. It's a story that deals with mourning over a lost loved one, so grief and healing are important parts of the story. Also, although Sarah is a gorgeous, confident, plus-sized woman, the story does include a small subplot that reflects the fatphobia in society and especially in size-zero Hollywood. It also includes alcohol use, discussion of past infidelity, and open-door sexual intimacy.

You don't have to have read *Always Never Meant To Be* to read this book. I certainly recommend it because I think it's excellent, if I do say so myself. (Hey, if I don't say it, who will?) And because experiencing the first part of Sarah and Joe's journey can only make this part richer. However, like all my Magical Seattle stories, this one is written as a standalone tale. All the essential magic from book one lives in this one, plus some new, wonderful, magical moments that I hope will fill your heart.

But if you did read and love *Always Never Meant To Be,* prepare to dive even deeper into the beautiful, enchanting, messy world of Sarah and Joe. And grab a tissue before you start because *Uncrossing the Stars* is absolutely the book you want it to be. Enjoy!

PART ONE

FATE

Just to be absolutely clear, Fate always does exactly what She wants. She's whimsical, mercurial, and entirely unpredictable. She's generally benign, but that doesn't stop Her from dealing out harsh fates now and then. And She always gets Her way. Don't like the fate She deals you? Don't bother fighting. She will find you eventually. Fate giveth and She taketh away.

The good news is, occasionally – if She's in a good mood – She also giveth second chances.

Chapter One

The Job

Sarah's slow walk to the short-notice meeting is inevitably paved in existential dread and abstract, greige carpet squares. All hands meetings are typically planned at least a month in advance. With treats and ice breakers. Not to mention colorful swag and fun gadgets to fiddle with. No good could possibly come from a same-day demand to assemble at 11 AM in the lobby no less – not even offsite at one of their go-to theatrical venues – for an important announcement.

Sarah contemplates the possibilities. None of them make her heart sing with hope, that's for sure. They've only had two other short-notice all hands like this in the seven years she's worked at the film commission. Five years ago, they assembled everyone on fifteen-minutes notice to say a water main break in the street meant they had no water and everyone could go home for the rest of the day. That wasn't be so bad. But surely another water main break in the same spot is too much to hope for.

The second happened only six months ago in the aftershocks of the new administration taking office. By then Sarah had been promoted to the Seattle Arts leadership team, a mixed blessing at best as the budget cuts hit. For the first few years, she'd only been in charge of film commission operations, which had been challenging enough, but at least she could still pass the buck back then. Stepping up to Executive Director, however, was considerably less fun when severe slashes from the state and feds resulted in an immediate halt on all non-essential projects. They'd all spent a solid week reaching out to grant recipients and program administrators to break the bad news. Oof. That had been awful. But at least she had warning before the bad news hit that time. This time, Sarah hasn't heard so much as a whisper.

Gabi's text pops in. *Did you say you were booking the car? Or should I?* She's asking this now? They're leaving for Los Angeles tomorrow for God's sake. Sarah pockets her phone and waves at Louise to hold the elevator. The sooner she gets to the lobby, the sooner she can find out what fresh hell awaits.

Could this be more budget cuts? But then, why wouldn't she be told? Would it be jobs this time? Her job maybe? Is that why she wasn't told in advance? Her pulse pounds into her temple. Hell, if it is jobs, let it be hers. Better that than being responsible for the cuts like she was at her last job. She can't do that again.

Ding. The elevator opens on the lobby where about forty people are assembled already. Sarah whispers to Louise, "Any idea what's going on?"

Louise shrugs in return and gives a worried squint toward the giant lobby windows shining bright sunlight into the space. A gentle murmur of people chattering echoes off the walls and high ceilings, disguising each conversation in the wash of them all. A current of nervous chuckles rushes through the crowd, everyone on edge awaiting what can surely only be bad news. Sarah's phone buzzes. Gabi again. *I can order it if you want. Only, I still have to pack. And write my presentation. And create my slides. But I'm sure I can find time.*

All that in one night? Sarah sighs and types, *Ten minutes.* She really can't deal with this right now. Hell, she might not even have a job tomorrow. And here she is planning a work trip with Gabi. It had seemed like such a great idea when it first came up. A nonprofit leadership conference they could both apply to their respective jobs and combine with a girls' trip. Now she might be losing the very job that's supposed to be paying. Great. Then again, if she's about to be unemployed, the professional development could come in handy. Excellent networking opportunities as well. There's an upside to everything, after all.

She feels sweat pooling at her temples. She runs her fingers lightly over the wedding ring hanging at her neck, then opens her boss Pilar's text thread and types, *What's going on? Should I be worried?* There's no response for a moment, then the three dots appear as Pilar types her response. Sarah braces for whatever is about to pop onto her screen, but the dots disappear. Well, that's not a good sign. Maybe it's nothing, but—

Ding! An elevator opens and another dozen people pour out, followed closely by the other elevator. The crowd's getting big now. Eighty or ninety people. Must be about everyone. Everyone but Pilar, that is. Sarah checks her phone, but Pilar is not writing back. Then another ding, and Pilar walks out with two other members of the city's arts leadership team. Sarah's used to being part of the group and sidles quickly up to join them. "Pilar, what's going on?"

"Catch me after," Pilar says. "We'll talk." She gives Sarah a half smile, then presses her arm in a gentle stay-put gesture, then sweeps off toward the stairs without her. The others follow the chief, but stop a step behind, granting her the clear, top leadership position. Suddenly, she's not "Sarah's friend Pilar," but "Pilar Alvarez, Seattle Arts Czar." The way she assumes control is magnificent, but Sarah's supposed to be part of the King's Council, nobly standing on the dais at her side. Suddenly being cast out among the not-so-blissfully ignorant court and commoners, as lovely as they all are, is unsettling. Her hard-earned privilege erased in one soft arm squeeze. She brings her hand back to her neck and furtively fiddles with her ring as the other three turn to face the crowd.

Well, if she was hoping Pilar would quell her anxieties, mission very much failed. Thanks for that. Pilar's signature strawberry blond afro reads extra red in the sunshine, commanding attention as she prepares to speak. She's always been so masterful as a leader. Well-spoken, insightful, both compassionate and pragmatic. And freaking gorgeous. Even at 60, her warm brown complexion is virtually flawless. She practically glows. The kind of woman who can command any room. In other words, the perfect leader.

Sarah takes a deep breath and prepares to face her destiny. If she's back on unemployment, so be it. She can handle it this time. She'll be okay. She'll freaking hate it, but she'll manage. There's doubtless still a lengthy laundry list of things that could shatter her life completely, but losing a job isn't one of them anymore. Fate's been unkind to her lately. She could use a win. But if this is what's coming, fuck it, she's ready. She closes her eyes, counts slowly to ten, then opens them as Pilar clears her throat. Let the games begin.

"Thank you for taking time out, everyone," Pilar says with enough volume to instantly silence the room. "This isn't how I wanted to share this news, but certain factors have come into play, which make this necessary."

Here goes, Sarah thinks, her head suddenly pounding. The crowd, which was already stiff with anxiety, goes positively rigid at attention. Sarah twists her ring round and round and wonders how she'll explain this to Ben – if it's true. She's tried so hard to prove to him that she's okay without him. That she's thriving even. But it's hard to claim you're thriving from the unemployment line.

Pilar continues, "As you all know, it's been a difficult six months, but in my opinion, we've weathered the budget cuts to date and necessary operational demands with aplomb. Thanks to all of you and your hard work... for which I am so grateful."

Pilar pauses a moment, visibly choked up. The job cuts theory is feeling righter by the moment. She loves her team. What else would make her this emotional? Even with her own job hanging by a possibly imaginary thread, Sarah's tears well for Pilar. This must be devastating for her.

"I'm proud of everything we've accomplished together, both over the last six months, and over the past ten years I've had the honor to lead you." Pilar turns and looks directly at Sarah with a kind smile. Sarah sucks in a deep breath and forces it to her stomach where she holds it as Pilar goes on. "And I know you will all continue to do great things for our Seattle arts community." Sarah slowly blows out her breath. "But I will not be with you for the journey."

A collective gasp washes across the room. *What?!*

"I am delighted to share the news that I have decided to retire early. I have grandkids to mind and books to read and a garden that desperately needs attention. And I am in a very blessed position to be able to step away from work knowing I've led this organization through extraordinary trials and tribulations and left it stronger than ever. With an amazing leadership team in place, even before my successor is chosen."

Retirement? Good news then. The energy in the room gurgles and bubbles over as everyone bursts into relieved cheers and applause. Sarah discovers her own hands clasped over her delighted smile. Pilar continues, "I hadn't intended to announce the news quite yet. I was still working out my exit strategy and just began a conversation with the board last night. However, we received word about half an hour ago that the Evergreen Arts Blog somehow got a hold of the story and they're posting it this afternoon. And I wanted you all to hear it from me first."

People giggle and the chatter grows. So why is Sarah's body still wound tighter than a drum? Louise leans over and whispers, "Who's going to take over, I wonder?" Ah, there it is.

***

Waiting patiently next to Pilar's door, Sarah taps furiously at her keypad. *I registered us both for the conference, booked the hotel, booked the flights, ordered our meals for the plane, and pre-paid the airport parking. In what world would I not also book the car?*

Gabi's response comes only a moment later. *There's no need to get snippy.*

Sarah spots Pilar making her way toward her office through congratulating crowds. *I'm in the middle of something.*

Dana says hi.

Pilar gets a few steps closer before being grabbed into a hug from Barry from finance. Sarah smirks as she types. *Tell your beautiful wife she deserves better.*

Gabi doesn't miss a beat. *She knows.*

Sarah types quickly attempting one last good-natured stab of the knife before Pilar reaches her. *And I love her.*

But Gabi doesn't take the bait. *She'd leave me in a hot minute for you.* Sarah giggles. She wouldn't have gotten through the past couple years, or any of what happened with Ben, if it weren't for Gabi and Dana. She stashes her phone and follows Pilar into the office. At Pilar's gesture, Sarah closes the door.

"I'm sorry I didn't get a chance to tell you before," Pilar says as soon as the door clicks.

"You don't owe me that."

Pilar drops in her seat and sags with the exhaustion of the unexpected communications emergency. "I had planned to tell you today. I was going to tell you before anyone. Well, besides the board. The others only knew because we were in a budget review meeting when the message came in about the blog."

"I get it. I'm excited for you!" Sarah takes her spot opposite Pilar and reaches across to squeeze her hand. "Retired. That's amazing! Although I expected you to go another fifteen years."

Pilar pulls her hand back and rubs her face in a dramatic show of horror. "A decade of my life is long enough, thanks. I love this job and this community, but I'm tired. It's time for someone younger with more energy to step in."

"Well, they'll never fill your Louboutins."

Pilar purses her lips pointedly at Sarah. "Someone like you."

"Sorry, what?"

Chapter Two

Big Shot

The old couple tip-toe toward Joe in the unmistakable manner of nervous autograph seekers. The halting eye contact alternating with sideways glances, wanting to make a connection without putting him on the spot. The gentle shuffle, the slouching shoulders as they ease his direction, nearly folding in on themselves trying not to be seen until the last moment. They always want to make themselves small, as if Joe is too big for them, as if they are mere mortals who dare not disturb such divinity as Joe's celebrity affords him. Until they summon the courage before him to offer their meager supplication for a photo or signature. The older folks usually want the photo and/or autograph, while the young ones want the selfie for socials. These two will probably want both.

"Excuse me," the woman says softly, brushing a loose strand of her gray behind her ear as her balding husband straightens his back proudly behind her now that the moment has come. She dips down toward Joe's table as if she might whisper, and Clark smirks at Joe with a knowing wink. After twenty-five years as Joe's agent, he's seen Joe through the lean times and fat. He enjoys these moments of hard-earned recognition. More than Joe does, to be fair. "Are you...?" The woman trails off as if she doesn't dare speak his name.

"Joe Parker, hello," he says, easing the way for her even as his own hand tightens on his fork.

"Joseph Robert Parker, yes! We thought so!" The woman beams and glances back at her husband who's gone ruddy with excitement. "Could we bother you for a photo?"

It strikes Joe once again how very disproportionate this has all become. Fans, photos, celebrity. All too big, too much, too posed. None of it feels like he dreamed it would when he was young. When he thought fame would mean fabulous award shows, glamorous parties, and sexy photo shoots sandwiched between one starring role after another. When he imagined every day off-set would be sunshine, beaches, and convertibles, and it would all be perfect. When he thought "perfect" was actually perfect.

Joe smiles warmly and stands, making a conscious effort to release the tension in his shoulders. "Of course," he says. He reaches for their phone since folks tend to cut his painfully tall head off if they take it. "Shall I take it?" They gladly hand over the phone, which he arcs high and aims down at all three of them. Clark is in the background looking amused. Joe opts to leave him in. *Click.*

By the time he finally achieved this current, outsized level of fame a few years ago, Joe knew enough to know it was all a farce, one he'd gamely signed up for in exchange for the opportunity to do the kind of work he'd always dreamed of. It wasn't real then and it's not real now. It doesn't matter. It's not who he is. But this couple deserves their moment, like they all do. So, he hands the phone back to them and hopes the end is near.

The old man nudges the woman and she takes a quick gulp before saying, "Oh, sorry, but would you mind signing this?"

She holds out a pen and piece of paper, which Joe takes as he settles back into his chair. It's their receipt from the lunch they've just eaten. He flashes an "of course" smile and flips it over. Quick scrawl of his celeb signature and he sets them free. "Thank you so much. Have a great day." They giggle and bow obsequiously as they wander off and Joe expels a relieved breath.

"You really hate that, don't you?" Clark says as he digs back into his steak salad.

"They were nice."

"Yeah, but you hated it."

Joe pinches back his smile of recognition and returns to his tilapia. "Hate's a strong word."

"Do you remember when we came here seven years ago? Right before you went to Seattle."

Joe glances around at the familiar alcoves in the walls, the heavy sconce lighting fixtures, and the bright arched windows. "We've been coming her for at least a decade. Why would I remember that particular visit?"

"Because that older woman came up to you, remember? I'll never forget it. Just like that couple now, and we thought she recognized you. It wasn't so frequent back then, so it was still fun." Clark pauses and starts to laugh. "And you were pulling out your pen to sign something, but it turned out she just thought you were her daughter's boyfriend." Clark busts into a full guffaw at the memory and Joe smiles at the reminder of his humiliation. Clark sips his water to wash down his mirth, then finally says, "No one's mistaking Joseph Robert Parker for anyone else these days."

"For better or worse," Joe chuckles and sighs. "Anyway, what was I saying?"

Clark chews as he speaks. "Goldblum."

"Oh, right." Joe chews a bite and swallows before continuing. "So, they said 'Jeff Goldblum will be offer only,' and I was like, obviously."

"Dude hasn't auditioned in decades."

"But if we can get him..."

"Goldblum is gold!" Clark chimes in, on the same page as always.

"Right?" Joe's phone buzzes in his pocket and he lights up when he sees the screen. "Sorry, I've gotta get this," he says as he clicks the green button. "Hey, honey. How's New York?... That's great! Oh, amazing." As Joe speaks, he watches Clark eyeing someone over Joe's shoulder. Clark nudges his head that direction in warning. "Absolutely. You get in at 4:15, right? I'll pick you up curbside. Okay. Have a safe flight. Love you!"

As Joe hangs up the phone, a skintight white dress over deeply tanned skin sidles into his peripheral view. Sitting atop the dress and camera-ready curves is the face of a gorgeous brunette with highly glossed lips and thick eyelashes. Joe tilts up at her and smiles. "Hello."

"Hiiii," she purrs. "You're Joe, right?"

Joe stifles a sigh and smiles as his shoulders tighten anew. "I am."

She bends deeply to his side, showing off her generous cleavage in the process, and holds out her phone before she speaks. "Okay if we take a picture?" She snaps the photo before he can answer, making sure her cleavage shows in the shot reflected back at them both. "My name is Amber. I'm an actress. I love your work."

"Thank you so much," he says blandly.

"I know you're producing a lot now, too. I'd love to hear about what you're working on sometime."

"Oh, well, I...." Joe rattles through his standard responses in search of something appropriate for the likes of Amber.

She slips a piece of paper onto the table next to him before he comes up with it. "Call me." She smiles again, nods at Clark with a "just in case" bounce of her brows. Clearly, this is a woman who intends to work every angle. Then she glides away with a careful sweep of her shapely bottom intended for Joe's personal entertainment.

Joe glances at the show, but it's one he's seen countless times before. He plops his elbows on the table and drops his face into his hands "I've got to get out of here, Clark. I can't do all this today."

"What else is new?" Clark says as he gnaws on a piece of steak. "Fine, fine. We're about done anyway."

"You got this?" Joe asks as he tosses his napkin on the table.

"That's what the expense account's for. But read the script!"

Joe rises and picks up the slip of paper with Amber's number. He crumbles it and drops it into the tilapia's lemon butter sauce. "By the end of the day, I promise. Thanks, buddy." He taps Clark on the shoulder and heads for the door.

***

It makes no sense to drive home via the Pacific Coast Highway, but Joe detours over to the ocean anyway. Driving the PCH with the top down, shades on, and the sun shining always does wonders to clear his head of the celebrity dog and pony show. And he needs to be clear if he's going to get through that script this afternoon as promised. The gentle roar of his vintage Mustang combined with the battering wind rushing around the windscreen silences his buzzing brain and gives him room to breathe. To think.

Not that he's unhappy. Not exactly. In many respects, his life is better than he ever imagined. At least since Seattle, where he once imagined a very different life, but all that's just a dream now. Still, things are so good, and he's so grateful. Two films out this year, three in development, and another set to start shooting in a few weeks. He's so goddamn blessed. It's totally worth the mild inconvenience of occasional fan encounters and painfully repetitive press junkets. And sure, some days the games may manifest more like a grind than a godsend, but he's been on the other side. He was on the other side for nearly twenty years. Now, he borders on overworked, and the paychecks border on astronomical, but that's surely better than scrounging for every role and worrying about paying the electric bill, let alone the mortgage. Those days are long gone now, thank God. Even if the glare of the spotlight does get a little too bright now and then.

Yet, sometimes he needs to escape everything and reconnect with the part of him he loses when he's not paying attention. To hold close all the things that help him feel whole. All the things he discovered with *her* help. To remember.

The phone rings through his retrofitted Bluetooth interrupting his reverie. "Mel, hi!" he says loudly over the wind. "What's going on?"

Melanie booms through the speaker as Joe rolls the volume button up to out-blast the high-speed road noise. "Hey, I found a house I think would be perfect. Can I send you the listing?"

"Perfect how?" Joe shouts.

"On the beach, four bedrooms, great pool. I think you'll love it."

"Okay, send me the listing," Joe says with a glance out at the water. Living on the ocean would be nice, but is it really what he wants? "I'll take a look."

"If you like it, we can go see it tomorrow," she says hopefully.

"Let's just start by sending it to me."

"You know we have to move fast in this market."

"I have script feedback due this afternoon. I can't think about this now. But I'll check it out and we can talk about it tonight. How's that?"

"You're a prince among men, my dear!" She ends the call by making a handful of kissing noises before the silence returns. Joe smiles to himself. Melanie's a whole different person these days, happier, more joyful, more like she was when they first married. How did that happen? How did any of it happen, really?

Yeah, a beach house might be nice.

***

Joe reads the final page of the script, then flips it closed. He takes a moment to reacclimate from the 1950s New York elite world he was just in to his poolside lounger, staring out at the glimmering water. Clark was right. That was a hell of a script. Smart, check. Funny, check. Surprising, check. And his final criterion, the one no one else knows about, but the one that's always his dealbreaker if the answer is no. *Will Sarah like it?* Absolutely.

Technically, he'll never know if she likes it, of course, since he's neither seen nor spoken to her in seven years. But he still carries her with him every day. She's the voice in his head helping him choose his projects, the invisible scene partner when he runs his lines, the soft voice that sings him to sleep. Sure, he's moved on in a very real way. Embraced every opportunity, loved the people closest to his heart. But she's still always there. In truth, every movie since the day he left Seattle has been for her.

And this one... If they do it right, get the right people, it's in Oscars contention, no question. This is why he got into the business, to do work like this. Maybe down the road, the same frustrations and disenchantment will settle in on this project that seems to plague everything these days. But at least for the moment, the possibilities gurgle happily through his brain.

The glass slider opens and his assistant Randy emerges with a tall pinkish-yellow concoction in hand. "Made you a smoothie," he announces as he hands the glass over.

"Aw, thanks. You didn't have to."

"I wanted one myself," Randy says. "Making yours gave me an excuse."

Joe chuckles, "Good man!"

Randy sits on the neighboring lounger and leans in. "So, how was it?"

"Good. Really good."

"Yeah?"

Joe holds back his smile, then lets it leak out as he says, "I think it could be great."

"Amazing!"

Joe takes another sip. "We've got to lock it up now. And get the right team in place. Would you get an email out, or a text, or whatever magic it is you do, and get a meeting set up with Marty?" Joe couldn't shake the thought as he read. This script has Martin

Scorsese written all over it. If they can get his attention to detail and fanatical passion pointed at this project, they'll take it all the way. Plus, they've been looking for the right project to do together.

"Marty, huh? Gangsters?"

Joe laughs again, this time at Randy's gangster obsession, his giddiness over the project spilling out. "Closer to The Age of Innocence meets The Aviator."

"Well, alright. Get it, Parker! I'll set something up."

As Randy moves toward the house, Joe calls out, "Hey, isn't it your anniversary today?"

Randy slopes his shoulders sheepishly. "Yeah, Carlos is setting up some kind of crazy surprise for me tonight. I'm terrified," he giggles with an appreciative smile.

"Ahh, young love!" Joe teases. "After you get the Scorsese thing sorted, why don't you get out of here? Go find a way to surprise him back."

As Randy disappears into the house, Joe returns his attention to the pool. The large umbrella shades him from the grueling late afternoon sun, but he's feeling the heat nonetheless. And the nervous energy bubbling inside him needs an outlet.

The door glides open again, but this time it's his son Nathan leaning out. "Hey, dad."

"Nate! How was your day?" Joe beams at his son, grateful for a place to focus the almost nuclear energy building up inside him.

"Ah, you know, just another day in customer service paradise."

Joe points to the lounger beside him. "Come talk to me."

"Can't. Gotta go call a girl."

"You really do talk like a movie, you know."

Nathan grins at his father. "Learned from the best," he says before disappearing back into the house. And Joe is left alone again.

He stares at the pool, then tosses the script to the side and pulls off his tee-shirt. He dives in, launching into as many laps as he needs to exercise and exorcize his excitement away. They're short laps, the attractive, organic, yet inconvenient curves of the pool drastically limiting the straight lines he can follow, but he keeps going until exhaustion finally takes over and calms him.

When he climbs out, he grabs his towel and phone where he finds yet another text from Melanie pinging him about the listing. Oh yeah. He slurps the remains of his smoothie, then settles in for a good scroll. Photo after photo of what can only be called a dream house. Huge rooms. Cathedral ceilings. Immaculate finishes. A bathroom for every bedroom plus two powder rooms. A screening room. A bowling alley? And, of course, the pool. The pool's perfect. Long and straight and ideal for laps. Not that this pool isn't nice. He'd just like something a little less kidney-shaped.

The house is right on the beach and he can practically hear the waves in the photos of the view. Mel was right. It's the perfect house. A man in his position should want this house.

Chapter Three

Funny You Mention It

SARAH STIRS HER SOUP on the stovetop, then returns to her seat at the island to stare at her laptop, which is still loading the conference offerings. She should be reviewing the upcoming film shoot reports and starting her employee evaluations. She really can't afford to take two days off work for this trip, even if it is ostensibly for professional development, and she'd planned to use this evening to get as far ahead as she could before she left. But with the new job prospect in play, she's rethinking her conference plans. Unfortunately, continents have shifted faster than this website has loaded.

Her anxiety over going to Los Angeles – not the conference, but the city itself – grows as she waits. There's no logical reason to be nervous, of course. She's assured herself of that repeatedly since she and Gabi first discussed the possibility of going. It would be fun to spend the weekend together, get a little professional development, then see the sights. Venice Beach, the Getty, The Last Bookstore, the Walk of Fame, then eat some good Mexican food. It would be great. And no reason in the world to expect to run into *him*. No reason whatsoever.

Finally, the grid-style table appears with the three tracks from which to choose. The Nonprofit and Public Administration Conference is designed, with relative success, to be all things to all people, with one track for Gabi's nonprofit management, one for public administrators like Sarah, and one for everyone. They'd mostly be split up on their separate tracks, but they'd found two courses they thought they could take together, courses that might actually be fun. Hell, compared to most of the sessions, "Fostering Better Morale for Better Performance" sounded like a night at Giggles Comedy Club.

Now, with the opportunity of a new dream job hanging over her, she's rethinking everything. She'd assumed Pilar would be around forever, and Sarah was glad to have her. But with Pilar leaving, the possibility looms that Sarah could lead not just Seattle's film commission, but the whole of the city's arts community. It's a mind-boggling opportunity, a dream bigger than any she'd ever imagined. But now that it's here, she can't stop thinking about it.

Pilar promised they'd discuss the prospect of Sarah's application next week when Sarah returns, and under the circumstances, maybe fun sessions are a luxury she can't afford. She scans the Public Administration track again, considering her options. Sacrifice "Better Morale" for "Working with City Officials: A Step-by-Step Guide to Communicating Value Beyond the Data"? Sarah sighs. Plucking her eyelashes out one by one sounds slightly more appealing, but anything to get a leg up.

Her soup boils. Sarah fills her bowl, slices a piece of sourdough, and returns to her grid scroll.

Bleep bleep. Bleep bleep. Bleep bleep.

The noise bursts into her brain and she quickly taps off the alarm. The horrible, piercing tone she'd chosen for her Wednesday at 7:40 alarm. Unlike most of her various alarms and ringtones, which greet her with perky tunes and gentle melodies, somehow she couldn't let this one be too pretty.

The conference will have to wait. She shoves a bite of bread into her mouth, then clicks away from the slow-loading website and over to her Gmail. She clicks into her folder labeled "Ben" and there it is. The email.

The folder itself is full of random and assorted messages from Ben. Not everything he ever sent her, of course. That would be crazy. There were a few old things that had been special enough to save originally, but the folder is mostly filled with every message since they first got the leukemia diagnosis. Since she first realized her clock with Ben might be ticking down, running out. Since it became clear every word was a precious measure of a dwindling resource. On that day three years ago, every email and every voicemail became priceless. And from that day forward, she saved absolutely everything. Even the shopping lists.

And there on top, the last email he ever sent. A week before he died. "Open after I'm gone" the subject line says. And so she had. But then she'd closed it right back up again. That had been a Wednesday night, too. She'd looked at the clock. It was 7:40. She wasn't ready. She decided she couldn't yet read whatever Ben wanted to tell her. So she saved the email as new and decided she'd come back the next week to read it. She set an alarm as a way to hold herself accountable. And yet, when the week passed, she came back and found she still couldn't do it. So, she reset the alarm.

And now, nearly two years later, she's still setting that damn alarm. At some point in the past year, she finally forced herself to read the relatively short message. But it more or less just says to click the embedded link to a file in their shared drive, and that she hasn't been able to do. Yet. Maybe tonight is the night?

The inevitable flutter taps a rhythm in her chest. Fear and grief commingling in the same old song. After all this time, the weekly routine is as familiar as a favorite movie playing for the hundredth time, but considerably less comforting. She mouses over the link, willing herself to click it. To finally face whatever's behind the link and process the last of her unresolved emotions. Not that she hasn't coped. She's had therapy and grief groups and mostly made peace with the Ben she'll never have again, and the Ben she still has. But there's something about clicking that link. It's her last little, unseen bit of him. As long as she has the link, he's still there, waiting for her. Like maybe, he's not really gone. Not entirely.

A text pops in from Gabi interrupting her reverie. It's a photo of Gabi holding up three silk caps. *Which bonnet should I bring? Carmen, Iris, or Monique?*

You named your headwraps?

Sarah watches the dots as Gabi types. *Yes, for the personality I assume when I'm wearing them.*

Sarah chuckles. She studies the photo and the caps. One a hot orange and yellow pattern, one blood red, and one in abstract black and white. *Can't Dana help you pick?*

She can, but you might not like who you end up sharing a hotel room with.

Sarah quickly taps back, *You may be genuinely shocked to hear this, but I have no preference on your bonnet. Surprise me!*

She returns to her computer, clicks away from the email of torment, and selects another email. An equally familiar part of the dance. Choosing another message, something silly or unimportant she's read dozens of times. Revisiting his words without surrendering that last gasp of hope. They used to make her cry, but not anymore. Now they mostly bring sweetness. This one's about work that needed to be done around the house that he didn't want her to forget with everything going on. Work that's been done by now. Old news. But for a moment, she's back there reading it for the first time. Vibrating with panic about how much there is to do and how she'll ever manage it all without him. The pain of it pulses through her, but at least that Sarah still had him in the flesh, unlike today's Sarah.

She doesn't always go back to the old emails. In recent months, she's found herself more and more willing to click away without the review. A good sign, her therapist Libby says. Her patterns and rituals are changing as she releases the past and embraces the present. Maybe she can even make way for a future. But sometimes, the need still hits, like tonight. Tonight, she's extra needy, and she thinks she knows why. She closes her emails and resets the alarm. Maybe next week.

After dinner, she settles into her favorite chair with the photos from the mantelpiece. She's slowly removed Ben from the walls and shelves where he was pictured during their life together, but she's held on to this last remaining frame. A triptych of images, with her on the left, him on the right, and a couple photo in the middle. She considers them together, then folds the hinged frame so she can focus on Ben.

"I'm going to Los Angeles tomorrow, honey. A work trip. A conference. But Gabi and I are also going to make it a girls' trip." She pauses and thinks about her next words. "It should be fun, but I'm a little nervous. Not sure why."

She stops again. Of course, she knows why. It's always *him*. Joe. Like Ben, Joe is always with her. The man who loved her enough to heal her and let her go back to her husband. He haunts her as much as Ben. He's haunted her since the day they said goodbye, but then Ben died and her quiet, background longing for Joe shifted from a loving memory to a painful reminder of her betrayal. It had been tolerable when it was a beautiful blip that helped her find her way back to Ben. But when she lost Ben, she lionized him, and her guilt over Joe grew into an ever-lingering wraith of regret. She can never regret Joe himself. Dear, wonderful Joe. But she can hold *herself* accountable and atone for past sins. Which means keeping Joe in his box, even if he's just a memory.

But if she can't even admit Joe's at the root of her anxiety to herself, she's certainly not going to tell Ben. Even the ghost form. Ghost Ben doesn't need to know all her secrets. "Oh, and guess what! Pilar is retiring, so I think I might go for it. We'll see. At least she wants me to. Anyway, wish me luck! And take care of us while we travel, huh?"

She kisses her fingertips, then presses them to Ben's face. He'd removed his glasses for the photo, so she can really see his warm, brown eyes. And his sweet, ruddy cheeks. It's a good face.

***

Every city appears sprawling from directly overhead, but the next day, as Sarah gazes out the airplane window at Los Angeles, she's absolutely staggered by its never-ending immensity. It goes on forever with no boundaries of any kind, least of all in her mind. The city is infinite. So, why is she so worried that her fingers are digging a hole into her leg? In a city this large, surely, she'll be safe.

Gabi reads her mind. "It's going to be fine."

Her voice draws Sarah away from the view. "What is?"

"Sarah, have you ever seen sprawl like this anywhere? It's a massive, sun-soaked, glammed up soup of like *four million* people going about their business and living their daily lives. And we're going to a professional conference, and tourist traps." When Sarah still doesn't click to Gabi's meaning, Gabi goes on. "These aren't places locals go."

"What? I'm not worried about—"

"The day you're not thinking about Joe Parker I will shave my head bald."

Sarah glimpses at Gabi's afro, which is less dramatic than Pilar's, but still represents years of effort and care. "After all that work? You'd sooner tattoo your face blue."

"I'll do both if it ever happens. Which I can safely say because that day will never come. But I'm telling you right now, you have nothing to worry about. The chances of running into Joe are like a million to one."

Sarah turns back to the window. A million to one. Those were the odds last time, too. A billion to one probably. Yet, it happened. The earth shook and the stars re-aligned and the man of her dreams literally stood on a street waiting for her. Waiting to knit his soul to hers, heal her head and heart, and then walk away again.

"Sarah, you're not going to run into him."

"I know," Sarah snaps back, her irritation evident in the way she refuses to meet Gabi's eyes, instead watching the fast approach of the runway.

"Do you?" Gabi needles.

The plane hits the ground and the loud rush of brakes against runway briefly halts the conversation. When the plane slows and the noise drops back to a more reasonable level, Sarah turns to her friend. "I'm sure you're right," she says.

***

Sarah breezes out to the curb with her carry-on and searches for the Uber sign as Gabi slowly drags her massive, checked bag behind. When she arrives at Sarah's side, Sarah points up. "There's the sign for the rideshare pick-ups. That way." She turns her finger across the road and to the right.

Gabi gazes down the long walkway and considers her bag. "Don't think they'd get us here, do you? I'd pay double to get in right here." She opens the app on her phone and gets ready to order the car.

"You really need to learn how to pack," Sarah says, smirking as she leads the way into the crosswalk. But Gabi lingers behind staring at her phone. When she notices Sarah has taken off, she shoves her suitcase into motion and charges into the street, met by the angry horn of a giant red SUV. Gabi makes a less than friendly gesture back, which is greeted by another even angrier horn blast as she reaches the other side and trudges after Sarah.

***

As Joe pulls up to the terminal, he rolls his eyes at the garbage truck sized, red SUV ahead of him blaring his horn like a foghorn. "Jesus, dude, calm down. It ain't that serious," he mumbles as if the guy leaning on his horn can hear. A frazzled woman with a giant suitcase drags it onto the curb on the other side of the street as the dude blasts her again. "We're all going the same place. One minute more or less won't make difference." Joe steers to door six where Avery waves happily. She tosses her bag quickly into the back seat then hops in with an eager hug. "Welcome home," Joe says. "How was your flight?"

Avery grimaces, then lights up. "Uneventful, which is exactly how I like my flights. But I have so much to tell you about NYU!"

Joe's heart bubbles happily at Avery's glow. She and Nathan are the only things keeping him sane some days. "Was it very artful?" he asks, alluding to Avery's chosen course of study.

"Oh, yes, very."

"Excellent!" He checks his blind spot and pulls out. "Am I taking you to Chip's?"

"Home," Avery says decisively. "Chip and I are done."

Joe's not sad to learn his beautiful, brilliant daughter is no longer dating a guy with both the name and the IQ of a cookie ingredient, but he's learned to keep his mouth shut. "Oh, I'm sorry to hear that."

"No, you're not," she quips.

Joe chuckles. "So, does that mean we'll see you for your birthday tomorrow night?"

"I already told Nate I was coming over. He didn't tell you?" She digs out her gum and offers Joe a piece.

Joe takes it and holds it in the air. "I love that kid, but I'd barely trust Nate to pass on a piece of gum, let alone a message."

"Fair. So, I'm spending the morning and lunch with mom. Then I'm coming for dinner tomorrow night – surprise! – but I thought maybe you and I could do something in the afternoon? If you're free?"

"For my darling daughter, I will move heaven and earth to get free."

***

A mid-afternoon coffee is probably a terrible idea, but Sarah takes a cup from the courtesy table and pours herself some caffeinated jet fuel anyway. She'll need it to stay awake for her last Friday session. It's only three-quarters through her first full day, plus last night's welcome session, and her brain is already shutting down from information overload. And she still has another full day tomorrow. She settles in for her next presentation then texts Gabi. *We need to decide where to eat tonight.*

Depends what else we want to do, Gabi pings back.

Exactly, I think we should eat downtown somewhere and go to the Last Bookstore tonight.

Gabi's reply comes quickly. *I thought we were doing that over the weekend.*

They had talked about doing it over the weekend, but isn't it more efficient to do it as a stand-alone since it's so far from everything else? *Makes more sense to go today. Plus, if we go right at four when we're done here, we'll beat the weekend crowds.*

Weekend crowds? Wtf? Gabi replies.

The speakers begin to assemble up front, with the session host taking her place at the podium. Sarah glances quickly down again at her phone where Gabi has added, *Is this a bookstore or an amusement park?*

She contemplates the question as the woman at the front begins her greeting. *You know how I hate shopping at Christmas. Because I hate crowds. Same thing. Besides, I want plenty of time to shop unbothered.*

Gabi's dots appear, then disappear. Sarah waits, debating whether to put her phone away as the first speaker is introduced. But then Gabi's dots reappear, followed by the words, *This doesn't have anything to do with you know who, does it?*

It's a bookstore, not a movie premiere, Sarah types with all the nonchalance she can muster. But of course, Gabi knows. Gabi always knows. Sarah does hate crowds, and it's just one random bookstore in a city the size of a small state, unlikely to attract any particular celebrities. Plus, she's been dying to go to this shop for ages, so it makes sense to go when they have time enough to enjoy it without rushing other activities. What she's saying is almost, practically, more or less, actually true. Still, better safe than sorry.

It was seven years ago, but it could have been this morning. Every moment seared into her brain, even after all this time, like an endless encounter happening in a loop. It's not a loop she enters often. She has – has had – a good life. Except for that two-year blip into jobless oblivion, of course, but that was so long ago. And since then? Even through Ben's illness and all the pain and grief, she knew she was one of the lucky ones. She may collapse under the weight of loss and uncertainty for a minute, or a month. But she would get back up and carry on. And when she did, she still had so much. What more could she need? Nothing. What more could she want? Well, that's not a question she asks.

But it's a loop that's always there, always available for her to jump into when she's waxing nostalgic or lonely. When she needs to remember who brought her back to life in her darkest days of unemployment and depression, who made her whole. Who – even in his absence – kept her rooted though the loss of Ben, when the grief was so deep it ripped through her life like a possessed chainsaw, destroying every ounce of peace, safety and joy she'd built with Ben. Her wonderful husband who she'd found again, thanks to *him*. Yes, even then, even in the pits of despair grieving the man who filled every day with love, *Joe* was there in her heart. Alongside Ben. On the loop that never ends.

Usually, the loop is safely tucked away in her mind, however, and that's fine. There it's safe with no real-world ramifications. But now, she's in L.A. Closer to his world than she's ever been, and somehow the comfort of the memory, laden with guilt though it is, has mutated into the threat of possibility, however remote.

Gabi's text pops in. *Fine, we'll go from here. But don't think I don't see you, sister.*

***

Ever since she first saw The Last Bookstore on bookstagram, Sarah's been dying to go. Admittedly, she's never met a bookshop she didn't like, but this one looked positively enchanting with magical discoveries at every turn. Now, as she and Gabi approach giant, heavy, old entry doors, she's brimming with excitement.

Her eyes take a moment to adjust as she steps from the bright L.A. sun into the blackness of the entry foyer. A guy at the desk stops Gabi and asks her to check her bag before they enter. A moment later, they're gazing up at the enormous, modified Doric columns and ornate, coffered ceilings so high they're practically celestial. The building used to be a bank, the old-school, traditional kind with massive proportions designed to impress and awe, and the bookstore has lost none of that colossal magic. It has, however, added personality for days. Where should they even start?

They begin with the art books room with its wall crammed to the gills with a weird mishmash of art hung salon-style, another wall featuring the most insane black and white, surrealist train mural, and books so pricey they are kept behind glass. Next, they land in the old bank vault. The massive, deeply ornate vault door is extraordinary, leading to a dark room inside with deeply scuffed wood floors and vintage leatherbound book collections like 1970s tax records and an Old West history series that someone must have once ordered from television back in the day. Sarah couldn't imagine anyone would actually want these books – were they even for sale? – but they were indisputably cool. Maybe for movie sets, she finally decides. They'd make good set dressing.

They meander through the funky, rock'n'roll tees, where Gabi finds a shirt with The Runaways, which she absolutely must have – despite never having listened to The Runaways in her life – because it's just that cool.

When they reach the second floor, a ceiling high book sculpture welcomes them to an entire level of quirky art, interesting nooks, glam chandeliers, surprising reveals, an Egyptian sarcophagus, old radios, endless weird angles and shelves, and another vault. Inside the vault, Gabi poses on the radiator chair and Sarah gamely snaps her photo.

All of this is already well worth the visit, but when Sarah turns the corner, she spots at last the piece de resistance, the very thing she most wanted to see. The illuminated book tunnel. She gleefully walks through it, down and around, and through it again. Then she walks back. The book tunnel is truly a thing of beauty, even if her camera apparently can't capture its magic in any satisfying way.

Gabi bumps her with her shoulder. "Is it everything you dreamed of?"

"So much more," Sarah sighs happily. "I shall keep it in my heart all my days."

They wander through the mini art galleries to complete their upper floor circuit, then return to the ground floor and split up. Gabi wanders off to the vinyl section at the front of the store while Sarah peruses the architecture books and pulls out a giant white tome of Old Hollywood homes. She climbs onto a platform at the middle of the store and takes a seat to flip through the photos. Page by page, she gets lost in the magic and glamor of each home, beautifully decorated, immaculately designed, perfectly maintained. And every single one has a pool. And now he's back in her mind. Joe. Who swam every day. Who once sent her a photo of his hotel pool, just to let her know he was thinking of her. Who wore his lean, long swimmer's body like a god. Joe.

Suddenly, the air around her begins to vibrate, which is impossible. She briefly wonders if this is an earthquake, but none of the books around her are shaking. And no one else is even looking up. It's not the air or the earth. It's her. Her hand shakes on the book and an electric quiver races from her vocal cords down to her toes. Oh, no. Can simply thinking of him bring back the inevitable vibration? It never has before. In the past, it had only happened when he was nearby. She'd learned to tune it out back when she was spending every day with him, to normalize it into a new rhythm in her heart. But the first time, every time they'd been long separated, she felt him. And every time, it felt exactly like this.

It can't be.

Then she hears it. The low rumble of a voice booming down from above. She can't distinguish the words, but the timbre, the vibration echoing in her ears is unmistakable. This can't be happening. A hot poker of sharp anxiety jabs directly into her gut. Slowly, she closes the book, then forces herself to turn her head and cast her eyes up to the second-floor walkway. And there he is, walking behind a shapely redhead with perfect hair. Sarah can't see the woman's face, but she saw enough family pictures back in the day to know who it must be. His wife Melanie. "Oh my God," she mumbles to herself.

Even if she could somehow handle seeing Joe himself, she certainly isn't ready to meet his gorgeous, red carpet-ready wife. She's in no way prepared to chat with Joe and his wife like a totally chill, absolutely normal, we-definitely-never-had-sex old friend. She jumps up as discreetly as she can, drops the book on the table, and rushes over to Gabi, who's found a Runaways record to go with her shirt. "I think I'll become a fan," she announces proudly.

"We have to go. Now," Sarah whispers, tugging on her arm.

"What? Why?"

"Now," Sarah repeats. She senses the wildness in her eyes when she adds, "Please."

She watches Gabi's face processing her desperation, preparing to relent, but before Gabi can agree, a low, distant voice calls out, "Sarah?"

"Oh my God," Sarah says again and turns to run for the door. Gabi drops her stuff and runs after her. Sarah darts straight outside just as she hears what she thinks is her name being called again.

Gabi has to pause long enough to collect her bag from the front desk, then dashes after Sarah who's halfway down the block when Gabi calls out, "Sarah, wait!" Sarah pauses, frantic with terror as her friend catches up. "What's going on?" Gabi asks.

"It's Joe. He's here."

Gabi's jaw goes slack, then a slow smile creeps onto her face. "Maybe it's a sign. Maybe it's Fate telling you—"

"It's not a sign. His wife's here."

"Oh, shit."

"I have to get out of here. Now."

She turns to run again, but three steps from the corner where she could turn and be safely out of sight, his voice reaches her. "Sarah! Please!"

Sarah freezes, uncertain what to do, genuinely torn between the two strongest sensations she's ever felt in her life. The desperate urge to run around the corner and into a safe, Joe-free oblivion. And the nearly suffocating need to turn around and look at his face once again. Not on a movie screen or television. Not on the internet or in a magazine. But here, right now, before her very eyes. The man of her dreams... who saved her reality once upon a time.

"I know it's you," he says so softly she shouldn't be able to hear it from this distance. But as always, she's tuned to him like a radio transmission and his words reach her heart like they were whispered in her ear.

And with those four words, all her resistance and fury drain away. Her shoulders drop along with her chin. Gabi stands sideways, looking at him, then back to Sarah who doesn't yet have the courage to face him. Their eyes lock and Gabi squeezes her hand. Sarah releases her breath, then turns. "Hi, Joe."

One look and the world disappears. Suddenly every car, every bus, every person, every dog evaporates. Even Gabi. They're on a busy downtown street, but with Joe standing before her, it could be an abandoned beach. Or a mountaintop. Or a personal cloud in Heaven. He's still as tall as a tree, and as handsome as ever. More lines around his eyes and forehead, a bit more gray in his dark hair, but still the same Joe. Still her Joe. Still *not* her Joe.

He stares a moment, an effusive grin exploding across his face. He looks like he might cry, but instead he runs to her and grabs her in a hug as warm, delicious, and comforting as climbing into her own bed after a long, exhausting journey. As if she might never want to leave. As if she can finally sleep again. Because she's home at last.

When they finally let go, they pull back and stare at each other again.

"Hi."

"Hi."

The silence envelopes them, and for a moment, it's all there is. No one speaks, and really, what can they even say? Words are unnecessary and unequal to the moment.

And yet, Gabi, who's not in on the magic, can only stand the silence for so long and jump starts the conversation. "Hi. Don't know if you remember me. Gabi?"

He recovers himself and shakes her hand. They'd only met the once, and briefly at that, but Joe's not one to forget anything. "Gabi, of course, I remember you. Nice to see you. So, what are you two doing here?" he asks, looking back to Sarah, drinking her in as if he might get drunk on the sight of her.

"Conference," Sarah stutters out like her brain's stuck. "We're here for a conference."

"And to sightsee," Gabi adds cheerfully.

Sarah shakes her head. "Well, just this shop, really. No time for more." She feels Gabi's eyes burrowing into her at the lie, but Gabi remains silent.

Joe nods slowly, clearly calculating his next words. "So, how are you doing? Everything at home...?"

"Good, yeah," Sarah answers too quickly. She suddenly remembers her wedding ring hanging at her neck and as casually as possible, she lifts her hand to tug her top over it. "Everything is good, really good," she says before adding, "You?"

"Great," Joe says. His eyes are bright with wonder. "It's amazing to see you."

"Yeah, crazy timing." And by crazy, she means the worst timing since the moment the Titanic crew saw the iceberg. But Joe's glow suggests he has a different take.

"Or Fate," he says. Sarah recognizes the spark of certainty that Joe always had. He never doubted Fate was at play from the moment they met. He'd been right, of course, the first time. But surely Fate doesn't come knocking twice. Joe tilts his head as he stares at her, as if he's replaying every moment of their movie as he plans his next words. "So, how long are you here?"

"Tomorrow," Sarah answers instantly, but not fast enough.

"Sunday," Gabi answers at the same time.

Joe swivels between them. "So, is it tomorrow or Sunday?"

Sarah flushes with the heat of the gaffe, but Gabi chimes in to save the day. "Tomorrow, right after our last session. Sorry, I was thinking about home." She smiles carefully, the smile of a woman who knows how to lie. "We fly tomorrow, which means I have Sunday at home."

This logic makes no real sense, which Joe can surely see, but Gabi has left him no choice but to accept it. He tries anyway. "Well, maybe while you're here..."

Sarah's eyes flit up to the window above. To her horror, behind the gold "Buy, Sell, Trade New and Used" lettering, she catches the distinctive silhouette of the redhead, Melanie, walking decisively through the vinyl section. She's searching for Joe, obviously following his trajectory, which followed her own trajectory through the records to nab Gabi before running out the door. Which means, she only has moments before Melanie will also walk out that door.

"Sorry, we've got a dinner tonight, and then I've got to prepare for my presentation tomorrow."

"*Your* presentation?" Gabi says with shock as she swivels her head to Sarah. Sarah hits her with a hard stare before Gabi turns back to Joe. "*Her* presentation."

Sarah clocks the redheaded silhouette moving toward the exit. "And unfortunately, we're already late for the dinner. But it was so nice to see you," she says with a sincere nod of her head before grabbing Gabi and darting around the corner out of sight as the large black door to the bookshop swings open.

***

"Dad, what's going on? Why'd you run out like that?" Avery says as she steps outside.

Joe stares at the now empty corner Sarah just disappeared around. All the traffic and noise has returned, but it's drowned out by the noise in his head. She was there only moments ago, and now she's gone. Like a magic trick. There one moment, gone the next. Poof. Or maybe she was never really there at all.

"Dad?" Avery says again.

Joe stirs from his trance. "Sorry, honey. Just saw an old friend."

"Oh," Avery replies with mild interest. "Where'd they go?"

"Had to run," he says, pressing his lips together in resignation. As usual. Sarah always has to run.

Chapter Four

Camping (Age 12)

SARAH WATCHED HER MOM kick dirt on the fire as her dad tugged a tent pole from the ground. It had been a good trip. The fishing was boring and gross, but everything else was great. Lawn darts and cornhole. Campfire songs and stargazing. Hot dogs and smores. Hikes and animal watching. They'd seen six deer, including a mom and her baby! But even that wasn't the best part. The best part had been the stream. Or was it a brook?

They'd only successfully crossed it once, at the start of their trip when it wasn't flowing too fast, but it had raised quickly from just a light sprinkle while they were on the other side and they'd "barely made it back alive." At least, that's how Dad described it with a laugh to Mom when they returned, and Sarah liked to think it was true. It was a real adventure, even if they only got a tiny walk into the woods on the other side before they had to hunker down under a tree to wait out the brief shower.

It must have been raining upstream somewhere because the water line had continued to rise since then and they hadn't been able to cross again, but it became Sarah's favorite spot. Like the impossible crossing to another world where unimaginable wonders were waiting. The fact that it was really just another campsite on the other side didn't stop Sarah from imagining magical things. She decided the rain had been a warning to turn back before they roamed too far into the enchanted forest. Still, she went to the creek every day, twice a day, and sat there for hours imagining some mystical creature was going to walk out of the woods and up to the stream to change her life. A unicorn coming for a drink maybe. She knew she was supposed to be too old for unicorns, but was she ever really too old for unicorns? Or a fairy. Or a troll perhaps. Or a wizard! Or maybe a perfectly ordinary boy drawn to the waterside just like she was, both of them reaching the stream at the same moment, only to discover they've been charged with a wondrous journey and a noble mission. She was absolutely certain those woods across the way were full of magic she could not understand.

"Can I go back to the creek before we go?"

Her mom poured a bottle of water on the last of the glowing embers. "Have you packed up all your things?"

"Yes."

"Your clothes, your sleeping bag, the cornhole?"

"Yes," Sarah repeated impatiently.

"And you put it all in the car?"

"Yes, Mother!" She said it with a hint of irritation, but then eased off. That tone wouldn't do her any favors and she really needed to get to the stream now. She could feel it. This was her moment.

Her mother shot her a face that was half annoyance and half indulgence. "Why don't you pack up the snacks and camp chairs and put them in the car?"

"Mom!" Sarah begged with her most desperate plea, sure her fervor would turn the tide.

Sarah's father pulled the last pole from the tent and collapsed it. "Let her go. I can take care of that."

"This is supposed to be a family activity," her mother said with dismay.

"She's done her part," he replied before winking at Sarah. "Go on, run. But make it fast. We need to get on the road."

"Thanks, Daddy!" Sarah shouted as she ran for it.

"Ten minutes or less!" she heard her mother shout as she charged off. And two minutes later, she was at the stream. The water was the highest it had been. Far too high to cross as it rushed by. So high it could almost be a river. Had her little crick become a river overnight? Was that part of the magic? She stared at the water for a minute, dropping to dip her fingers in the cool flow. She reached down with both her hands and immersed them, then pulled her two hands full of water up to splash her face, baptizing herself in the mystical torrent she'd decided it was.

Part of her knew how silly this all was. She was getting too big for games like this. She never played these kinds of imagination games anymore at home. All of her friends acted like they'd outgrown them. But she quietly held onto the magic as long as she could. She knew it was slipping away day by day in her regular life. This might be the last time she'd ever get to play like this, and that sucked. But today, for a few more minutes, she had a magical river and a be-witched forest just across the way. The enchantment of the moment buzzed through her in a literal vibration, which slowly grew stronger and stronger. She felt it in every inch of her body.

Suddenly, something flickered in the distance. Her eyes darted to the spot where she thought she saw movement, but the cause had already moved on. Her eyes darted all around the woods. Could this be her unicorn? The hum and buzz in the air grew until she felt dizzy. She watched the woods awaiting the miracle. And then it came, dressed in a blue and white striped shirt. It was a boy.

So, maybe not a miracle. He looked like an ordinary enough boy – brown hair, on the tall side, about her age. But while he didn't appear to possess any special powers, there was something about him. He was cute for one thing. Not that she really cared about things like that. But she liked looking at him. He was staring down at a compass as he walked, but as he reached the stream, he stopped and looked up. He shielded his eyes a moment as if he couldn't see her from a glare, though she didn't know where the glare could be coming from with trees hanging heavy overhead on both sides of the water.

Slowly, the buzz in her head died down until the bubbling, rushing flow beneath her returned to her ears, and the boy lowered his hand at the same time. They stared at each other, seemingly both enchanted. Perhaps they were indeed destined for a great journey. But how could she start a great journey now when she was about to go home?

"Sarah," her mother called, right on cue.

Sarah and the boy continued to stare. He offered a sweet, shy smile, which she returned in-kind. Gosh, he really was cute. Slowly, she raised her hand to a stationary wave, and he did the same.

"Sarah, now!" her mom called.

"Come on, kiddo! We've got to get going," followed up her dad.

"Hi," Sarah said. And though she didn't say it loudly, she knew he could hear her somehow, even above the gushing torrent between them.

"Hi," he said back.

"Don't make me come get you!" her mother shouted from the distance.

Sarah looked back to the direction of her parents' voices and sighed. It was time to go. "Bye," she said to the boy with a resigned droop.

"Bye," he said as he slowly dropped his waving hand to his side.

So, she would have no great journeys after all. At least not today. But she got a bit of magic to take home with her. That was something.

****

Joe watched the girl walk away and felt something inside him tug after her. If there weren't a river in the way, he would have run after her. She was so pretty with rosy, round cheeks, her frizzy blond hair pulled into braids, and her sun-kissed summer skin. But there was something more than that. She shone like the sun, which was totally weird, but also totally cool. It made him want to stare at her forever. But that was never going to happen now because she was gone. The prettiest girl he'd ever seen was gone. And he didn't even know her name.

So far, their trip to Pittsburgh, where his parents were from – and where he himself had been born – had been pretty boring. Mostly visiting his parents' old friends who he didn't remember and staying with family who usually came to visit them. What was the point? But his parents had promised him they could go camping at the end as a reward for good behavior. Camping was one of his favorite activities and he'd been excited to explore a new spot. So, they'd borrowed his aunt and uncle's stuff and headed out to this little alcove by a stream his uncle recommended. Joe had been thrilled to arrive and strike out on his own to search out the wonders of an all-new wood. Now, he knew why.

He found a giant rock big enough for his bottom and dropped onto it to watch the water cascade downstream. He loitered as long as he could, hoping maybe she'd return, but she never did, and eventually he knew his parents would start to worry. He'd have to come back tomorrow and try again. He climbed off his rock and made his way back to camp where his dad was piling sticks to make a fire. "Find anything good out there?" his dad asked as he arranged the sticks.

"Yeah, a girl," Joe replied without an ounce of hesitation or self-consciousness.

Joe's mother climbed up the hill with a giant cooler and set it by the tent as his dad stopped what he was doing and looked at his son with a knowing smile. "A girl?" he said. "You don't say! What's her name?" His mom's head twitched toward her son with interest.

"I don't know. She had to leave," Joe grumbled as he flopped onto a camp chair.

Joe's dad leaned over to his son and mussed his hair affectionately. "Oh well," he said, "there will be lots of other girls."

"Not like this one," he said.

Joe's mom shot his dad an amused smile, which Joe caught, but he didn't care. So what if he's the butt of their jokes? He knew what he knew. "She was the most special girl in the world."

"Until the next one, sweetie," his mom said as she planted a quick, extremely unnecessary kiss on his cheek before his parents both giggled. Well, let them have a hearty laugh at his expense.

"You guys don't understand."

His dad sobered up and asked him softly, "What don't we understand, bud?"

Joe sat up straight in the chair, looked his dad in the eye, and nodded decisively. "I'm gonna marry that girl."

Chapter Five

Back to Normal

THE SIZZLE OF VEGETABLES in the pan fills the air as Joe tosses them around with a spatula. "Nate, could you get me the soy sauce and sesame oil?"

Avery leans on the kitchen island and watches her brother head to the cupboard. "Thanks for cooking, Dad."

"How could I deny you your favorite stir-fry on your birthday?" he says as he takes the oil from Nathan and splashes some in the pan. "But wait until you see the dessert I got."

"Avery doesn't eat dessert anymore. Didn't you hear?" Nathan says with a smirk. "After twenty-five years, she's finally realized she's a woman in L.A. She's surviving on a green salad, a carrot stick, and a breath mint a day."

"Shut up!" Avery says with a punch to his arm. "Just because I don't eat like a fifteen-year-old boy bulking up for the wrestling team."

Joe turns his back to the stove and grabs a swig from his beer. "Avery, please tell me your brother is full of shit and I don't need to worry about you."

"You don't need to worry. I eat plenty! He's just mad because I mocked him for eating a *whole pizza* last week when I wasn't hungry," Avery says before shooting her brother a dirty look. "Just for that, you're not getting any of my dessert. I'm eating yours." She sticks her tongue out at her brother, then redirects. "So, what are you working on these days, Dad?"

"I just got a new script I'm excited about, but I can't say too much yet."

"Not even to us?" Nathan says.

"Not even to you," Joe replies. Avery is usually a vault and Nathan would probably forget by tomorrow, but it's still too soon to talk about the Scorsese thing. "Right now, the big one is the Seattle Center film, which is about to start shooting on location."

"Right," Nathan says. "Are you in that one?"

"Just a cameo, which I'll shoot on the soundstage in London after I get back from Bora Bora and my well-earned break."

"Obviously, Bora Bora sounds amazing," Avery says. "But I'm surprised you're not going to Seattle. I remember how much you loved it there." Her voice sounds pointed and he notices her watching his response carefully, though for what, he has no idea.

He answers his daughter with a wordless shrug. He did love it, she's right. Enough to make a whole movie about it. Enough to ensure at least part of it would be filmed on location even though, since it's largely a period piece, most of it would be on the soundstage. But as the shoot drew closer, he decided that maybe he didn't need to be there after all. Or more accurately, maybe he needed *not* to be there. But that's not a conversation he needs to have with his kids.

Joe pulls down plates and hands them to Avery. She takes them to the table as Nathan pulls out silverware and they begin to set three places at the table like a well-oiled machine. Their family nights are a well-established tradition. Joe checks his rice and returns to his stirring as he says, "How was your mom?"

"Good," Avery says. "Still mom, per usual. Did you know she's been the top producing agent at her office for three months in a row?"

Joe nods with pride. "Good for her! She's really found her calling."

"Speaking of which, she said she showed you a house yesterday. What did you think?"

"Where?" Nathan asks as he grabs the napkins.

"Malibu," Joe answers. He thinks about the place with its high ceilings, great view, and perfect blend of Hollywood glam and coastal chill. And the incredible pool. "It was nice."

"Yes! Let's get a beach house," Nathan says.

Joe chuckles as he dishes up the food. "You planning to live with me forever?"

"If you get a beach house," Nathan replies proudly.

"If Dad gets a beach house, you could learn to surf," Avery offers as encouragement.

"Dad, I could surf!"

Joe places the serving bowls on the table and takes his seat between his kids. "You could surf. But I'm not sure it's the house for me."

"What are you talking about?" Nathan balks. "It's a beach house!"

"I think I might be more of a lake house guy."

"There are no lakes around here," Avery mumbles as she dumps veggies onto her rice.

Nathan mumbles back, "You can't surf on a lake."

Joe takes the stir-fry from Avery, scoops some onto the plate, then passes it to Nathan. "You like this house, right?"

"Sure, yeah," Nathan nods. "I mean, the price is right. For me, anyway."

Avery swallows, then turns her eagle-eyed gaze on her father. "This place is fine, but you've been renting for four years. This isn't a decade ago. You're a huge movie star now."

"And big-time producer," Nathan interrupts.

"Living in a rental house," Avery continues. "Isn't it time you settled on a place?"

"Your mom is always on the lookout."

Avery rolls her eyes. "It's been years. And you never like any of them."

Nathan nods. "Seriously, Dad, what's the hold up?"

It's a good question. Joe shuffles the veggies on his plate, then reaches for the soy sauce to stall. He can't tell the truth obviously. That's far too complicated, and under the circumstances, there's really no reason his kids ever need to know. He will probably need to make some decisions eventually, however. Avery's not wrong. It does seem odd, at least from the outside, that he's still renting this house. But there's no answer that will satisfy them in the moment. "Avery, tell us about NYU."

***

On Monday night, Sarah's not quite ready for the silence of her empty house after a weekend of constant company, so she heads to her home away from home at Gabi and Dana's. She trails like a puppy as Gabi carries her basket from the laundry room back to her bedroom. When they arrive, Gabi drops the basket on the bed and pulls out a sheet, handing the other end to Sarah as they shake it out. Dana emerges from the bathroom and grabs a tee-shirt from the basket to fold.

"Okay, go back," Dana says, "and start again. So, you didn't tell him about Ben?"

"Nah, that would have been too easy," Gabi says as she walks toward Sarah and matches their corners.

Dana hadn't been privy to the whole Joe show. Gabi witnessed every brutal plot twist from start to finish, but Sarah had only just met Dana when it was all going on originally. And even once Gabi and Dana got married, Gabi probably would have taken it to the grave if Sarah herself hadn't let it slip one drunken night after Ben's death. And so the whole story came tumbling out, and Dana carried it like a trooper, giving Sarah all the love and support a newly widowed, drunk woman needs when reminiscing about the dead husband whom she loved with all her heart – and about the very much alive, but never-to-be-seen-again love of her life. It was a testament to Sarah's trust that she let her biggest secret, and biggest joy, out to Dana, even drunk, but it was a story almost impossible to convey in the telling. So, Dana's still playing catch-up. "Did you consider it?" Dana says, running a hand through her newly cropped fire engine red hairdo before reaching for another top.

"No! What was I supposed to say? 'Oh, hi, Joe. Nice to see you. By the way, Ben's dead and I'm available if you still want me'?"

Gabi pulls out the fitted sheet and shakes it at her. "That would be a good start."

"Babe," Dana says with a pointed look at Gabi and a gentle shake of her head. Dana lost her first wife a year before Sarah met her, and she went through much the same journey as Sarah, just a few years earlier. She has seen Sarah through some of her toughest moments. Gabi is Sarah's oldest friend, and she loves her like a devoted, straight-talking sister, but sometimes Dana instinctively gets things in a way that only personal experience can teach.

"Have you ever had a normal conversation in your life?" Sarah says to Gabi as she takes the edge of the next sheet.

"When were you and Joe ever normal?" Gabi shoots back. Well, she's right there. She and Joe were always the farthest thing from normal imaginable.

"*Were* being the operative word," Sarah says. "Besides, I'm not really sure I am available. I'm not there yet." It seems strange to be saying this nine whole months after her first post-Ben date. She'd thought she was ready then, and Nick was a great guy. He'd been kind to her in the aftermath of Ben's death, and he was patient and sweet when they began dating. But when she looks back now, it's clear it was never going to last. It had only been a little over a year at that point and she must have been crazy to think she could do it. She faked it pretty well for a while, and she did have some much-needed fun, but it was more the company than the specific man that attracted her. And eventually, she knew she had to get back to herself.

"It takes time," Dana says. "Grief isn't a straight line."

"Fine. Okay, I'm sorry. But she dated Nick for six months," Gabi protests.

"Dated. It was never serious. And as soon as it got serious, I bailed." Gabi stares at Sarah like she's got a third eye or an extra nose, awaiting a more credible response, but it's Dana who chimes in.

"Sometimes we try things and find out we're not ready." Dana says the words softly as she presses her hand to Sarah's arm in a comforting squeeze. "And that's okay."

Not one to be left out of the lovefest, Gabi drops the socks she was pairing and steps in to hug Sarah. "I'm sorry, hon. It's just hard to see you walking away from Joe when I know what he meant to you." She stops, looks to Dana who nudges her with a nod before she adds, "But I get it. You need to take the time you need, and I support you in that."

When Gabi releases her, Sarah plops flat on the bed and thinks. She considers Gabi's words, and what happened with Nick. Admittedly, she might have felt different if she'd been dating Joe instead of Nick. It's possible that not getting serious was more about the guy in question than about her readiness. Maybe Nick just wasn't right for her. Sure, he was sweet and easy to talk to. He was handsome in a nerdy, middle-aged way she really dug, and was pretty good in bed, too. Honestly, he ticked all the boxes on paper. Yet she hadn't been able to commit to him. When he said, *Sarah, I think I'm falling in love with you,* she said, *Nope.* Well, not in so many words, but that was the gist. Just like that, it was over. And it wasn't even a little bit his fault.

No, she was right in the first place. The problem was her.

She wasn't ready then, she's not ready now, and she's certainly not ready for Joe. "Besides, however ready I may or may not be, Joe is still married. Remember?"

***

The next morning, Sarah kicks her foot nervously against Pilar's desk as she awaits her boss's return. Waiting to discuss the job opportunity of her dreams, to be in charge of the whole Seattle arts scene, feels like waiting for an audience with the Dalai Lama. Thrilling and terrifying at the same time, with the potential to change her life forever. The room is vibrating at an ultra-high frequency, like the lights are dancing, the computer keyboards are singing, and any second now, every piece of glass in the office will shatter into tiny shards. Or maybe it's just Sarah's nerves electrifying the air. Probably that's it.

This is the first chance she's had to talk with Pilar since she returned, and terror and exhilaration tussle for supremacy in her chest. Pilar marches in and closes the door behind her with a quick apology for being waylaid near the printer. She drops a copy of the position description in front of Sarah. "This will be posted online by Friday, but here's a hard copy for your reference. Start getting your materials ready."

"I have some time, though, right?" Sarah says as the skims the first page. No one can ever fill Pilar's five-inch stilettos, but the chance to become the Arts Czar for all of Seattle is a delectable temptation if she can summon the guts to try.

"Not as much as you think," Pilar says. "They're willing to open it to the public if necessary, but they'd prefer someone with direct city experience."

"An internal hire?"

"They're going to start with an internal search and only open it up if they don't find who they want. You need to make sure they don't get that far." Sarah nods as she processes the news that everything might change much faster than she imagined. "Now listen," Pilar adds, "you've got my vote. I'll pull for you, but I'm on my way out and they're not going to let me wave a wand and pick my successor. The city is required to do a fulsome search, and you're going to have to prove yourself."

"Of course," Sarah says. Her hand flies to the ring at her neck, her fidget focus, and she twists absentmindedly as she leans back in a concerted effort to appear relaxed and under control. "Any suggestions?"

"As a matter of fact, yes. They want someone with city experience, which you obviously have from running the film commission. Check. Leadership experience, good with customers both internal and external. Check and check." Pilar twists her bracelet as she speaks. "And they want someone who can make the city look good." She pauses dramatically in a way that rattles Sarah.

Sarah glances down at her vintage-style plaid vest and matching bell bottom slacks. She was proud of this outfit when she put it on this morning. She thought she looked cool. "Is there something wrong with how I'm dressed or..."

"No, no, nothing like that. Listen, they also want someone with a Masters, which you've got, but in the wrong discipline, and they prefer someone with a PhD."

"That I don't have."

Pilar regards her seriously. "Which is why you need to shine even brighter where you can. So, I have an assignment for you."

Sarah's eyes dart around the office as if everyone is listening in on her secret mission. No one is even looking, let alone listening through the glass walls. "Okay. What is it?"

Pilar taps on her computer, opens a file, then swings her monitor to show Sarah. "You know Monica's about to go on maternity leave. Hunter will be filling in for her, but let's face it, he's one step above an intern. And that film starts shooting soon. I think you should step in for Monica and act as our liaison to the shoot."

Sarah leans in towards Pilar's monitor to read the treatment for a film with the working title "Seattle Dreams." "Sure, I'm happy to. But isn't that just a ceremonial welcome gig?"

"Not this one. It's a big film. Haven't you looked at the brief?"

Sarah sighs. She meant to get to it last week, but got so caught up getting ready for her trip to L.A., and fretting over the meeting with Joe that surely would never happen – and then did happen – that she never got to it.

"It's a huge budget, huge stars. Milo Penn is starring." Jesus, Milo Penn? They don't get much bigger than him at the moment. Ever since his dystopian teen saga and 60s popstar biopic blew up the same year, you can hardly find a movie he's not in. "Terry Blanchard," Pilar adds.

"Really?" Sarah says in amazement. Terry Blanchard, damn!

"And Kelsey Cartright," Pilar says.

Ugh. Well, you can't win them all. Kelsey Cartright may be the large breasted, up-and-coming toast of young Hollywood, but something about her rubs Sarah the wrong way. "Well, yeah, that's a huge cast."

"And they're going to be on location in Seattle for three weeks. All over the city. It's a big, high-profile moment for the city. The mayor wants everything to be perfect."

"Okay?" Sarah says. She tries to hide her hesitation, but she really doesn't understand what this means for her.

"They're going to need a lot of hand-holding. You'll need to check in every day. Anything they need, you make sure it's handled."

"But don't they have producers for that?" Sarah remembers when she worked on Joe's indie movie all those years ago. "Jazzman's Blues" was a tiny production, and they still had producers to troubleshoot. Usually. Except when Sarah herself had to step in and save the day, but that was a fluke. Okay, a couple of flukes. She happened to be in the right place at the right time and got lucky. But that was then and this is now, and this production dwarfs that little indie by several city blocks. There are people whose entire job is to make sure things run smoothly all day every day. People besides Sarah, surely. "I mean, Pilar, I have a full-time job to do. How am I supposed to do this on top of everything else?"

Pilar taps her desk for emphasis. "Sarah, this is your chance. The decision-makers want someone who reflects well on Seattle. Who can stand in the spotlight and shine. You do this, and you do it well, and they will notice."

Sarah does a mental run-through of her long to-do list. Adding this, which is at least a couple hours a day, maybe half a day – well, the math isn't mathing as the kids like to say. She's already been working herself silly the last couple of years. Ben's death had turned her into a bit of a workaholic. At first, it was just an escape from the pain, but eventually, she realized that she was trying to prove something to Ben. That she was okay. That she could handle it. That he didn't need to worry about her. It was an unfortunate habit, but one she hadn't quite figured out how to shake. And now she was supposed to add still more to her plate? "It's not that I don't appreciate the opportunity," she finally says. "I just don't think I have enough time in the day."

"Learn to delegate," Pilar says firmly.

Not the warm, fuzzy response Sarah was hoping for. But warm, fuzzy probably doesn't get jobs. "Can I think about it?"

"Of course," Pilar says. "But if you want the job, this is how you get it."

***

When the elevator doors open to the lobby, she's greeted by the smiling face of her ex Nick. Of course, she's not sure he's really an ex. How long do you have to date someone to call them an ex? But she attempts to position her hug right in the safe zone of true, trusted friends who she's definitely not trying to rekindle anything with.

"Hey, stranger," he says. "I'm surprised to see you anywhere but glued to your desk. I thought you never left before 7 PM."

"Yoga," she says. "But I'll be back online as soon as it's done, rest assured. You?"

"Taste of Seattle meeting."

"Yum." They make a minute of polite conversation before they both excuse themselves for their respective commitments and Sarah makes her way toward her car. Why is it so easy to talk to Nick without guilt or hesitation, yet she could barely manage ten words to Joe without combusting? After all, she'd slept with Nick just a few months ago, while her relationship with Joe was the better part of a decade in the past. Then again, her memories of Joe have a way of getting all timey-wimey and immutable at the same time. She barely remembers what she had for lunch, but she remembers every night of her time with Joe like it's her favorite movie on replay. A

Joe movie, obviously. Maybe that's why she's been talking to Ben nonstop since she saw Joe in L.A. Guilt is a powerful motivator.

As she climbs into her car, she forces herself to shift from Joe to the job. There are pressing matters at hand. She starts her car, but sits idling as she rolls her ring on its chain. "What should I do, Ben? I wish you were here to talk it through."

Ben would want her to go for the job. Even if it means working more for a while. "It's not forever," he would say. "Short term pain for long term gain," he would say. "You can do anything you put your mind to," he would say. It would make him so proud. It *will* make him proud if she gets it. Getting this job would be proof absolute that she's okay, better than all the twelve-hour days combined. And nobody thinks the twelve-hour days are actually good anyway. It's just been easier than going home to an empty house most nights.

Perhaps if she's smart, if she listens to Pilar and delegates, she could do this without adding hours to her days. Skip out on her monthly and weekly appearances at all the chamber and 4Culture meetings, send Louise in her stead to the cross-community liaison meetings, and pull out of the current grant selection committee. Maybe take a few weeks off from yoga. She could easily recoup seven to ten hours a week. It might actually be manageable, if she plans well. And, of course, if she doesn't do it, she can kiss the promotion goodbye.

She stares into the mid-distance and gives her ring one last spin. "You'd tell me to go for it, wouldn't you?" She nods as if listening to the voice in her head, sighs, then pulls out.

***

Joe turns his back to the golf cart buzzing past his window and pours himself a glass of water as his two o'clock cadre marches in right on time. His small bungalow of offices on the lot came with his five-picture deal, and it's great to be on the lot, but he's never really gotten used to the constant whirlwind of executives, writers, actors, and assistants. It's not so bad when he's shooting. That's the creative community he loves. But when he's writing, or planning, or just trying to think, the chaos is, well, chaotic. And it seems to have seeped inside him lately. Nothing feels easy anymore. Or even fun most of the time. He never could have imagined feeling this way when he was just starting out. Acting, making movies, that was all he ever wanted. Yet now, the joyful moments are so brief, and regularly eclipsed by the frustrations and irritations. It used to be fun, didn't it?

Randy walks in, shuts the door, and grabs a chair by the wall to listen. That's Joe's signal to begin. Joe takes his seat at the table and makes eye contact with each person individually, his way of making sure they feel seen and welcome. "Thanks for coming, everyone. We have a lot to cover," he says. "I want to talk about the New York project. Marty's interested, so that's in motion. And we need to check-in on Seattle."

"About that," Naomi says, followed by a heavy pause. "A couple things. First, they've added two scenes for you."

Joe purses his lips. "I'm just doing a cameo."

"Well, they want you to do a bigger cameo now. Beltran says you're too valuable to waste on a single scene. He wants to 'maximize his Parker time.' His words, not mine."

Joe sighs and rubs his temple. He's been excited about this film. He's the one who found the story of how Seattle Center was built for the World's Fair and developed it from the start. It would be his love letter to Seattle, and well, all the city represents to him. *Who* it represents to him. He'd wanted to write it himself, but he didn't have time, so he handed it over to his team, but he still loves the project. From a safe distance anyway. "Well, as long as it can wait until I'm back. Bora Bora waits for no man."

"That's the other thing," Naomi says as she brushes her black bob behind her ears. "The studio is pulling me and sending me to London for the untitled Glen Powell vehicle."

"They can't do that!" Joe protests.

"They can and they have. They've exercised their privilege of riches on a poor producer, and I'm leaving tomorrow, which means I can't be onsite in Seattle when the shoot starts."

"Then who are we sending to Seattle?"

"I was thinking you maybe?" Naomi studies him with a brow raised even higher than her normal Botoxed elevation.

"Not me. I've got my trip. And my scene is on the soundstage, not on location."

"They've moved your existing scene on location in Seattle, along with the two new ones."

Joe is fighting hard to maintain his composure, but his irritation is pushing hard for a place at the table. Yes, this definitely used to be fun. Those were the days. "Why is nobody talking to me about these decisions?"

"I'm talking to you right now," Naomi says.

Joe gulps his water to buy himself time. There's a reason he wasn't going to be on-set in Seattle. A reason he chose to take his first vacation in three years while the Seattle film was shooting. And that reason wasn't because he didn't like Seattle. And yet, that reason had just walked back into his life, hadn't she? Of course, then she'd walked right back out again. "So, they want me in Seattle?"

"Yes."

"For the whole shoot?"

"You know how far Beltran went over on his last film. They want someone there to keep him in line."

"Someone else can keep him in line," Joe grumbles.

"They don't trust anyone else." Naomi's eyes dart to the others at the table, then she looks pointedly at Joe. "Joe, they're serious about this. If you don't do it, I think they'll pull the plug."

"Fuck," Joe says under his breath. He gazes up at the three giant movie posters on his wall from three of his biggest movies so far. His eyes linger on the poster for "Jazzman's Blues," the first movie he made in Seattle. The movie that Sarah worked on, which changed his life in more ways than one. Seattle was certainly lucky for him once. Joe mumbles to himself, "Apparently, Bora Bora does wait."

"Sorry, what?" Naomi says.

"Fine," Joe says after expelling a slow, careful breath. "I'll go."

***

Joe and Randy climb out of the golf cart and walk into the commissary. "I really could have brought you something, you know," Randy says as he steps behind Joe in the line.

"I know," Joe says. "But I needed to get out of the office." They eye the menu as they work their way through the line and Joe sizes up the guy in front of him who is dressed as an Old West saloon bartender. "Working on the Costner film?" he says to the man.

"Nah. Jordan Peele's thing."

"Really? Jordan Peele's doing a western? Guess I haven't been paying much attention."

The guy leans in conspiratorially and lowers his voice. "Well, not exactly. But..." He stops speaking and mimes zipping his lips shut. "You understand." Joe nods that he does indeed understand before the guy adds, "By the way, if you've got anything going, I'll be free next week."

Joe laughs. "I'll let you know." He appreciates a bit of good, old-fashioned hustle. It's been a long time since he felt that. He and Randy order, and as they wait, he watches the western barkeep take a spot across from an old-timey banker who already has a giant napkin tucked into his costume to protect it while he eats. Joe should eat in the commissary more often. The vibes are immaculate. It reminds him why he got into the business in the first place. For the fun and fantasy of it all. Before it all became PR and fake smiles in front of the camera – and endless meetings and headaches behind-the-scenes. There's no doubt about it. Joe is burned out.

They find seats at the end of a table and Randy jumps back to the topic at hand. "So, we're heading to Seattle?"

Joe takes a bite of spaghetti. "Are you up for it?"

"Yeah, I loved Seattle last time we were there."

"That's right. That was our first movie together," Joe says with an appreciative smile.

Randy sips his Perrier. "Back when I was a lowly production assistant PA instead of a lowly personal assistant PA."

"You're not remotely lowly," Joe says. "And you know I have a spot for you on the producing team any time you're ready to take it."

"I know," Randy says. "But I'm not quite sure I'm ready to jump into the fray again." Randy's previous venture into producing had ended in a catastrophic bomb, and when the powers-that-be needed a fall guy, Randy got burned. Low man on the totem pole and all. Joe can't blame him for being gun shy now.

"Fair enough," Joe says through a mouthful of garlic bread. They pause to watch a pair of gladiators in full armor clang noisily past them. Their swords sway in their sheaths and knock several innocent bystanders on their way out. "Damn, I love this place."

"It's good, right?" Randy takes a bite of his chicken, chews patiently, then continues. "You love Seattle, too, though. Right? That's why we're doing the film. I thought you'd be excited to go back."

"I am." Joe shrugs. "I guess. I mean, I do love it. It's just…" Joe trails off seeking a word that doesn't reveal every ounce of the dread, desperation, and glorious anticipation currently swamping his thoughts of returning to Seattle. "Complicated," he finally says. "I have a lot to figure out." He hopes Randy will take this as a reference to his trip and personal plans.

Randy stares at him a moment too long, then says, "I'll take care of everything. I'll cancel what I can, reschedule what I need to. You don't have to worry about anything but learning your lines."

"For three scenes? I think I can manage it," Joe laughs. "So, you're looking forward to it, then?"

"Yeah," Randy says before his face pops with excitement. "Oh, I should call Sarah!"

Joe chokes on his spaghetti and coughs his food back onto his plate. Randy jumps up as if he might need to give the Heimlich, but Joe calms himself and reaches for a drink of water. "Sarah?" Joe says when he's finally calmed both his throat spasm and his inner churning. "Sarah who?" Surely, Randy can't mean *his* Sarah.

"Sarah Abbott. From 'Jazzman's Blues'? Remember, she was the other on-set PA with me?"

Joe takes another swig of his water. Of course, Randy knew Sarah. Why hadn't he thought about that? They'd worked together. They'd even gone to karaoke together. "Right. Of course. I didn't realize you'd stayed in touch."

"We did. For a while. We had a group text for several years, anyway. Eventually, we lost touch. It's been a couple years now. But it would be great to see her again."

"Yeah," Joe agrees with a smile tighter than his constricting chest. "That would be great."

Chapter Six

Resistance

Sarah paces frantically back and forth in the small, brightly lit room, ignoring the tasteful brown leather couch in favor of wearing out the carpet. Her therapist watches wearily, then asks, "Did something happen?"

Sarah doesn't stop moving. "I have a lot on my mind. This job, you know? It's a big deal."

"It is a big deal," Libby agrees. "But you got promoted a couple years ago and you weren't nearly as agitated that time. Do you feel like you're not ready for it?"

Sarah stops and looks at Libby. "What? No. That's not it," she says before the pacing resumes. "I just don't know how I'm going to manage this whole extra job on top of my regular work if I agree."

"Do you have to do it?" Libby asks.

"Only if I want the promotion."

"Okay, so we can talk about that. Make a plan. And is that all that's bothering you?"

Sarah's mind flashes to Joe yet again. He's run on that endless loop since she saw him. She used to be able to turn the loop off and only summon it occasionally when she most wanted it. Now she can't stop it, like a haunted television that keeps playing even after she's yanked the plug out of the wall. Everything that was beautiful and perfect – and impossible – replaying like an endless rerun. Which has seared her with so much guilt she's been talking more and more to Ben. Every night since she got home from Los Angeles, in fact. She hasn't been like that since the early days. But now she swings like a pendulum almost hourly from dead Ben to impossible Joe back to dead Ben. "Nope, just the job," she says.

Libby watches Sarah pace a few more seconds. "Sarah," she says calmly. "Please sit down."

Sarah stops and stares at the floor before finally, reluctantly taking a seat. "Sorry," she says. "I don't know what's gotten into me tonight." Except she knows exactly what's gotten into her. Why can't she say it? She told Libby about Joe a long time ago. Why can't she say it now? Is she afraid to speak it into existence? Sarah stares at the wall for a solid minute, her frantic energy draining away into nothingness, and Libby lets her. Libby's never one to push. She prefers to let Sarah bring things up when she's ready. Finally, she says, "I've been talking to Ben a lot lately. Every night."

"Is it helping?"

"I think so. At least, it seems like it in the moment."

"Then good. Sarah, you've come a long way over the last couple of years since Ben died, and you're doing so well. But we've talked about this before. Grief is nonlinear. Sometimes when it feels like you're almost on the other side, your resistance will pull you back one more time. Setbacks are part of the process." She stops and waits for Sarah to acknowledge the well-worn truth they've come back to repeatedly. "If talking to Ben is every night is helping for now, then talk to him. There's nothing wrong with that."

Sarah shrugs. "I guess."

"What might be helpful to explore, however, is why you feel the need to talk to Ben so much these days." Libby watches Sarah studiously avoid eye contact before speaking. "It feels like something's off tonight." Sarah turns her head slowly to face Libby who adds, "Is there something going on, more than the job, that we should be talking about?"

Sarah looks down at her body, her arms now pulled around her legs, folded in like a catatonic armadillo. She releases her legs and spins them around to lower her feet to the floor. "Sorry."

Libby smiles kindly and says, "What haven't you told me?"

Sarah clasps her talisman of Ben at her neck and slides her finger into the ring. It's an awkward gesture at that angle, and of course, the ring won't go all the way down with the chain in the way, but she slides it up and down the finger it once lived on anyway. Finally, she forces herself to say it. "I saw Joe in Los Angeles."

"Joe? You mean the illicit-love-affair-that-changed-your-life-and-saved-your-marriage Joe?"

"That's the one," Sarah says.

Libby sets her pen down on her pad and removes her glasses. "Maybe we should start from the beginning."

***

Joe leans back in his chair and kicks his feet up onto his desk. His long legs protrude out over the corner of the desk and he adjusts himself until he's comfortable. He stares at the "Jazzman's Blues" poster and thinks of Sarah. He'll be back in Seattle. And Sarah will be there. And Randy will be in touch with her. And they'll be a hair's breadth away from each other. It's not a stretch to imagine they could cross paths. There are a million ways it could happen, even without trying. Hell, if Fate is playing the game he thinks She is, then running into Sarah is a sure thing. He doesn't even have to lift a finger.

Not that he wouldn't. He'd lift a mountain for her if she was free. But she chose to go back to her husband and he can't really argue with that. She said she was happy when he saw her. She looked happy. Well, actually, she looked deeply panicked, but in a happy way, he thought. And beautiful. Her face had a couple more lines. Her blond curls were a little less wild. Her curves were every bit as delicious.

He can feel her right now. The way she felt in his arms. Beneath him in the bed. Wrapped around him while they slept. Holding his hand. God, he loved just holding her hand. The softness of surrender as her hand folded into his, the certainty that no two hands ever fit together more perfectly. It was fucking glorious.

He snags the baseball from the stand on his desk and tosses it in the air. The ball is signed by Shohei Ohtani and should be under glass, but Joe likes handling it. He plays catch with himself until his phone pings with a text from Avery. *I met a woman.*

Congratulations, Joe types back with a smile. *I hope she makes you happy.*

Not for me, dummy. For you.

Avery...

Dad, you'll love her.

Joe places the ball back on its stand and rubs his face before typing, *Not interested.*

I met her at the salon while getting my highlights.

Here we go. Yet another attempt to convince him someone else, anyone else, could actually fill his Sarah-shaped hole. That settling for any other woman, no matter how beautiful or accomplished or kind she may be, is possible when you've met your actual soulmate. It doesn't matter if he can't be with her. That's not the point. That kind of connection can't just be written over by a pretty face and good conversation. Not that he hasn't tried, but in his heart, he's known since he first laid eyes on her.

Of course, he can't say as much to Avery without admitting what happened. Without copping to the biggest shame of his life, despite the fact that he could never regret it. But telling Avery would break her heart. So, his devoted daughter keeps trying. He types back, *A hairdresser?*

***

Avery begins to type her response, then stops. It's too complicated. Instead, she clicks over to her phone and calls her father. "A hairdresser?" he repeats as he answers.

"There's nothing wrong with a hairdresser," she says.

"Of course not," he says. His voice is sincere. Her father is not a snob. The farthest thing from it. But he is a stubborn, old mule. He goes on, "But what would I have in common with someone who spends their days making other people look good?"

She fights her frustration with her dad and searches for her angle in. "Don't you always enjoy chatting with your hair and make-up people?"

"Sure, but that's different," Joe says. "They're creative, and in the business."

"She's creative and in the business." she says. "Who do you think her clients are? Industry people." She's not letting him get away so easily this time. Val is gorgeous, smart, the right age, and single. He'd be stupid not to at least meet her. "And she owns the salon, Dad. She's more than a hairdresser, she's a businesswoman. And trust me, this is a very nice salon. She has two locations, including the one in Beverly Hills." Her father sighs, but says nothing, so Avery continues. "Why are you always saying no? You haven't given any woman more than a second date since the divorce. What's the problem?"

She scribbles a floral doodle on the envelope in front of her while she waits for Joe to finish his annoyingly dramatic pause. "Ave, I'm just not in the market. It's as simple as that."

"But why? Do you want to get back with Mom? Because that would be great!" She already knows the answer to this question. She long ago accepted that her parents' divorce was both real and permanent. But it had fairly well sliced and diced her life for a long time, so some small, unrealistic, wildly optimistic part of her still clings to the dream of a reunion that she can't help floating now and then.

"No," he says too quickly. "Your mother and I are never getting back together. We're much better as friends."

Standard reply. But it was worth a shot. "Then why not meet Val? She's terrific."

"I'm not interested."

He'll be alone forever if she lets him get away with this shit. She expands her doodle into a complex latticework at the top corner of a building she begins to sketch. "How do you know if you haven't met her?"

"I know what I want."

She rolls her eyes. This again. "And what do you want?" she asks as she scratches hashmarks into the corners of her building for shadows.

"What I want is not in your power to obtain," her father says pointedly.

Well, that's definitive. He's wrong, of course, but he sure is certain about his wrongness. "So cryptic," she mumbles as she draws in an ornate window.

"What can I say?" he says. "Your dad is a cypher."

***

It's Wednesday at 7:40. The computer screen glows bright white at Sarah as she mouses over the email. "Open after I'm gone." Ben's final request and she can't do it. Well, open it, yes, but not to click the damn link. She lets the mouse float over the link in her little, ritualistic dance that allows her to pretend for up to sixty seconds at a time that she might click it this time. Like maybe she's healed enough. Maybe she's ready. Then she clicks away and closes the computer. There's always next week.

She makes herself a cup of Sleepy Time tea, then climbs the stairs to her bedroom. Since she's been talking to Ben nightly, she's moved his picture upstairs. It reeks of regression in her mind, but Libby says it's okay, and she needs him right now. She takes a sip of her tea and sets it down on the coaster. She stares at Ben a moment, then pulls the photo to her chest and flops flat on the bed. She holds the frame close and stares at the ceiling. She waits until the words come. They always come eventually.

"How are you doing tonight, Ben?" she says after a few minutes. "I hope you're okay. I'm... okay. I guess. My brain is running about ten miles a minute lately. I know that's not exactly new, but I'd gotten better, you know. But now I can't stop. I'm like a merry-go-round with no off button."

Libby suggested in her kind, gentle way that perhaps Sarah's need to talk to Ben was related to having seen Joe. Sarah had laughed. As much as she's always appreciated Libby's guidance, this was never a tough case to crack. Sarah's known from the start exactly what's going on. Pure, unadulterated guilt. And she didn't really even do anything. Not this time anyway.

Libby also suggested that maybe she should come clean to Ben. It couldn't hurt, could it? At least, no more than whatever this nightly torture session does. She stares at the ceiling awhile, deciding what more, if anything, she wants to say. Deciding if she has the courage to say the words tonight. She takes a deep breath, then releases it in a sigh.

"I saw Joe..."

There, she's done it.

"I think that's what I've been afraid to tell you. Why I keep talking. I keep trying to find the courage to tell you.... Do you know who Joe is? I think you do... I'm afraid you do. But it was nothing, I swear. Just ran into him. It wasn't, like, planned or anything. And I'm not seeing him again. You don't have to worry about that. He is definitely in the past.... Of course, so are you, but that's different."

She smiles sadly, then rushes to add the reassurance, "You're always with me, you know."

Never mind that Joe is also always with her. She doesn't need to mention that part.

"Anyway, I guess I thought you should know. And also, I love you."

Her message delivered, Sarah takes a beat, then lifts the frame from her chest and gazes again at Ben's face. That lovely, warm face. She sets him by the bedside and goes to brush her teeth, leaving the tea nearly untouched.

Chapter Seven

Fate's Way or the Highway

Joe slams the trunk closed on his rental car and climbs into the front seat. His stomach lurches with an unexpected bolt of nervous energy - the uneasy see-saw of Seattle. He presses the Start button and listens to the quiet hum of the engine. "Seattle, I'm back, you gorgeous beast," he says with determined bravado before moving the car into drive. He pauses before hitting the gas, allowing the uncertainty to gain ground against him. "Maybe let's try to get it right this time?"

Once he's on the road, he lets his mind wander. He thinks a bit about the film, who he needs to check in with when he arrives, what his schedule holds. But he's had nonstop meetings about the production for days now, so he mostly wanders backwards in time, to the Seattle of the past. Sarah's Seattle. To the city he saw through her eyes. And to Sarah herself. Not that she is ever far from his thoughts.

As the city skyline comes into view, he flips on the radio in time to hear the end of a Sam Smith song as the deejay intones, "93.7. Old, new, and just for you! Now here's an oldie, but a goodie from our favorite local rock star. It's Brandi Carlile with 'Right on Time.'"

The mournful opening notes play and Joe laughs. "Of course." The song that started it all. The dance. The kiss. The everything that came after. He turns it up and sings for all he's worth.

Sometimes he hates how he still feels so much for her, even after all these years. He knows it doesn't make sense to be holding on after so much time. To imagine a future with her when she chose to go back to her husband whom she loved. Good for her. It was the right thing to do.

Just as it was the right thing for him to go back to Melanie and the kids. And he really tried with Mel when he went back. He gave it his best again for the first time in a long time, and she responded. They were softer with each other, more patient. They talked more, and not just talked, they actually communicated for the first time in years. Ironically, it was by being kinder and more present that they were finally able to admit to each other that it was over. Sure, eventually they divorced, but it was years later and they did it on their own terms – because it was time. Like Sarah had wanted. He had to choose it for himself, not for her. Sarah couldn't be the reason. That's what she'd said – and she was right.

And he knows Sarah has been happy. The couple times they texted in the early aftermath, she said as much, reassured him they'd made the right decision. She was truly happy. That was all he ever really wanted. Yet, he couldn't let her go. Not then, not now. No, maybe it doesn't make sense, but when did anything about them ever make sense?

He'd been blown away from the start when she told him what she'd found on Wikipedia, that they'd been born the same day in the same city. That was an already an extraordinary connection, yet it was more than that. Eventually, they'd discovered they were born in the same hospital, no less. How could he ever ignore such an astonishing coincidence? Two babies born the same day in the same hospital, sharing their first night together in the same nursery, finding each other and falling in love decades later? It was like something out of a movie.

Then he'd seen her that New Year's Eve in college. He knew it was her, even when he had no idea who she was. He'd taken one look at the blonde girl by the streetlight at midnight and felt the pull of deep familiarity before she'd been yanked away by her friend. He hadn't technically known her then, of course, but when Sarah told him she'd gone to Pitt, which is right next to Carnegie Mellon where he went, it hit him like a lightning bolt. She was the girl he never forgot.

And then there was the museum in Asheville. The blonde woman sitting in front of the painting called "Destiny," the woman who looked exactly like Sarah, both on the canvas and sitting before it. Not *like her*. It was her. He just knew it. Sure, that sighting had never been confirmed anywhere but in his imagination, but technically, neither had the New Year's Eve sighting, and he had absolutely no doubt about either one. Their lives had been intertwined from the start, intersecting again and again. Tethered, as she'd called it. Soulmates.

And yet, somehow, he was supposed to just move on. He glances down at the tattoo on his left forearm, the one he got for her. A boy crow and a girl crow holding a golden cord that twists and turns around a globe, keeping them connected. Always connected. No matter how far, no matter what happens. He's come to think of them as always never meant to be. Always tethered, but never able to be together. Not really. Still, she's always with him, tattooed on his heart as clearly as the ink on his skin. His Sarah.

The song ends, and instead of waiting through the commercials for the next song, he switches off the radio. He wants to sit in the quiet magic of Brandi Carlile and the feelings that song always wrings from his heart. The memories continue to swirl and Joe decides to let them. He's fought it long enough. Tonight, he might just set up camp in his memories and roast some marshmallows because he's not going anywhere for the time being. It's becoming increasingly clear that he's exactly where he's meant to be.

Joe's always believed in Fate and Destiny. He knew the truth about Sarah from the first moment he saw her on that street corner. Despite how it ended, they'd been destined to meet the first time. They healed each other. They went back to their lives better – *because* of their time together. And now, with all these freaking signs piling up one on top of another, it's damn hard not to believe something amazing is brewing again. As if maybe they get a second chance. But what's he going to do? March up to Sarah and steal her away from her husband?

No, for all the signs blazing in neon along this road, he's not going to make the turn on his own. Losing her last time hurt too much. It may have been the right thing to walk away at the time, but he can't do it again. He'll wait. He'll trust in Fate wherever She takes him. If Sarah really is his destiny – and she goddamn better be – then Fate will bring them together again. Right?

***

Sarah stands in the Chihuly garden and marvels at the purple glass spirals shooting into the air like tropical flowers. All around her, plant life and glass flora are woven together into a fantasyland almost as fanciful as an "Avatar" movie, and considerably less dangerous. She's attended a lot of events at this museum. Probably a dozen receptions or more since she's been with Seattle Arts. It's a go-to location for artsy folks and the perfect spot for the "Seattle Dreams" launch party. The film is, after all, about the building of the Seattle Center where this museum now stands. And besides, every room and every vista summons inspiration. But right now, Sarah's not looking for inspiration. She just wants to enjoy a glass of wine and the quiet before the storm. Tonight, it all begins.

Nick sneaks up on her and gives a gentle "Boo" from behind. She figured he'd be there with the mayor's team tonight and she's happy to have a friend at hand. She turns and gives him a hug, the wine softening the edges of her usual awkwardness with him.

"Nick," she says warmly as she wraps her free hand around him. "How are you doing?"

"Oh, you know, another day, another major infrastructure emergency." He laughs and scans her up and down. "You look incredible!" he says with enough heat to warm her blood.

Sarah has made a decision. Tonight, she will tell Pilar she's going for the job and will serve as the liaison to the film. And since, as director of the film commission, she's been tapped to make the welcome speech this evening, she decided she should amp up her star power. Hence the deep-cut black dress taking full advantage of her generous cleavage, and the sexy zipper all the way up her back. It clings to her every curve, of which she has many, and she remains self-conscious when she shows it all off like this. But she's embraced the width of her waist, the thickness of her thighs, and the not insubstantial curve of her bottom, and she's learned not to hide it. Still, now she's here with the Hollywood folks, she's remembering how narrowly defined their beauty standards are. And although their relationship ended months ago, Nick's appreciation is the confidence boost she needs.

"How about you?" he asks.

"Good, yeah. Some big things on the horizon, I think. I hope."

Nick surveys the garden for spies, then leans in. "Really? Do tell."

It occurs to Sarah, too late, that as a member of the mayor's team, Nick might actually be a part of the selection process, which could complicate things enormously. Can she still talk to him about it? Would he have to recuse himself? In any case, she should probably tell her boss first. Fortunately, Pilar is approaching. "I'd love to tell, but can we pick this up after my speech?"

Nick spots her and nods. He cheek kisses hello with Pilar, then wanders off to schmooze, leaving the women alone. Sarah's insides roil perilously, her body vibrating in a way that's disorienting and weirdly familiar, but she chalks it up to her nerves. This is a huge moment. She gives the broadest, most confident smile she can summon and says, "Good news."

***

The way the kid's face lights up when Joe steps out of his car at the Space Needle valet station gives Joe pause. Maybe he should have gotten a driver after all. Fewer direct interactions that way. He normally prefers driving himself, but he forgets he's not the same more-or-less anonymous dude he was the last time he shot in Seattle. And this isn't L.A. where you can't throw a stick without a celebrity's dog running after it. In L.A., valets don't even blink when you pull up. But not here. Here, they may be used to bigwigs in fancy clothes, but celebrities are a thrilling novelty. Especially ones as big as Joseph Robert Parker.

He makes the short walk to the Chihuly museum where the welcome event is being held. He stops on his way in at a rack of Seattle activities brochures and spots a flyer from the Seattle Art Museum promoting their current special exhibition. And the painting on the cover of the flyer? "Destiny" by Trenton Freed, the very painting he'd seen Sarah sitting in front of in Asheville all those years ago. "Fuck," he mumbles quietly under his breath. He shoves the flyer in his pocket and heads for the check-in.

They've shut the whole place down for the private event, so he's set loose to roam freely and find his way to the reception. He's immediately dazzled in the very first room by a stunning ceiling of bright colors and organic shapes, which evokes a glowing undersea wonderland, despite the incongruent location overhead. And that's only the beginning. One room evokes a magical forest of glass, another a convoy of lost boats full of wild glass shapes, escaped from a circus perhaps, on a pristine, black sea of glass. There are extraordinary chandeliers and spectacular bowls and so many fabulous colors, both natural and unnatural in form, that Joe's brain runs out of adjectives as he wanders. He's never seen anything like it.

Until he remembers he has. Well, not quite like this, but suddenly he's flashing back to his very first morning with Sarah when she showed him the gorgeous glass art at a souvenir shop and told him about Chihuly's connection to Seattle. And then they took the

Monorail to the Seattle Center and came out right next to this very building. He remembers it like it was yesterday. How is it all roads always lead back to Sarah?

Joe finds his way to the large, glass atrium where the reception is being held. The party is already in full swing and bubbling with activity, so he grabs some food from the buffet, and joins a group of cast and crew chatting near the band. Terry Blanchard's there, looking dapper as always, and he reaches out for a jovial handshake and pat on the back. This is their second movie together and he can't wait to see what Terry will do with the role.

Within seconds, Kelsey Cartright pops up and grabs Joe for an overly familiar hug. She's got her breasts on bold display and she angles them directly at Joe as she speaks. "It's so great to see you, Joe! Isn't this exciting?" she says as she tosses her long brunette locks over her shoulder and shoves her boobs out a bit further. Joe's not a great fan of Kelsey's, but she's hot right now and is expected to bring eyes to the project, so Joes greets her warmly, and they all fall into the usual Hollywood small talk.

Joe peruses the room looking for their leading man, Milo Penn, but he's nowhere in sight. Instead, his eyes land on Randy, who sidles discreetly up to him. "We have a problem. Well, it's not that big of a problem, but Milo's not going to make it."

"Why not?" Joe asks.

"His flight got delayed."

Joe is still happy enough to fly commercial, but he knows that's not Milo's style. "How does a private flight get delayed?" Joe counters.

Randy winces. "Well, he got to the plane and discovered he was almost out of his protein whey gummies. Apparently, he pops them like Pez."

Joe sighs and repeats, "His protein whey gummies?"

Randy goes on. "So, he sent his people to get them."

"We could have gotten them here, had them waiting for him."

"And that would have been quicker," Randy agrees, "but he said he couldn't fly without them. So, get this, he sent two people to get them, one to a store and one to his house, to see who could get them faster. Except by the time either of them tried to come back, it was rush hour. And you know L.A. at rush hour."

"Thirty minutes turns into two hours."

"Every time," Randy says with a disenchanted nod.

The band stops playing just as Joe turns back to the others and there's a quiet tap at a microphone on the podium. A young fellow in all black taps again, gives the thumbs up to someone at the back of the room, and then steps away from the podium. Thirty seconds later, he's watching her glow as she steps into the spotlight where she belongs.

Sarah slinks up to the podium in a skintight black dress that hypnotizes Joe. Okay, she probably doesn't actually slink. She walks normally, like a woman with a mission actually, but somehow Joe takes her in like a slow-motion sexpot scene. Her golden waves perfectly styled. Her lips red and tempting. And dear God, those breasts! She's nothing short of stunning. And she's right there.

Fate never misses.

***

Sarah clears her throat and begins, her voice confident and strong. She's done this a million times. She's got this. She welcomes everyone and talks about how pleased she is, on behalf of the City of Seattle, to host such an esteemed group of talented artists in her beautiful city. "I may be biased," she says, "But I think Seattle is pretty special and it's always a great pleasure to show it off to the world."

She goes on to introduce a handful of key players who wave from the audience, then shares a few interesting snippets about Seattle's vibrant cultural community. She's killing it. She even gambles on a couple jokes and the whole room laughs. Not polite, courtesy chuckles, but big, unfettered belly laughs that say, "This woman's got it! She is a leader. She could be an Arts Czar, for sure!" At least, this is what Sarah thinks as she rounds the corner into her final remarks.

Then her eyes fall on the incredibly tall, dark-headed figure at the back of the room. She stutters. He's in shadow and it takes her eyes a moment to focus on him, but once they do, her stomach jumps. Her stutter peters out to momentary silence as she stares, followed by uncomfortable hems and haws. Her mouth turns to sand. A couple people in the audience glance backwards, though they don't know what they're looking for. Sarah vaguely notices Randy standing at Joe's side, sees him looking first at her, then to Joe, whose mouth is hanging open.

Sarah recovers herself, swallows a couple times to get her juices going again, and quickly presses on. She finishes with as much flourish as she can manage under the circumstances as she hands the podium off to the film's director, Matt Beltran. She stands at the side of the podium waiting for the remarks to end. Nick eases up to her and wraps her in a hug. She's not sure if it's intended as congratulations or commiserations. How much did she just fuck up? But she gratefully receives the embrace, and then they stand arm-in-arm listening to the remainder of the director's comments.

***

Not one word of Beltran's speech penetrates because the blood in Joe's ears drowns everything out as he stares at Sarah, and the man who is holding her. The man with his arm wrapped cozily, comfortably around Sarah's waist. And she's got her own arm just as comfortably around him. Fuck. That must be her husband Ben.

Sarah glances back at Joe and for a moment, and they lock eyes. Her mouth drops open as if to say something from all the way across the room, but then she darts her eyes away and refocuses on the stage. With her free hand, she snags a glass of wine off a passing tray and gulps it. She laughs when everyone else laughs, putting on a good show of normalcy, though Joe can tell she hasn't really heard what was said any more than he has.

When Beltran finishes, everyone applauds and conversations begin to bubble up anew around the room. Sarah talks to Beltran at the front and smiles graciously. Playing host. His eyes are glued to her, but slowly he becomes aware of Randy's gaze at his side. Randy hasn't said anything yet, but he's definitely looking at Joe. Finally, Randy speaks. "God, she looks great, doesn't she?"

Joe shakes himself out of it and pivots to Randy. "Sorry, who?"

"Sarah," Randy says as if it's the most natural observation in the world.

"Sarah?" Joe says with genuine surprise before taking a new tack. He can hardly blurt out their secret after all this time, especially to someone who actually knows Sarah, someone who knew them both while it was going on. Joe may be free now, but he wasn't then, and Sarah still isn't. So, he plays dumb instead. "Oh, is that... was that Sarah from 'Jazzman's Blues'?" He says the title with too much emphasis to play as well as he hoped. If only he had another take to get the line reading right.

Randy smiles and says too carefully for Joe's comfort, "Yeah... that was Sarah."

"Huh," Joe says. "How about that. It's been so long, I barely recognized her." He attempts an innocent and perfectly normal, not-at-all-in-love-with-the-woman-in-question chuckle.

Randy smirks. "Yeah, how about that." Randy hesitates a moment, looks at Sarah and then back to Joe. "Why don't I go fetch her so we can both say hello?"

Oh, no, that's not going to work. Joe is not ready to actually talk to Sarah. Not when Sarah's husband is right here in the room with her. Joe will still talk to her. He must. But he needs a minute to regroup because Fate has just gotten a whole lot messier. "You go ahead. I need to make a quick call. Catch up later."

Randy nods slowly, then wanders off, leaving Joe to regroup the fuck out of this thing.

***

After a joyful reunion with Randy and promises to text and get lunch scheduled in the next day or two, Sarah grabs another chardonnay and heads for a quiet spot in the garden. She should have recognized that vibration the moment she felt it, but she'd chalked it up to nerves. She chugs the wine in one determined go and contemplates her options. Joe being here was not part of the plan. She hadn't seen his name in the cast list, apparently because he's only making a secret, unannounced cameo. Randy said he's producing, too, so he would have been on the producers list, but she hadn't bothered to review that. It never occurred to her she'd know any of them. It never occurred to her one of them would be the long lost and recently found love of her life.

Libby had reassured her it was okay to have feelings about Joe. That it was normal and healthy for those feelings to flare up after seeing him, given the way it had ended so definitively back then. They'd had closure, but none of the small markers or quiet ceremonies that normally signify and cement a separation. No coming by to pick up their things. No forwarding mail or passing on messages. No arguing over custody of the kids or the dog. No relapse sex and final goodbye. No divorce papers to sign. Nothing but their brains to tell them it was really over. Forever.

Which naturally led to the lingering sense that it wasn't over. Not really.

Libby said Sarah should allow herself to experience whatever came, accept it, and pay attention to what it could teach her. But right now, all the unholy knot in her stomach is teaching her is that she should have eaten something before she downed her fourth glass of wine thirty seconds ago. She's a lightweight in the best of times, and with Joe Parker right inside, she's skewing way more topsy turvy than she'd hoped to be tonight. This was her night to shine. Now the prospect looms that she's on the cusp of losing whatever's left in her belly.

"You did a great job in there." His deep grumble of a voice comes from behind. That voice. Oof!

"Thanks," she says, inhaling deeply for the courage to turn around. "Wasn't my best moment, but I guess I managed."

"I don't know," Joe says, "You were pretty dazzling to me."

Sarah sighs and smiles at him. "Hi, Joe."

"Hi, Sarah." He returns her smile, then holds out his arms in invitation. She accepts as she steps to him and they sink immediately back into the world that is always only their own. When she pulls back, Joe immediately jumps into safe, catching-up mode. "So, you're director of the film commission now? That's great!"

"Yeah," she says with an embarrassed shrug. "It's been a couple years, but I'm going for another promotion now, so we'll see." Joe beams with automatic pride, but before he can say anything else, she shifts the topic to him, eager to avoid her own messy life. Her stomach can't take too many more feelings at the moment. "And you're producing this film. I didn't realize."

"Yeah, it's kind of a passion project actually. I didn't expect to be here, though. Naomi – you remember Naomi? – she was supposed to be onsite, but she got pulled off to another project and I ended up here."

"You didn't text or let me know."

"I wasn't sure if I should, after last time."

The bookstore. She'd acted like a blooming idiot at that store. But what else was she supposed to do when his wife was only seconds away. "Sorry if I was a complete idiot that day."

Joe emits a gentle smirk. "Just the right amount of idiot."

The gentle ribbing sends her emotions tumbling with her stomach. "Well," Sarah says, "that's great." Except she says it like it's very much not great. Like it might be the worst news she's had all year. And it might be, if her gut is any indicator. It's sloshing angrily, as if in protest of the torment she's currently shouldering like a hair shirt.

"Listen, Sarah. I know this is a big work night for you." Joe pauses to line his words up just so. "And I know you're not here alone." Sarah glances inside at Pilar and Nick and wonders who he means. "But there's something I should tell you. I want to tell you."

Dizziness overtakes her, like her brain is shutting down, like her whole body is shutting down.

"And I don't want you to feel any pressure from this..."

The world narrows almost to a pinpoint as Sarah raises her hand to her stomach. This is too much. Too much pressure, too many feelings, too much wine. This night started off so well, but now she's seriously unwell. Sweat beads at her temples.

"But I do think you should know... And you may know already, but..." Joe pauses to take in Sarah's rapidly flushing face. "Are you okay? Maybe you should sit down?"

He walks her to a nearby bench and sits her gently down. He stands above her and places a hand on her hair in comfort. "I'm here."

She gazes up at him gratefully, warm from the heat in her cheeks as she takes in the tiny, new crow's feet that surround his beautiful blue eyes. Then she falls forward and vomits on his shoes.

Nick is the first to spy the scene from inside and he comes running out with Pilar on his heels. "Sarah, are you alright?" Nick says with a quick glance at Joe before he returns his attention to Sarah.

Pilar kneels at Sarah's side, but Sarah just mumbles, "His shoes" in a quiet cry. Pilar jumps up and runs for napkins.

Joe reassures her, "It's okay. It's okay. Don't worry about the shoes." But Pilar is already gone.

"Come on, let's get you home." Nick lifts her from the bench and wraps his arm around her shoulder. "Sorry about that, Mr. Parker," he says as he hastens Sarah away.

Chapter Eight

Ignorance Is Bliss

Low-key Mexican music hums in the background as Sarah scoots her seat in at the vegan taco restaurant that sits along the water past the Montlake Cut. Randy is eyeing her suspiciously before she even takes a drink of water.

"So, what's with you and Joe?" Randy says without hesitation.

Sarah spews a literal spit take of her water and coughs for a solid thirty seconds before wiping herself with her napkin and signaling the waiter for another one. This was not how she envisioned this conversation. She and Randy had gossiped endlessly when they were PAs together on "Jazzman's Blues," but she'd studiously avoided the topic of herself back then. Randy would talk about guys he'd hooked up with and Sarah would occasionally mention Ben when not mentioning him would be too weird, but she basically listened as much as possible. She never wanted the focus to turn to her in such a way that she'd have to lie about herself and Joe. She didn't want to lie to Randy then, and she doesn't want to lie to him now. But she also doesn't want to put Joe on blast for what happened. She can take it if she must. After all, she's a widow now. Whatever pain she caused is long in the past, but it's not fair to sully Joe's reputation, or his marriage – least of all with someone who works so closely with him.

When Sarah has regained her composure and apologized, she hopes the topic has floated away with her coughed out germs, but Randy is not so easily distracted. "So, Joe?" he says.

"What do you mean? Joe Parker?" she says. "I didn't even know he'd be there last night." Absolutely true. "I haven't even seen him since the last movie." Almost true. "Nothing's up with Joe." Not remotely true.

"Come on, you guys hooked up, right?" Randy asks. He's not going down without a fight.

Sarah musters her most aghast face. "What? No... What?" So smooth.

"I'm not stupid, Sarah."

"I honestly don't know what you could be talking about." Bold-faced lie. "I don't know what you think you saw, but you clearly got the wrong end of the stick." Now she's pushing it. "I barely remember that shoot." Biggest lie ever told?

"I'm not talking about the 'Jazzman's Blues' shoot. I didn't notice anything back then. But I didn't know Joe then like I do now. I'm talking about last night."

"Last night...," Sarah says. "You consider vomit a romantic gesture, do you?"

"Vomit, no," Randy says. "But the way he looked at you? Fuck yeah."

"What? When?"

"While you were speaking. He couldn't take his eyes off you. But not like he was listening, more like he was overwriting the speech with the swelling violins of Rachmaninov. He practically swooned."

Sarah tries to imagine Joe swooning. All six foot, three of his lean, sturdy, muscular swimmer's body. He was always Sarah's rock, the strong one, the one with the courage to do the hard thing. He wasn't weak. Gentle, loving, earnest, yes. Weak, no. He wasn't a swooner.

"I know Joe really well and I know what I saw. And I saw your face, too, by the way."

Sarah chafes at the observation. It's bad enough to know that she's so transparent to the people who know her, but worse than that, the obviousness of her emotions feels like yet another direct betrayal of Ben. Her persistence of feelings for Joe was never in doubt. She knew she'd carry him with her forever, but she had a responsibility to her husband to put him first. She loved Ben deeply. Was it different from her love for Joe? Of course, but she chose to make a life with Ben, a good life. The least she could do was push her lingering devotion to the man she'd never see again into the deepest, quiet crevice of her heart.

And she thought she'd done that successfully. Admittedly, she'd set Google alerts for Joe's name when they first parted. It made it easy to track the progress of his film from auction to release. It almost felt like she was still in his life. But after about six months, she realized she was relying on them too much. To fully embrace Ben and find their way back to true happiness, she needed to let Joe go all the way. Well, she would still go to his movies and watch his shows, of course. But the Google alerts had to go.

She felt proud of how definitively she'd closed that door after that. Tightly enough that no one but Gabi and Dana would ever know. And Libby, of course. But all three were sworn to secrecy, two by the best friend code and one by professional ethics, so she thought she was safe. Yet here's Randy sitting across from her telling her in no uncertain terms that she basically stood at a podium under a spotlight and put that lingering devotion on display for the whole world to see. At least to anyone close enough to see the signs.

Sarah drops her head in a flash of silent prayer for guidance. Libby said the truth would set her free, so Sarah takes a deep breath and jumps in. Besides, he apparently already knows anyway. "Okay, fine. We had something. But it was over when the shoot ended and we both went back to our lives to live happily ever after. And you can't tell his wife, please. It was a long time ago and I don't want to fuck things up for him. That's the last thing I would want. You know as well as I do, he's a genuinely good man. He doesn't deserve that." Sarah sips her water to soothe her suddenly bone-dry throat at revealing her long kept secret to someone who actually knows Joe. It is perhaps a sign of progress that she's willing to come out of the shadows herself, but the reality is her truth puts Joe at risk.

Randy drops back against his seat and begins to laugh. Sarah's stomach clenches. There's nothing remotely funny about this, yet his quiet chuckle at first grows into a full-blown guffaw, which he must actively suppress to speak. Finally, he says, "You know, don't you? That Joe's divorced?"

The words clasp hands and do a ring-around-the-rosie in her brain. Joe's divorced. Joe's divorced. Sorry, did he say Joe's divorced? "I... what? How? I thought..."

"They split a few years ago. It was in all the celebrity news at the time. I assumed you'd seen it."

Sarah had most assuredly not seen it. She'd pointedly stayed away from celebrity gossip after deleting her alerts in a concerted effort to erect a firewall around her life with Ben. She kept an eye on new movie releases, but movie star divorces definitely weren't part of her algorithm. She'd even asked Gabi and Dana not to tell her if they happened to see anything, though the chances of that were virtually nonexistent. They couldn't care less about Hollywood actors. Dana loved movies, but was too busy to pay attention to celeb lives off-screen. And Gabi didn't even know who Joe was when Sarah first met him.

"So, Joe is..." Sarah stops. She can barely manage to think the words, let alone say them out loud. And processing what they actually mean? That's at least a week's work. A month maybe. A year is not out of the question. But for now, she forces herself to say them anyway. "Joe is single?"

Randy tilts his head thoughtfully. "I mean, you wouldn't know it to see how he turns down every woman who so much as shoots a sideways glance at him. But something tells me you might have more luck."

Sarah's lungs expand too fast. Her heart drums out her anxiety and she begins to hyperventilate. When she can't catch her breath, Randy jumps up, then kneels at her side and takes her hands. The waiter comes by to take their orders and Randy shoots him a "not now" face before calmly saying to Sarah, "Hey, it's okay. Nice and slow. We're fine. We're just sitting here having a pleasant lunch on the water." Sarah's breathing begins to slow and she meets Randy's eyes. "Nice and slow," he says again. "Easy. Slow breaths. We're fine. Yeah?"

She's still locked on him, but her heartbeat has dropped from her ears back to her heart, which she takes as a good sign. She nods at Randy. "I'm okay. Sorry."

"No worries," he says as he moves back to his seat. "But that was a lot, hon. It seems like you might have some feelings about this."

"Gee, ya think?" she says aloud. She should have kept that in her head, but her boundaries are erasing themselves faster than she can erect them.

"So, what about you then? Still happily married? Or happily divorced?"

Sarah steadies her breathing and prepares to say the words she always hates saying. She knows Ben's gone. She's come to terms with it. Mostly. It's no longer the cataclysmic, world-slicing, sob-inducing admission it once was. The pain of saying it out loud after two years has dulled to a quiet thud, like dropping a small stone on her foot. It's a sharp, momentary jab of pain followed by a quiet ache for a few minutes, but it's tolerable. "Third option," she says. "Widowed."

This leads to the usual flurry of horror, belated sadness, and sincere, but tongue-tied condolences, followed by the inevitable, "So, how are you doing now?" and "Gosh, you're so brave." Sarah doesn't feel brave. She doesn't really feel weak anymore, but she does feel like a more-or-less typical mess of a human being who's just carrying on day after day the best she can under a set of shit-heap circumstances she wouldn't wish on anyone. If that's their definition of bravery, so be it. She prefers to think of it as survival. She survives better some days than others, but she never thinks of her basic continuation to draw breath on the daily as bravery.

"Listen," Sarah says. "I need to ask you not to tell Joe about this."

"About you being a merry widow?"

"I know it's a lot to ask, but I need time. I'm still grieving, you know?" Randy nods and Sarah continues, "And I'm not really sure how to process whatever this is with Joe."

"So, there *is* a 'this' with Joe?" he asks.

"I don't know. I just know I need time," she responds. Yes, *so very brave.*

Randy stares intently at Sarah for a moment and purses his lips before answering. "Okay, listen, I don't like it. I don't like hiding things from Joe. I don't lie to him."

"Okay..."

"But I can *not* mention it for now. You were my friend first and it's your news to share, not mine. So I'll keep my mouth shut – as long as you promise you'll tell him at some point." Sarah sags appreciatively, finally ready to relax, until Randy goes on. "On one condition."

Sarah's heart picks up speed again. "What's the condition?"

"Carlos is coming up this weekend and I want you to meet him," he says.

"Ahh, amazing!" Sarah giggles with relief.

"Come to dinner with us."

Sarah grins broadly, her previous anxiety in the rear view at last. "I'd love to!"

***

The moment Sarah closes her car door, she texts Gabi. *Joe's divorced.*

Girl, comes Gabi's quick reply. Followed by, *The skies opened and the angels wept with joy.*

Sarah chuckles because how can she not? Gabi always comes out with the craziest shit. But this is serious. *It's not that simple.*

Gabi types briefly, then her response appears. *Why not? You're single, now he's single. Go smash that man with your sweet, sweet love and mighty yoga thighs.*

I don't even know if he's still interested. It's a copout of an answer. Gabi will call her on it, but she's learned if she doesn't give voice to her tiny sparks of doubt, they can occasionally turn into infernos. So, she hits send anyway.

Yes, you do, Gabi snaps back. Sarah can practically hear Gabi's eye roll in the response. *So what's the real problem?*

Sarah takes a deep breath, then taps her answer. *Ben.* It's the one thing Gabi can't argue with. At least not over text.

You better come over tonight. We'll order Thai.

***

Dana walks in with three beers, handing one each to Gabi and Sarah before sitting on the arm of the sofa behind Gabi and taking a swig. "Food should be here in twenty."

Gabi squeezes Dana's knee and says, "I was just telling Sarah about our travel debate."

"Sarah, you agree with me, right? A vacation should be a time to rest and do nothing," says Dana.

"Doing nothing does sound nice," Sarah agrees.

"But you want to have some fun, too!" Gabi says. "A little adventure. A little danger."

Sarah winces. "I don't know about danger, but adventure sounds good."

"We have this argument every year," Dana sighs. "Anyway, we have more important things to talk about. This Joe situation."

"It is a situation," Gabi says leaning back against Dana. She sips her beer, then says, "So, let's get into it. You dated Nick for six months and that was fine. It didn't work out, but you tried. But you can't even try with Joe. Is that where we are?"

"That's not exactly what I said. Only..." Sarah trails off and Gabi and Dana lean in like it's a ghost story just before the jump scare.

"What?" both women say together.

"With Nick, there was never the possibility of it being real. He's a sweet guy, but the spark was never there. At least not for me." Sarah shakes her head as she clarifies the complications swirling around her head. "There was no real danger with him. But with Joe—"

"It could be real," Dana says.

"It *is* real," Gabi says.

Sarah nods sadly, then adds, "And I never cheated on Ben with Nick. So, there's that."

"Ahhh, right." Dana sips again and contemplates the stickiness of the situation. "The cheating part."

Sarah sighs and flops back. There are way too many layers to this cake. Grief. Cheating. Guilt. Desire. Obligation. A terrible recipe, the sweetness of desire far outweighed by the sourness and acidity of the other ingredients. And yet, somehow she keeps eating at it, day after day. Or allowing it to eat at her. A carnivorous cake? Sarah laughs at the notion. Sounds like some bizarre, anime-inspired horror movie.

Dana draws her attention back. "Honey, it's okay to need time. Give yourself as much grace and time as you need." She smiles kindly at Sarah who receives the smile like a burst of sunshine that warms her through. "There's no right answer, you know?"

"And no wrong answer either," Gabi quickly adds.

"Gabi..." Dana says with a gentle warning and a firm hand to Gabi's shoulder.

"No, I'm saying, take care of yourself first. And we'll support you no matter what you need. But baby, don't forget, I saw it all firsthand. I know how you felt about Joe."

"Seven years ago," Sarah says. As if time could dampen Eternity in any way.

"You and I both know the truth. And you can choose to walk away and that's one hundred percent okay. We'll support you whatever you decide. But it's not wrong to choose love. It's never wrong to choose love." At this, she looks up at Dana and they quietly beam at each other. Dana had been the first woman Gabi was even attracted to, and now they're happily married and perfect together in a way that just doesn't happen every day. All because Gabi had the courage to say yes.

Sarah tries to take in the truth of Gabi's words, but her resistance is still working overtime. "The truth is, I feel like I'm betraying Ben every time I even think of Joe. And yet, I think of Joe all the time."

"Okay, so it's messy. But you don't have to decide anything right now. Just take care of yourself, that's enough," Gabi says.

"This is about you first," Dana adds. "Not Joe and not even Ben. You."

"Absolutely," Gabi agrees. "But when you're ready... Sarah, this is Joe we're talking about here. Do you really want to say *never* to Joe?"

Sarah doesn't have an answer. How can she say no to Joe? Not that he's even offered anything, technically, but he's Joe and he's free, and as soon as he knows she's free, the clock will start ticking. She'll have to make a decision. A decision she's definitely not ready to make.

Fortunately, they're right. She doesn't have to decide anything tonight, and there's blessed relief in that knowledge. Unfortunately, that glorious relief only lasts about thirty seconds until another thought rudely bulldozes into her frontal cortex. "Oh fuck!" she says.

"What's wrong?" Gabi asks.

"I just realized, Randy asked me out Saturday night. He's having a little dinner party with his visiting husband."

Dana makes a weepy face. "Sweet."

"Except, he works for Joe," Sarah says. "They're good friends. Joe's almost certainly going to be there." Her blood drains from her face and rushes to her fingers and toes, perhaps protecting her from the bitter cold of the realization. "I'm going have dinner with Joe on Saturday night." Her brain pops and whirs with the unsettling knowledge that the clock may already be ticking. And weirdly, she's no more ready to make a decision than she was sixty seconds ago. This has disaster written all over it.

"You need a buffer," Gabi says with a decisive nod before taking a self-congratulatory drink.

"Someone to help keep Joe at bay," Dana adds. "I like it."

Gabi smiles proudly. "Ask Randy if you can bring a guest. I'm sure he'll say yes."

"Then one of you will come with me?" Sarah flickers between them hopefully.

"You want the funky, cool realtor or the badass homeless shelter director?" Dana says with a riffle of her fingers through her funky, cool cherry red hair.

Gabi shakes her head. "We don't make sense. You can't roll up with a bestie. Like, why?" She pauses, sips, then smiles. "You know who you should take? Nick. He works for the city, so it even kind of makes sense."

"He was at the party, after all," Dana adds. "And he took you home that night when you were sick. It will just look like a date."

Gabi is getting excited now. "You might even make Joe jealous!"

"I do not want to make Joe jealous," Sarah says.

"Okay, fine," Gabi relents. "But he's still a good buffer. You can't be expected to talk about anything heavy if you're there with a date."

"But if I bring Nick..." Sarah can't bring herself to finish the sentence, but her meaning is clear enough. If she brings Nick, then where is Ben? Her secret will be officially out and the protective barrier that the mere idea of a living husband has provided will be stripped away. Joe will know the truth.

Gabi frowns sympathetically at Sarah. Gabi always understands. "One way or another, you're going to have to tell him about Ben," she says. She leans forward and takes Sarah's hand for support. "You don't want to hide that from him forever. Do you?"

* * *

Joe sits in his director's chair under a small canopy that protects him from the bright Seattle summer sun. He sips his Caffè Americano and watches the crew set up for the next shot. The first AD Geena talks into a walkie, then leans into the cinematographer Jeff's ear to be heard over the noise. Joe should be doing something, but he's already checked in everywhere and no one needs him for a damn thing right now. He had three phone meetings this morning and he just got off the phone with Naomi in London where they're wrapping up her shoot for the day. At the moment, he's feeling a bit "surplus to needs" as the Brits say. Why is he here again?

Then he catches sight of her, and suddenly, he remembers exactly why he's here. By the perimeter of their shooting location, Sarah pushes through a group of eager spectators to the security guy monitoring the rope. She shows him her pass and he lets her through with a disinterested nod. She pauses once she's on the inside of the rope to collect herself and runs her fingers through her hair as if she's assuming a role for her visit to set. Or simply a consummate professional making sure she's presentable for the task at hand. Judging from her face, probably a little of both.

Joe watches Sarah practically tiptoe onto set. She's been given permission to come and go as needed, yet she's clearly still finding her sea legs. Trying to figure out how to help without stepping on anyone's toes. Of course, once upon a time, she'd been part of a set like this. Well, not quite like this. "Jazzman's Blues" was Lilliputian compared to the scale of this monster, most of which will be filmed on a soundstage after the location shoot ends, but Sarah certainly knew what to do back then. Still, she's in a different role now, and Joe watches her lean forward and back like a racehorse waiting for her moment to burst through the gate as soon as Geena and Jeff stop talking. Sarah has clearly learned one of the most important lessons in the movie world. Timing is everything.

When they finally break apart, Sarah jumps in with greetings. They chat and Joe presumes Sarah's asking if they need anything. Geena holds up a finger in a "just a minute" gesture and Sarah responds with a smile and a nod. Geena runs off, and since Jeff has already redirected elsewhere, Sarah is left standing alone. She places her hand on her gut, her brow furrows, and she inspects her surroundings with a quick scan. Her eyes land on Joe and he smiles.

He hops up to meet her as she comes his way, her expression growing more sheepish with each step. "Hey," she says. "I want to apologize about the other night. I'm so sorry. About me. About your shoes."

"The shoes couldn't matter less," he says. "But how are you? Are you feeling better?"

"Much. I fear I consumed a little too much liquid courage that night." Her face goes pale like she's reliving the whole thing. "But I drank a bunch of water when I got home and I barely felt it by the next morning. Plus, I think the…" she waves her hand in a half-circle from her mouth out, miming the vomiting incident without having to face the horror of the words. "I think getting it out did most of the work. But I really am so sorry."

Joe can't wait another moment. He has to tell Sarah the truth. It won't change anything, and he refuses to be the guy who chases another man's woman. They made their choices once before and he's obliged to assume Sarah's going to stick with her decision unless she tells him otherwise. Of course, she partly made the decision for him, so she wouldn't come between Joe and his kids. She understood from the beginning how much his kids meant to him. But she also said she loved Ben and promised she'd be happy with him, and judging from their few communications, she'd kept her promise. Joe isn't about to fuck that up. No matter what he wants, he would never willingly disrupt her joy. If she's happy, he's happy *for* her. Period.

But Fate still brought him directly to Sarah. Fate has intervened again and again and made damn sure Joe didn't miss his chance to tell her how he feels. Or, at least to tell her that he's free. She already knows the rest. Neither of them left in any doubt about their feelings. But he was taken back then, and now he's not, and he needs her to know that. He won't even consider making another move if she's happy, but he at least wants everything on the table. Let her do with the info what she will.

"Sarah, I need to tell you something. It's something you may already know, but just in case, I—"

"You're divorced," she says without letting him finish.

"You knew," he says. His heart breaks a little more than it should because somehow he'd been assuming she didn't know. He thought when she found out, she'd throw herself into his arms and swear to be his forevermore. It was a silly fantasy, and one he hadn't really admitted even to himself until this very instant. But she already knows, and she doesn't appear to be throwing herself into his arms yet.

"I just found out, actually. Randy told me."

"Ah." Joe breathes a sigh of relief. If she just found out, well, that still leaves some wiggle room on the throwing herself into his arms thing. She could still be processing.

Sarah taps at her chest below her neck a few times, then clutches what must be the pendant on a necklace he hadn't noticed before speaking. "Actually, I have something to tell you, too." He recognizes the tapping for what it is, one of Sarah's coping mechanisms for her anxiety. And if she's feeling anxious, then whatever she's going to say has some heft behind it. *If* she says it, of course. Sarah has a longstanding habit of running from her feelings until she can't run anymore. But he's here and he's ready to listen. He tilts his head inquisitively and gives her his best "open and receptive" face. He marks the terror in her eyes as she opens her mouth to continue, but before she can speak, she's interrupted.

"Sarah!" Geena calls from her perch by the camera rig. She's found the director Beltran and she waves Sarah over. "We have a permit question."

"Oh," Sarah says. "I guess duty calls." She casts a forlorn glance his way, a glance weighted with the unspoken words.

"I guess so," Joe says with a sad shrug. "But that thing you were going to tell me?" He really needs her to finish. Whatever it is, it's important. If she needs to tell him, he needs to hear it.

Sarah regards the directors, awaiting her patiently. "Sorry, I better go do this. I'll talk to you later, okay?" And she's off. Per usual.

***

Sarah nearly collides with Nick on the way into the building. Apparently, he's been in meetings with the arts team to discuss the hiring process and how the city's team will be involved in the process. He tips his head forward and gives her a pointed look. "A birdie tells me you might be in the mix," he says.

Sarah scratches her neck and checks her environs before answering. "Yeah, I think so. Are you on the selection committee?"

"Undetermined at this time."

"So, would you have to recuse yourself from discussion of me or…?"

Nick holds open the door for another incoming person, then returns to Sarah. "I don't think so. Since we're looking internally, it's presumed we'll all know the candidates, so I don't think our past will matter. Not many folks know about it anyway, and it's all squarely in the past, right?" The question hangs there like half-deflated balloon, too heavy to fly away, but without the courtesy to drop to the ground where it can be crushed and thrown out forever.

Sarah squints an apologetic smile and nods. "I think so," she says in a tone that is far more definitive than the words themselves.

Nick nods amiably past a slight hint of bashfulness. "Well, there you go then."

"Actually," Sarah says. The timing couldn't be worse really, after Nick's trial balloon of an inquiry, but she has no choice. The dinner is tomorrow. She can't really wait.

"Actually?" Nick says with an intrigued smirk.

"I was wondering if you could do me a favor." Sarah shoves her hair nervously behind her ears and summons her courage, then says it. "Would you be my date tomorrow night? Or really, my fake date tomorrow night?"

"Fake date? Like in all those books you like to read?" He lights up with a mischievous grin. "Don't the fake daters always end up falling in love?" He moves in teasingly close and brushes her arm flirtatiously.

"In books, yes." She steps backwards and laughs. Two more people come into the building, so they step together over to the wall before she continues. "But this is definitely not *that kind* of fake date."

Nick is chastened, but not hurt. "Then what's going on? Are you trying to make someone jealous?"

"No, definitely not. The opposite. I just need to be taken for a night or two."

"Well, why didn't you say so? That I can do." He bounces his eyebrows seductively her way.

"Not taken like that," she says with a roll of her eyes. Sarah could be annoyed with all Nick's flirting if she didn't know how genuinely sweet he is underneath it all. He didn't hide the fact that he carried a little torch for her after she ended things, but he really has seemed over it for a while. At this point, it's just friendly flirtation, which he would immediately stop if either got involved with someone else. At least, she's pretty sure he would. "I need to *appear* taken. As in unavailable. Very much not available."

"Why?" he says, and it's a fair question. But it's not one she's ready to answer, least of all to Nick.

"Can I remain a woman of mystery on that front?" she says. Nick doesn't say anything, but his face has gone more serious, his mirth wiped away by serious contemplation of what is, to be fair, a pretty strange request. Sarah can't bear the thought of going to that dinner alone, but maybe this isn't kind to ask of him. "But, look, I don't want to lead you on," she says after a painfully long pause. "If it makes you uncomfortable—."

"Fine," he says with a long sigh. "I will be your fake date."

Chapter Nine

Lies Both Large and Small

Joe stares at the door watching for Sarah. The room is dramatically lit with gothic sconces and chandeliers, and the heavy wooden table has deep grooves in it, which he nervously caresses with his fingertips.

As Randy's boss and the undisputed biggest star at the table, he's been placed at one end in a seat of honor. Unfortunately, he's been hemmed in on one side by two of Randy's local friends, who are strangers, but very nice, and on the other side by Kelsey Cartright. Joe can't quite imagine how Kelsey wormed her way into this dinner as Randy doesn't like her much, but when he glances at Randy, Randy offers an apologetic grimace that assures Joe he appreciates the sacrifice. Randy sits at the other end with Carlos at his left next to their friends. And between Randy and Kelsey, two empty seats. He knows from Randy that Sarah will fill one of those seats, but who is sitting in the other? Her husband seems a likely candidate. Joe begins preparing himself for the role he's likely to have to play tonight.

Kelsey leans in and says, "This is so nice, right? I wonder how Randy found this place?"

He smiles politely in return. "Pays to have local friends, I guess."

"It reminds me of this great spot in L.A. Blue Rosehips," she says. "Do you know it?"

Joe turns back to the door, but absentmindedly answers, "Don't think so."

"Oh my God, it's so great! We should go sometime. They're very discreet."

She bats her big, vapid eyes at Joe, but he tries not to notice. He winces a little at the very thought of a dinner alone with Kelsey Cartright, who's young enough to be his daughter. "I don't really get out much. Especially in L.A."

Kelsey puts her elbows on the table, which pushes her boobs together dramatically, then places a hand on Joe's arm and frowns sympathetically. "I totally get it. It's so hard to go anywhere without being seen, isn't it? But staying in has its advantages." She bounces her brows once and offers a smile that's so intentional and rehearsed that it should be onscreen. Joe smiles back, but returns his focus to the door.

He contemplates his options, still unsure how to manage his feelings and the weight of the evening to come. He's determined to play it cool, though not for Sarah's sake. He's never been able to play it the least bit cool for Sarah. But for everyone else, for the good of the order as it were. And if that empty seat is filled by her husband, then for him especially. Tonight needs to be an Oscar-worthy performance.

Outside the room, over the ambient clamor, the hostess chats with someone as they approach. He braces himself, but no one enters. There's a strange pause, as if the hostess and her charge have stopped just short of the room. The pause lingers, accompanied by complete silence, and then at last, the hostess leads Sarah into the room. And of course, she has a man in tow, the man he recognizes from the museum. Ben.

Joe leaps to his feet. He will be gracious. He will be mature, discreet, and respectful. As Randy hugs Sarah, Joe marches over to say hello. He nearly hugs Sarah, but her tense shoulders and half step backward stop him in his tracks. Instead, he sticks out his right hand. "You must be Ben," he says with a hearty grin.

Randy gasps, Sarah looks stricken, and the man wobbles with uncertainty. "I, uhh..." he turns to Sarah open-mouthed like he needs her to translate.

"Joe, this is Nick," she says.

"Nick?" Joe stares at the man, then at Sarah. Then he turns back to Nick and smiles anew. "Hi, Nick. Sorry. I must have gotten my wires crossed. I'm Joe."

"Hi, Mr. Parker. Joe," Nick stumbles out. "I'm a big fan of your work."

"Aw, thanks," Joe says, turning on his standard operating mode.

Randy hops in to introduce Nick to Kelsey and point him to the seat next to her while whispering to Sarah, "I'll give you two a chance to catch up."

Sarah retreats to the farthest corner of the room, away from everyone else and next to a giant potted plant, and Joe follows. "Sorry about that," she says.

Joe searches her face for an explanation. "That's okay. But who's Nick?"

Sarah fixates on the floor through a couple slow breaths, and Joe gives her a moment to get where she's headed. Finally, she says, "I tried to tell you the other day, but..."

Joe feels flattened with the confusion of the moment. "Tell me what?"

"Joe, Nick is my date tonight because... because Ben died. About two years ago. He had leukemia."

"Oh my God. Sarah!" Joe's first instinct is to grab Sarah and hold her as tight as possible for as long as possible. And he's not even sure if it's from sympathy or personal need, but the instinct is enough to raise his arms toward her before catching himself and looking around the room.

"It's okay. I'm okay. I mean, it's been a long road, but I'm okay. Most of the time."

"I'm so sorry," he says. And he means it. The last thing he would ever wish on Sarah is that kind of loss and grief. What she must have been through the past two years. It presses down and carves through him. One of Joe's greatest strengths as an actor is also his greatest emotional weakness. He feels things too deeply. And right now, all he feels pulsing through his body is sadness for her. "I'm so fucking sorry."

"I know," she says.

"Can I give you a hug?" he says. In normal times, a hug would be a given, but there are so many eyes in this tiny room and too few places to escape. If they attract those eyes, they may become the subject of a collective stare all night long.

Sarah glances around the room where everyone appears suitably distracted, then nods. Joe folds her in and she sways gently in his arms, as if she's been waiting for this much needed support. Her warm, full body is so alive and real in his arms, and it's the most alive Joe himself has felt in months, hugging Sarah about her dead husband.

A man clears his throat and Joe notices Nick staring at them from across the room. Joe releases Sarah and pulls back. He smiles politely at Nick, then says to Sarah, "Nick seems nice."

She regards Nick appreciatively and smiles. "He is."

"Have you been together long?" Joe asks, hoping for a "no." Maybe they just met this week. That's possible, right?

"We met years ago through work," Sarah says. She pauses, then adds, "And then we started dating about nine months ago."

Nine months is a long time. Damn. But at least that's a hopeful sign that Sarah is finding her way through her loss. That's a good thing. A cold comfort perhaps, that she's healing in someone else's arms, but at least she's healing. She says she should probably get back to her seat and Joe nods his acceptance, but he spots a glimmer of hesitation in her eyes that he can't quite read.

The rest of the evening passes in a frenzy of good food, bubbling conversation, and lots of laughter, Kelsey's uncomfortable attempts to ingratiate herself aside. Before Joe knows it, the night is ending and the complicated pain of it crackles through him. Because even though he's been three whole seats away from her all night and hasn't had a single private word since she first arrived, this is the first time Joe has spent more than five minutes at once with Sarah in over seven years. It's been a portal into a life he's imagined hundreds of times. The life where they were so linked they could be in the same room without talking all night and still feel their connection fizzing beneath the visible surface, knowing they were both there for each other, that at the end of it all, they'd come back together, take each other's hands, and go home to make love. That's exactly the night they've had tonight. Except now, Sarah is going home with another man.

As everyone stands and Nick says his starry-eyed goodbyes to Kelsey, Joe snags Sarah. "Hey, I'm off tomorrow. You?"

"We mere mortals tend to have Sundays off," she snickers.

"I was thinking of going to the Seattle Art Museum tomorrow. There's an exhibit I read about that I really want to see. Come with me?" He needs her to see that painting, to know for sure, for once and for all, that the woman sitting in front of it all those years ago was Sarah. He needs her to say it. And she will, if only he can get her there. Of course, he never would have tried had Ben still been in the picture. And he won't pressure Sarah in any way. But now, under the circumstances, he needs to know that they still share this one thing at least. That they share "Destiny."

Sarah glances at Nick who is hugging Kelsey. "I don't know. I have a lot of work to get done. And Nick...." She trails off, unwilling or unable to finish the thought.

Joe scans the room, keeping an eye on the goodbye-ing. "Please. It will give us a chance to catch up without all these prying eyes."

"I'm not sure it's a good idea."

"I'm not asking you to my hotel, Sarah. Just a museum. Public place." He smiles mischievously at her, hoping the subtle nod to their past will rekindle their connection.

She releases a reluctant giggle and whispers, "Okay."

Joe's heart does an enthusiastic flip. "I'll text you the details," he says as Nick approaches. Then he turns to Nick. "Sarah's a very special woman."

Confusion returns to Nick's face, but he agrees. "I know."

"Take care of her."

Nick puts his arm around Sarah's shoulder and pulls her in. "Will do," he says.

***

Sarah stares blankly at her computer screen, attempting to make the email she's reading make sense. Of course, it's not the email that's the problem. It's just some random update for Monday's meeting. It's the fact that every time she tries to focus on work, her impending outing with Joe sneaks back into her brain.

Despite her comment to Joe last night about having Sunday off, the reality is she does have to get some work done this morning if she wants to stay ahead for the week to come. Weekend work has been a pretty steady companion for the last couple years anyway, but now that the shoot has started, her time really is at a premium. She's cut back as much as she can to manage the extra tasks, but she was really hoping to clean up her inbox at least before meeting Joe this afternoon. But when push comes to shove, somehow Joe always pushes back. And now he's pushing into her brain like a locomotive with no intention of stopping.

She gives up on the inbox and instead goes upstairs to get ready for her date. Except it's not a date. She reminds herself again and again. It's just two old friends catching up. In a public place. Where nothing can happen. She tells herself she's not doing anything wrong. As long as they stay just friends. She can't undo the past, but she can do what she's promised Ben and keep Joe in that past where he can't do any harm. She didn't manage to stay true to Ben in life, but by God, she'll be true to his memory if it kills her.

At least, that's how she feels at the moment, but her emotions lately have been as unpredictable as a Seattle spring day. Later, she may want to climb Joe like a tree. But that would be entirely inappropriate and no, there's no chance she'll be doing that, thanks very much. Fortunately, they're going to SAM today and not REI. No climbing allowed.

When she's finished getting ready, she checks herself one last time in the mirror and heads for the door, but a text pops in before she walks out. It's Ben's sister Wendy pinging about dinner. It's been weeks since she's been over to see the family. Her nieces are probably taller than she is by now at the rate they've been growing. She takes a moment to promise Wendy she'll circle back soon to get something scheduled, then shoves the phone in her pocket. She really is overdue for a family visit, but it will have to wait until after the shoot. She turns back, walks to her bedside table where Ben's photo now sits, and transfers a kiss from her fingertips to his face. "Bye, sweetie."

***

Joe tugs his baseball cap tighter and runs his fingers through his beard as they step away from the ticket window, grateful for its protective cover in this very public locale. The woman behind the counter definitely looked at him funny, like she was deciding if it was really him. It's an expression he's pretty familiar with and he's glad to escape before she decides he is. Working in his favor is the fact that it's Seattle where people don't expect to run into celebrities. Most people don't really pay attention to the random strangers around them, so he can often sneak by in these situations. Still, he is Joseph Robert Parker.

They ride the escalator up from the foyer level to the first real gallery floor of the museum. Sarah stands on the step above Joe, bringing them closer to the same height, and they lock eyes, staring with an easy softness of two people who *just know*. Joe's heart swells with the certainty that today will change everything. Somehow, today will be the key, and the escalator is the first proof. But the ride ends too quickly and the link is broken.

Their timed entrance to the special exhibit is still half an hour away, so they wander through a series of contemporary galleries. They stop to admire some paintings, loiter to reflect on others, and pause long enough to scratch their heads at still others. It's simple. Easy. They're together as they stroll from room to room, which is all that matters. A giant, multi-colored installation of glass and steel that spirals across every plane fills half of one room. It's impressive and fun to look at, but neither of them really understands it. "I think I might be better at figurative stuff," Joe says. "Are we supposed to understand things like this?"

"I don't know," Sarah says. "I think maybe we're just supposed to consider it."

Joe takes a couple steps around it to the left to absorb it from another angle. "Well, consider it considered," he says as he casts his eyes upward to the ceiling where it attaches to another spiral in the form of a ceiling medallion. Sarah giggles and gazes at him softly, and he recognizes every bit of their history in her eyes. She's still in there. His Sarah. She sees him, just as he sees her.

A couple walks up to him, and the woman giddily says, "Excuse me, are you Joseph Robert Parker?"

Joe smiles and says yes as quietly as he can manage, hoping not to attract the attention of anyone else. He glances at Sarah who watches with part amusement and part consternation at the sudden intrusion into their outing. The last time they were together, Joe wasn't nearly as famous, and even though he knows how to get around discreetly, it's an imperfect science at best.

"Could we get a picture?" the woman asks, and Joe agrees, because of course he does. The woman stands next to him and puts her arm around his waist. He rests his hand lightly on her shoulder, very visible, very appropriate, and smiles for the man's phone. *Click.*

Joe thinks the interaction is done there, but the man turns to Sarah and says, "Would you mind?" Sarah smiles graciously as the man shoves his phone into her hand and takes his place at Joe's other side. Three, two, one, *click.* And then it's really over. There's only one other person in the gallery at the moment and he watches with mild interest, but keeps his distance, so Joe shuffles Sarah quickly away before others enter and notice the commotion.

"Is it like that a lot?" Sarah asks.

Joe isn't sure what to say. The truth is, he gets recognized a lot more than he used to, but he's learned to restrict his life in ways that minimize the fan disruptions. He can disappear pretty well when venturing into public, especially when he's bearded, but he also largely limits where he goes to places where he won't be noticed, or where no one cares. It makes his life smaller in that way. Sure, it's bigger in other ways, but it's a trade-off. A trade-off Sarah might not want to make. "Sometimes," he says.

Along the front corridor, they head toward the special exhibition and admire a series of vastly different portraits as they go. From hyper-realistic to cubist abstractions to an upside-down, all blue painting of a mother and child, Joe decides the portraits tell a story collectively of what it is to be human. "It's amazing how all of these, every single one of these, is just a picture of a person living a life," Joe says.

"And life is every bit as complicated as these portraits," Sarah responds.

Joe wants to disagree, to point out how wonderfully simple and clean and perfect life can be if they choose it. Together. Right now. But he knows the truth. "Yeah," he says. "It is."

The time has come, so they approach the ticket-taker for the exhibit. Joe presents the tickets and they walk slowly into the front room. They stop to read the intro wall about the exhibition entitled "Rejecting Modernism: Paint, Light, and a Time That Never Was." According to the wall, the exhibit explores the way certain 20th century artists steadfastly rebuked the changing times and rapid growth of technology by clinging to an idealized, long past, and often entirely fantastical vision of the world in their work.

"This sounds interesting," Sarah says as she turns toward the entrance, and Joe agrees, but he dares not say more. He dares not admit he's really only come for one painting. To share one painting in particular with Sarah. It was the featured painting in the exhibition promo on the way in, but Sarah doesn't appear to have noticed. At least, she hasn't said anything. And yet, his instincts scream at him to find that painting. If what he thinks is true, surely it will change everything. It must.

They roam into each new room with an easy pace that belies Joe's eagerness until they finally reach the gallery where it's hanging. "Destiny" by Trenton Freed. It's been over a decade since he last saw the painting in person, but his eyes fix on it instantly, exactly like before. It's incongruous to see it here, on loan in an exhibition, outside the context he's imagined it in all these years. Yet, in another way, it's exactly the same.

The first time he saw it, it was on the wall in the Asheville museum where he was shooting on location. He'd stumbled on it on break and been drawn to it like a giant-ass moth to the sun itself. He couldn't stop staring at the image. A man and a woman stand on opposite sides of a wooded lake, both staring up at the same night sky, both wishing on the same shooting star. Each alone, yet somehow together, united though they remained separate. *Separated.* He'd found the woman with her wavy, golden crown of hair, generous curves, and flowing white shift blowing in the wind to be unspeakably beautiful. He couldn't stop staring at her. He lost time staring at her.

Now, Joe stands unmoving in the doorway for a flicker as he eyes the painting from afar, but Sarah keeps moving. She doesn't make her way gently around the room, however. She makes a beeline straight to the painting and freezes in front of it, staring up. Like lightning, it flashes in Joe's mind, the exact moment he saw all those years ago in Asheville, the mysterious blond woman with wild waves and the flowing white shirt in front of the painting. The woman from the painting come to life in three glorious dimensions. Fifteen years ago, he'd stared at the painted woman like she was real, like he knew her. And when he'd come back to see the painting again on his next break, he'd seen Sarah sitting in front of it, staring at it just as he had done.

He didn't know Sarah then, of course. He never spoke to her. He never even saw her face because he was pulled back to the production before he had a chance. But the woman in front of the painting that day was Sarah. After Seattle, after what they shared, he'd gone home that very night and looked up at the poster of the painting he'd had framed and hung in his office. And for the first time, he knew it was her. He didn't know *how* it was her. He certainly didn't know how Sarah herself could have been in that museum that day so many years ago. He could never prove it. Anyone would call him crazy. And yet, he knew it. And now, she's standing there again, and he's more sure than he's ever been. It's always been Sarah. It's only ever been Sarah.

He steps up behind her, considering what to say, how to broach an impossible moment he's been dreaming about since the day he left both Seattle and her. He leans close to Sarah, too close to someone who's dating another man, but she doesn't move. An unmistakable energy radiates from her as he says softly, "What do you think?"

Sarah breathes heavily, takes her time, and finally responds, "It's beautiful."

Joe steps forward to take his position by her side. "I've seen it before."

"Oh?" And though she doesn't say more, Joe senses a dam breaking in Sarah. Or perhaps not yet breaking, but definitely straining.

"In Asheville," he says. "When I was shooting a film there many years ago."

"You saw it in Asheville?" She perks up at this news. Her eyes alight as she turns to Joe, and he returns her gaze directly without fear or hesitation.

He slides his hand gently into hers and she allows him to hold it. He will meet her wherever she is. This is, after all, exactly why he brought her here today. She's close. He can read it in her eyes. She understands. They were both there that day because of course they were. Because they're soulmates and Fate has been throwing them together again and again, and now it's finally their turn. She must see it, too. He gives her a warm smile of expectation and certainty. She smiles back, briefly, and then the smile fades and her lip quivers. It's barely visible, but to Joe, it may as well be skywriting. She returns her gaze to the painting. "What a small world that you and it both came to Seattle at the same time."

"Yeah," Joe says robotically, still monitoring Sarah's every micro-expression for proof that the moment isn't lost, but she is unreadable.

Her eyes flit to the empty wall between paintings, then she releases his hand and steps onward to the next work without another word. Sarah's dam has held, but Joe has broken open.

***

Sarah walks into her mudroom from the garage and immediately collapses back against the door. She rubs her face and breathes through her momentary panic. She needs to at least get all the way into the house before falling apart entirely. After a moment, she pulls herself upright, drops her purse on the built-in bench, and walks into the kitchen. She peruses first the kitchen, then the family room, debating where to go until her feet simply take her.

Like a sleepwalker devoid of any conscious thought, she makes her way to the stairs, slowly up the steps, and down the hall to the primary bedroom. She pushes the door open, tumbles onto the bed, and casts her eyes up to the framed poster on the wall. "Destiny" by Trenton Freed.

She'd bought it that day at the Asheville museum but kept it in the poster tube for years. She wasn't even really sure why she had to have it, but she did. When a painting basically hypnotizes you for the better part of two hours, she'd figured, you have to take a copy home, right? Still, their home was fully decorated and there was no obvious place to put it, so it stayed in the tube collecting dust.

Then Ben died. She wept and cocooned and hid from the world, leaving every single thing of Ben's exactly where it was for months. She didn't put his glasses in their case. She didn't remove his brush from the vanity. She didn't give away a single tee-shirt. For nearly six months, she pretended like he might be home tonight and he'd expect everything to be right where it had been when he left.

Until one day, she woke up and knew he was gone. Obviously, she'd known it in her head, and felt it in her heart, since the day it happened. But that day, for the first time, she felt the sad certainty in her nervous system. Ben was truly gone. And he wasn't coming back. As much as she loved him, it was time to begin slowly making the house hers instead of theirs. It didn't happen all at once, but it started with the poster. She took out the tube and went to Michael's to get it framed. And when she brought it home, she hung it above the bed because it felt right there. It was romantic, certainly, but it also bathed her in safety. There was comfort in that picture, in that tall, dark, and handsome man in the painting who felt like a safe place for her heart. The fact that he resembled Joe was incidental. It was just a painting, after all. And if it gave her comfort, well, she needed that.

Now, she gazes up and contemplates what just happened. She didn't know Joe yet, not personally, on that day in Asheville all those years ago, but had he really been there at the same time? The guy she saw and fleetingly mused about? She'd thought he looked like her favorite movie star, Joseph Robert Parker, but had assumed at the time it was her imagination. Why would Joe Parker, of all people, be at the Asheville museum, of all places? And yet, he just said he was there.

How many times had Fate crossed their paths? How many times had they seen each other, missed each other, longed for each other without even knowing each other? And if all that's true, why the fuck can't she just let go and embrace what Fate brings her?

She glances at Ben's photo. She grabs it, holds it to her chest, and turns her whole body away from the poster. She should take it down. She never felt disloyal looking at it until now, but as she holds Ben, she can't bear to lay eyes on it. "I'm being good, Ben. I love you. I still think of you every day. Every hour." Except, even as she says it, she knows it's not true anymore. She thinks of him daily to be certain, but nowhere close to hourly. She's had plenty of Ben-free hours. And eventually, she'll probably have an entire Ben-free day. And that's okay. It's normal, right? He would want her to move on.

Just not with Joe.

***

The bright orange food truck's line reaches down the block by the time Avery and Nathan's food comes out. Avery hands Nathan his burrito and then grabs her own gourmet grilled cheese and truffle oil garlic fries from the service shelf. She snags a few extra napkins and heads to the last open picnic table. She shoves the fries, which are thick, greasy, and perfect-looking, between them. *The family that eats fries together stays together* doesn't exactly roll off the tongue, but she's always found it to be true.

She allows herself the first heavenly bite in silence. The explosion in her mouth of three cheeses that are somehow both bitter and sweet, surrounded by the perfect hard crunch of the parmesan crusted bread, sends her synapses happy dancing all over her body. This is what food is all about. Despite Nathan's occasional teasing, Avery doesn't eat like most L.A. girls anymore. She refuses to deny herself the glorious, messy pleasure of BBQ ribs. Or the utter bliss of a thick cream lemon bar. Or the sheer perfection of a carefully composed, lovingly toasted grilled cheese sandwich. Her dad would approve. Her mom would not. But happily, art historians don't need the same waiflike figures that movie stars do, so she grabs another fry and chomps.

She and Nathan talk about his girlfriend, job, and whether he wants to go on with school, and it all makes Avery smile. Her baby bro is all grown up. Even though he's only two years younger, most of their lives, he seemed so young. She'd felt as old as the hills next to him, even as a kid. Especially as a kid. She was the big, smart, and always right sister and he was the goofy little boy tagging along behind her. He was always a child, even in high school. Sweet, but childish. And in college, he was a good kid, but still a kid. Now, for the first time, he's starting to act like an actual adult.

He tells her about the giant bouquet of flowers he got for his girlfriend's birthday, which must have cost a fortune. Not that their dad ever begrudges them anything as long as they're working toward their goals, or at least working. That's his rule, and fair enough. There would be no spoiled, over-privileged kids in the Parker clan, but there wasn't much off-limits as long as those requirements were met. Nathan pulls out his phone and shows her a photograph of the flowers. They're spectacular, and the next photo shows his girlfriend beaming next to them. Who wouldn't beam next to those things?

It would be nice to have someone to send her flowers, too, but that's a worry for another day. Today, Avery has an agenda, which she tackles when Nathan finishes his show-and-tell. "So, I want to talk to you about Dad."

"What about him?" Nathan says through a mouthful of burrito.

"I think he's stuck."

Nathan wipes his mouth and sips his soda. "Stuck how?"

"Why is he still in that rental house after four years? He's one of the biggest stars in the world."

"Maybe he likes it," Nathan offers helpfully.

"Then he should buy it and stop renting."

"Buy *that house*?" Nathan says.

"Exactly! It's a nice house, but you know as well as I do it's not a house fit for someone of his stature. And there's something else. Why isn't he dating?"

"Dad dates."

"He goes out once, maybe twice, with women. And then they're out."

Nathan holds up a finger, then hops over to the truck to grab the hot sauce, which he slathers on his burrito. When he finally sits back down, he resumes the conversation before taking a bite. "Maybe he just doesn't want a girlfriend." He swallows, then adds, "Or a house."

"But why? That's the point." Avery stares blankly at the slowly tapering queue as she thinks. "It's like, something in him is broken. Ever since the divorce. Or even before that. Years before they broke up." Avery pauses to take a fry and considers her next words. She's been hesitant to bring this up after keeping it to herself all this time. And maybe she imagined it and Nathan won't have a clue what she's talking about. Even if it was real, it was a long time ago, after all, and that was dopey teenager Nathan back then, not the sensitive, reasonably emotionally intelligent grown-up sitting across from her now. Still, after her latest failure to so much as tempt her father to go on one single date with a woman, she has to try. She can't let him stay stuck forever. "Remember when he came home from Seattle that first time?"

"You mean when he made 'Jazzman's Blues'?"

Avery nods. "He was different. Remember? He came home somehow sadder, but also like, more alive? And kind of happier?" Even after all this time, she's never figured out how to describe the change she saw in her father that summer.

Nathan's face curls into a baffled mask of loving, but distinct mockery. "He came home sadder and happier at the same time? Nah. Can't say I remember that," he says. "Sounds like a neat trick, though."

Little punk. Maybe he's not so grown-up after all. "Well, you were a child, what do you know?"

"What do I know? I was only the one at home living with him. You went off to college. But sure, you know better," he says with a light eye roll.

She runs back through the snapshots of the way her father has changed as they've fixed in her head, like photos in an old-school View-Master. How he was so sad when he first came home from Seattle, but with this strange, serene joy she couldn't understand. But then she left for school, and by the time she came back at Thanksgiving, he was a new man. He was so present and trying so hard with their mother. They'd been so perfunctory with each other for such a long time that she'd come to see it as normal, but when they were suddenly being kind to each other again, it jarred her out of her complacency. Avery still sensed an undercurrent of something with him, but she could never name it, and it was so great to see them both opening up that she'd embraced it.

Then a couple years later, seemingly out of nowhere, her more open, kinder, and she'd thought much happier parents suddenly announced that they were very amicably and with all due love divorcing. Just like that. Her dreams for her family were shredded, her heart was broken, and her Seattle suspicions bubbled back to top of mind. Somehow, Seattle had started the slow clock ticking and the bomb had just gone off in all of their lives.

Avery slouches in her seat and slurps her soda. "I'm telling you, he came back different. Something happened in Seattle. Something that broke our father. I think it's why he and Mom split up."

"I don't know, Avery," Nathan says. "But if there is something wrong, I think you have to stay out of it. It's his life. Let him live it."

"Oh, I know. I will," she says before taking another sip of her soda. She lies so easily. She must have gotten the acting gene from her father. "Hey, did I mention I'm going to Seattle for an interview?"

Chapter Ten

Road Trip

Joe pulls open the door to the Armory and is blasted with a wave of beautiful, painful nostalgia. They've been shooting around the Space Needle all morning and the production has special, private food trucks and tents set up on the plaza near the fountain outside for meal breaks. But Joe remembers his Seattle Center tour with Sarah too well and it drives him to wander up to the massive steel hanger of a food court for at least a gander. Not to mention another shot at that amazing falafel sandwich, which somehow embedded itself in his memory like a savory thumb print. Besides, he needs some time to himself.

He puts his head down to move unnoticed through the crowds and makes his way to the Mediterranean restaurant. Five minutes later, he's at a table reliving the first day he met Sarah in every bite. The falafel is still exceptional, but in the interceding years, it's become so intertwined with his thoughts of Sarah that Joe realizes his memories have perhaps aggrandized the sandwich beyond its natural limits. It is, after all, just a sandwich. And like everything else with Sarah, it might be time to let it go.

Joe stares across the space to the door they used the first time. He can almost see their ghosts walking in among all the tourists and local lunchers. Those ghosts have been haunting him for seven years, and he's welcomed their company. Sarah, the incandescent miracle of a woman who was born to share this world with him, to change his life, and apparently, to break his heart. And Joe. No, not the Joe he is today, but the Joe he was with Sarah, who vibrated at a level of pure joy and perfect harmony. The Joe who knew with absolute, unshakable certainty he'd found his person. That Joe has been with him all these years, perhaps in the shadows, but always there to comfort him and give him strength when he was low, because that Joe knew the only truth that mattered. He was a changed man – a happier man, a better man – thanks to Sarah.

Until now. Because when your soulmate chooses someone else, as she has apparently done for the second time, what choice do you have but to move on? Even if she's scared, even if she's confused, even if she's grieving, the bottom line is she's not ready. Ever since his marriage ended, he's quietly waited for Sarah to come back into his life. His instincts told him it was inevitable. And he would wait forever if he thought she'd come around, but yesterday she as much as told him she's not going to do that.

He was absolutely sure she'd been at that museum in Asheville. She'd seen that painting before. She walked straight to it like a tractor beam was pulling her in. And for one glimmering speck of time as she stood in front of the magical landscape, he saw her face alight with possibility, with the knowledge they were both there in Asheville. They were meant to be at that museum together that day. Just as they were meant to be together in Seattle the first time. Just as they are now meant to be together, today and forever. The undeniable truth that's so obvious to him flashed on her beautiful face for the tiniest of milliseconds, and it was perfect. Then she turned her back and walked away.

After that, she grew quiet and careful for the rest of the afternoon. She withdrew into herself and nothing he could say could bring her back. That's when he knew she was gone. She'd made her choice, and it wasn't him. So, he could keep hanging around playing the fool, or he could force himself to move on.

And yet, here he sits eating falafel. Fuck, moving on is hard.

His phone buzzes with a text requesting him back on-set to discuss a costume problem. He shoves the last of the sandwich down and heads back to the spot where they've been shooting, only to find Sarah arriving from the other direction at the same time, and she's walking with Nick. Joe watches her press a hand to Nick's arm as they say goodbye and Nick splits off. Joe and Sarah smile politely as they simultaneously reach Geena, but it smacks of wrongness. Joe and Sarah should never be polite with each other, they should be real. The brokenness rakes over him.

Geena hooks her walkie onto her waist as Joe reaches her and says, "We have a huge problem."

When don't they have a huge problem? His title should be "Executive Shit Shoveler" instead of Executive Producer for all the crap he has to dig out of these days. "Oh good," says Joe. "I love a huge problem after lunch. Helps the digestion." He glances at Sarah who giggles, but she keeps her eyes on Geena. "What's going on?"

Geena begins, "The rented costumes arrived—"

"Rented? What are we renting? We've been building costumes for months."

"For the cast, yes," Geena says. "But not the background actors for the World's Fair scenes. There are too many, and they're not in focus anyway, so the plan was to rent."

Joe crosses his arms and waits. "Okay?"

"Well, they arrived, only somebody must have typo'd because instead of 1960s wear, we got 1860s. Petticoats, bonnets, and breeches for days."

"That's a problem," Joe agrees.

"Beltran's on the rampage," Geena says. "And I don't even know where to begin on such short notice. Our costumers can't even go looking because all the extras are arriving right now to get sized for tomorrow's shoot. They'll be measuring people all afternoon. And then we shoot tomorrow."

Joe hangs his head and begins to rattle through his brain for solutions, but Sarah jumps in before he can speak. "I can help," she says. "I know people at all the local theaters. Fifth Avenue, Seattle Rep, Village Theatre. They've got huge costume warehouses. Give me ten minutes. I'll find what you need."

Geena's face lights up like an angel has landed on earth. Hope is a beautiful thing. Joe smiles appreciatively as well, but somehow the moment also hurts. It's too familiar. She saved the production repeatedly last time, and here she is doing it again. Everything's the same, yet entirely different. Because this Sarah isn't *his*.

Ten minutes later, they reconvene and Sarah announces there's a costume warehouse in Issaquah that should have what they'll need. "I'll be happy to escort the costumers out to take a look," she says with a delighted grin.

Geena melts in grateful puddle. "You are amazing! Wow! But like I said, the costumers are all swamped this afternoon with the background actors."

"Tomorrow morning then?" Sarah says.

"I think we need to go today," Geena answers, "in case they don't have what we need. We'll need time to pivot again." She turns to Joe. "Can you go with her to check it out and report back."

Sarah's face flashes with horror, but she covers it quickly with a smile. He should have known this would happen. Joe laughs to himself, but doesn't bother to explain to his two confused onlookers. "Sure," he says, "I can go with Sarah."

***

Sarah drives since she knows her way around better, and it's all so familiar, yet entirely different. Once upon a time, they'd basically fallen in love in a car as she showed him around Seattle. They'd spent two days tooling around one memorable spot after another, singing together, and by the end of it, they were wrapped up so tightly in their invisible tether that their hearts merged into one. This time, their solitude together hits different. The questions that linger now are less the delightful daydreams of what could be and more the leaden fear of what is. It's a terrible, exquisite pain.

"I noticed Nick came to set with you," Joe finally says to break the tension.

"Oh, yeah, we rode together," she answers. "But he wasn't coming to set. He was going to a meeting at MOPOP."

"Ah," Joe says. "The music museum," he adds, and then he leaves it there. MOPOP is a source of yet another Sarah memory, and honestly, they're all coming too fast now. They were fine, welcome even, when they were unsullied snapshots of a perfect time. But somehow, they're all beginning to blacken around the edges as the darkness descends. He needs to find something safe. "Oh, Geena said you solved our film permit issues like a champ. It's amazing how something that should be so simple can turn so complex."

"It was no problem. If I can't fix a permit issue, what am I even doing?"

"Well, thank you," Joe says before falling quiet again. Their silence no longer feels like the peaceful calm of two people basking in togetherness, but the awkward wordlessness of people who don't know what to say. He loiters in a strange limbo on the cusp of saying something real, something important, but never quite finding the courage to say it. Knowing there's someone else in the picture. Even if he's not Ben, Nick has technically been around longer than Joe was. And what Joe had with Sarah was years ago now. Their invisible string is eternal, to be sure – but there appears to be a hell of a knot in it at the moment.

Then Sarah switches on the radio and blessed relief comes in the form of Taylor Swift singing about "Opalite." Taylor has always been more of his daughter Avery's thing than his. In fact, she nearly fainted when he got them tickets to one of Taylor's L.A. shows and managed to get them backstage to meet Taylor. She was very nice, of course, and Joe enjoyed meeting her, but it was really Avery's moment. It's hard to hear Taylor now without thinking of Avery, but in this moment, all he can think about is how grateful he is for the musical distraction.

He happily sings along to escape the weight of his and Sarah's newfound awkwardness, and Sarah joins in with a giggle. They're singing together, their first love language, and suddenly, everything is fine again. Or if not fine, at least forgotten. Which is good enough for now.

***

Sarah leads Joe into the warehouse where they meet a contact from the theater. The scene is set in 1962, so he shows them to the late 50s/early 60s section. She watches Joe comb through rack after rack of costumes and smile. "How many do you have?" he asks the guy.

"I'd have to check for exact numbers, but a couple hundred easy," the guy says without hesitation.

Joe gazes up at the second packed layer of costumes on the racks overhead. He pulls a couple on his level at random and inspects them for quality and make. "Great! These are perfect. Thank you so much!" Joe leaves promising someone from the production will be in touch regarding contracts and specs right away and shakes the guy's hand gratefully before they hop back into the car.

Sarah says her thanks and waves as she rolls down her window and pulls out. "Happy?" she says.

"Very," he grins. He turns to her and shakes his head. "How is it you're always there to solve our problems?"

"It's my job," she says. He says nothing, but she catches the smirk that says he's holding back. Still, the light on his face lifts her own spirits despite her best effort. She's been trying diligently to keep everything friendly and professional, and to keep her own feelings in check, but seeing Joe so happy lifts a weight she didn't like to admit she was carrying. She knew, of course. The weight of her feelings for Joe could crush a mountain, yet so could her grief over Ben. And since she long ago learned to compartmentalize her grief to get through the days, she decided to do the same with Joe. Pack him away in that box and keep the lid on it. But each flash of that beautiful smile that *she* put there lifts the lid a little further until her feelings are flooding out in hopeful bursts of joy. She won't give into it. She can't. But maybe there's a happy medium.

"It should be your job," he finally says.

Sarah isn't sure what he means by this, so she changes the subject. "Hey, before we go back downtown, want to go visit a troll?" A little detour can't hurt.

Joe's face lights up. "Do you even have to ask?"

Ten minutes later, they're parked and walking down a long, wooded path toward the hiding place for a troll. The sun speckles through the treetops along the paved path and the wind jostles the leaves in a pleasant tune. They find their spot in the easy flow of walkers enjoying the day. A jogger runs past them. A couple with a baby crosses their path walking the other direction. They settle into the quiet peace and comfort of the woods like a warm blanket.

They don't hold hands, but they walk so close the inevitability sings. If they keep walking down this very path, eventually they'll take each other's hand, their hearts will merge once again, and all will be right with the world. It's everything Sarah could wish for, and everything she must resist. Still, her pinkie reaches for Joe and she doesn't resist in the least. But before she can make contact, Jakob Two Trees comes into view. "There he is," she says with relief.

Jakob is a fourteen-foot-high wooden troll who stands with his arms around a large tree to either side. He's a whimsical fellow with a birdhouse necklace, which invites woodland creatures to come visit, and a ponytail, the very first troll ponytail according to the online write-up they find. He's made entirely of recycled materials and he greets visitors with a warm smile that belies his size. He may be a troll, but he's no ogre.

Sarah and Joe snap photos, and then turn around to take a selfie together with Jakob in the background. "Send that to me," Sarah says and Joe happily agrees. He taps at his screen and within a moment, the photo pops into Sarah's phone. She opens it and stares at their grins. Two happy, glowing faces. Faces that fit so naturally side by side you'd almost think they were part of the sculpture. It's a beautiful picture.

Sarah tucks the phone back into her pocket and suggests they head back to the car. A couple of older women recognize Joe and ask for a photo, which of course he accommodates, and that in turn leads to another young woman noticing him and asking for her own photo op. The hat and beard are a fairly effective deterrent, but they fall somewhere short of Clark Kent's glasses on the disguise spectrum.

Sarah steps back politely and smiles patiently, but her insides convulse and her hands tighten to fists of tension. It's a relief in one way to have the interruption, to pop the membrane of the happy bubble that was forming around them exactly like it did when they were first together. It's a much-needed disruption. But on the other hand, she hates having to share him with all these people. Even if he's not really hers, it's nice to pretend for an afternoon. Yet they can't even have that. Sarah watches the interactions with dismay, despite how gracious Joe is. He will always be spotted at least a little. It's part of his life now, even on this remote, lightly traveled path in the middle of a weekday. It's such a different life from the one he was leading when they were together before.

As they walk, Sarah reminds herself of all the reasons why this can't happen. Not now. Not this time. And it's not just Ben, though obviously he's the biggest reason. But there's also Joe's increased fame, which plays more and more like an un-invited third party in their time together. And then there's the happiness. The terrifying happiness tells her everything is too fragile to last. It's the balcony that collapses under a hundred bodies who were joyfully celebrating only seconds earlier. It's the bungee cord that snaps in the middle of the most thrilling jump of your life. It's the transcendent joy that turns tragic. It's quite literally too good to be true. It was a perfect dream the last time, meant to last only for one magical moment in time. The relationship was never meant to last forever, even if the feelings did.

She walks further away from Joe now, establishing a bound-ary that he clearly senses because before they reach the car, he stops her and says, "Can we talk?"

Everything in Sarah screams "NO!" There's nothing Joe can say to follow those words that will be easy and painless. The only easy, painless way out of this is to say nothing, to drive home and pretend this was just another day on the job. No big deal. "Can we talk" is an invitation to real feelings that Sarah would very much like to sidestep. Yet, how can she deny Joe his say? Joe, who has always held her heart in his hands with the gentlest touch, who seven years ago led her out of the dark forest of her depression with the light of his love. Giving him the chance to say his peace is the very least she can do for him.

"Of course," she says as she steels herself for the inevitable. This is the talk that must come, even if she doesn't want it. When they will say what needs to be said and let the sweet dream fade into the past where it will remain the best memory of her life. It will always be perfect. And it will always be in the past. At least, this is what she tells herself as Joe steers her to a bench and turns to face her.

"Tell me about Ben," he says.

Sarah's heart seizes. "What?"

"Tell me something I don't know."

This is not remotely what Sarah expected. She was prepared to look Joe in the eye and break his heart. After the museum, after seeing how much he wanted her to say words she couldn't say – to admit she was there, that she saw him, that they were every bit as connected as he believed – she knew he still felt the same as ever. And, of course, he did. So, yes, she had been ready for that. That she could handle. But this? To talk about Ben? "But... we talked about him a long time ago. There's no reason to go into all that now."

"Sarah, there's every reason to talk about him now. What you've been through, I can't even imagine how painful it's been." He stops and reaches for her hand before he goes on. "Ben is part of your story, and your story has changed a huge amount since I saw you seven years ago. I don't want you to feel like you have to hide that from me."

The invitation floods Sarah's memory with flashes of her late husband that she hasn't entertained in too long. As she's healed, she's lingered less and less in the specifics, still welcoming particular memories here and there, but slowly settling more into the general idea of him. The concept of him. His love. His humor. His determination. But now, for the first time in longer than she can remember, she's seeing all of him at once. Ben healthy, Ben sick, Ben laughing, Ben vomiting, Ben taking out the trash, Ben making love to her for the last time. "I don't even know where to start."

Joe smiles softly. "How about you tell me one specific thing. One story. Something that makes you smile."

So, she tells him about the cake. A month or so before he died, he'd been weak, but he wanted to make her a birthday cake. He wasn't a huge baker, but it had always been a point of pride that he made her birthday cakes each year. So, with Gabi's help, he made her a cake. Chocolate with raspberry filling and white chocolate icing. It was so decadent and so delicious.

Joe nods his appreciation. "That sounds lovely."

"I still have one last piece in the freezer." She smiles at the memory. "I'm sure it's not very good anymore, but I can't seem to throw it away."

"Then don't," he says simply. He squeezes her hand and they sit quietly as an old man hobbles by with his walking stick.

Sarah watches him pass, summoning her courage to say what she needs to say. Of course, Joe would never pressure her. She should have known that. But that doesn't mean he's not feeling it. She was ready when she sat down on this bench, so she might as well push through. It's kinder to say it now and let him be free, isn't it? And so, she inhales deeply and blurts it out. "You know I can't be with you, right?"

"What?" Joe's face reddens with alarm. "No, we don't have to talk about that now. You need time."

Sarah shakes her head. "I don't need time. It's been two years. I mean, yes, I'm still coping with it all, but I'm mostly okay."

"Sarah, you get all the time you need to heal from a loss like that."

"But it's not about time."

He drops his head and squeezes his eyes shut. "This isn't where I intended this conversation go." Then he looks her in the eye. "I don't want this to be about me."

"But it was hanging in the air," she says. "It's always hanging there."

Joe speaks carefully and the desperate strain in his voice scratches Sarah's heart. "Look, I can't imagine how devastating this has been.... But at some point, when you're ready, it's okay to move on and live your life."

Sarah pulls her hand back into her own lap and sits up, her boundary returning "It's not that I can't live my life," she says. And when he still looks baffled, she finally says the words. "It's just that I can't have you."

Joe drops from the bench to a crouch right in front of her and takes her hands again. People could see him. Talk. Take pictures. But he doesn't seem to care. "You can. When you're ready, I'm right fucking here. I'm not going anywhere."

Sarah cups his face in her palm as a new kind of grief rips through her. It's one thing to feel these things, to share them with her friends even, but to say them to Joe summons a sense of finality that crushes her heart like a vise. "After what I did to Ben last time, with you..." She takes a deep breath and prepares to say the hardest words she will ever say. "Don't you see? You're the one person in the world I can't have."

Joe studies her eyes for a moment, and she in turn gets lost in the electric azure of his. How many more times will she get to look into those eyes for real? Not on a TV or movie screen. Is this the last time? Joe puffs out a slow breath. "Well, there's nothing I can say to that."

They drive back in silence.

Chapter Eleven

Trying Not to Try

It's Wednesday night, so Sarah spends about fifteen minutes on her ritual failure to click Ben's link before she gives up, puts a kettle on for tea, and calls Gabi.

It rings several times, before Gabi picks up on speaker, her voice straining. "What do you think of rock climbing in Utah?"

"I beg your pardon?" Sarah responds.

"Sarah, please sell her on the beauty of a quiet, country house with a porch swing." Dana says, followed by a tense grunt. "Maybe with a nice stream out back."

"What are you two doing?"

"We're competitive wall sitting," Gabi says.

"You're what now?"

"Dana and I are having a contest to see who can wall sit longer." Gabi's voice tightens as if someone's just pressed a hundred-pound weight on her chest. "We're up to two minutes and twelve seconds, thirteen, fourteen."

This certainly isn't what Sarah was expecting when she called, and while it's entertaining, she needs focus. "Okay, call me when you're done."

"No, we could use the distraction," Gabi grunts. "What's up?"

Oh well. She may as well get it over with. The sooner she puts this whole debacle behind her, the better. "Oh, it's no big deal, really. I just wanted to let you know Joe and I are officially over."

Over the phone comes the distinct tussle of two women's bodies collapsing in unison. The fall is accompanied by pained moans on both sides and a worrisome yelp from one of them. Maybe she should have waited after all.

"You said what?" Gabi says as she gasps for breath.

"I told Joe I couldn't do it."

"Why?" the women say together.

"It's not fair to Ben. No matter how I look at it, and I've looked at it from every angle, believe me," Sarah says as she pulls a mug from the cupboard. "I just can't do it. How can I be with Joe of all people? How can I do that to Ben?"

Gabi does not hide her disgust as she speaks. "Dude, I know you loved Ben. And he was a great guy. But you do still get to have a life now that he's gone. You know that, right?"

"Maybe not now," Dana says gently. "If you're not ready. But Gabi's right. You *are* allowed to move on."

"But not with Joe. Not after what happened."

"Don't make me come and beat you up," Gabi says, and the tone of her voice suggests she might actually do it. She's never chosen violence before in the past thirty years, but this might be enough.

"You can't beat up widows," Sarah says as she drops her tea bag in her mug and pours the boiling water.

"I can," Dana says, pulling her widow card. Dana's the kindest of souls and the most caring of friends, but they appear to have entered the tough love phase of the healing process. Of course, there's a piece of this even she won't understand.

"But it's more than that," Sarah says, but once the words are out, she's not sure how to proceed. Her irrational reasons will make no sense to Gabi and Dana, and she has no interest in being talked out of them anyway. Her reasons may be irrational, but that doesn't mean they're wrong.

"We're waiting," Gabi says.

Sarah sips her tea to stall and think, but she knows she can't hide from her two best friends forever. "Every time I get too happy, it's snatched away."

An annoyed huff escapes from one of them before Gabi says, "Explain."

Sarah has spun around this argument in her own head countless times. It's crazy, but she can't shake the notion that it's real, even though her friends are about to mock her viciously. "Okay, when we were in college, I was so happy, I had a great boyfriend, and I was doing so well at school. Remember?"

"I do," Gabi replies with an impatient clip.

"And then my parents got a divorce out of nowhere and my life completely fell apart."

"Yeah," Gabi agrees.

"So then I spent the next ten years either alone or in one terrible relationship after another because I stopped believing in love." Sarah pauses, but Gabi says nothing, so she goes on. "Until Ben. Then I fell in love, got a great job, everything was going so well, and then blam! Synergy fell apart and I spiraled into a two-year, jobless mindfuck of a depression." Just mentioning the darkness that followed Synergy's closing drops a stone in her gut.

"Which Joe saved you from," Gabi says. Gabi was there to witness it all. Sarah's depression, the way Ben pulled away over those years, and the way Joe brought her to the light again – which she's delighted to remind Sarah at this very inconvenient moment. "So far, you're not helping your case."

"Yes, sure. But those two years before Joe were hell."

"Okay. And?"

"Then I came back to Ben and we found each other again, and we were so good." Sarah stops as the emotion wells in her throat. "So happy," she repeats. The next words hardly need to be said, but her point needs a period. "And then he died."

Gabi starts to speak, but gets stymied mid-word and Dana jumps in. "So, let me get this straight. Your argument against being with Joe, *when you're ready,* is that bad things happen?"

"You guys, I can't do it again." Sarah takes another sip of tea and clutches the mug against her chest like a safety blanket.

"Okay, um, give me a second to gather my thoughts," Gabi says. After the briefest of beats, she continues, "Okay, pardon my French, but you're a fucking idiot."

Dana chimes in right behind her. "I don't speak French, but I agree. You're an idiot."

"Dude, everybody has bad things happen to them. Terrible, awful things. That's called life." Gabi sounds so irritated, Sarah finds herself glad they're not in the same room. Gabi really might try to beat her up. Lovingly, of course.

"Hello, I lost a spouse, too," Dana adds. "And it took me time to mourn and recover. Just like you."

Gabi finishes the thought. "But look how happy we are now."

Over the line, an "aww" from Dana is followed by the distinct sound of the women smooching. "Alright, you two, break it up."

Gabi sighs. "The point is, think of all those years of happiness when the bad things *weren't* happening. You get way more good than bad if you do the math."

Dana agrees, "At the end of the day, you can't refuse happiness because it might someday be followed with sadness. That way lies madness. I was utterly devastated when Chloe died, but it didn't stop me from trying again. And also, what if it's not followed by sadness? What if it's pure, unadulterated bliss for the rest of your life? Ever think of that?"

"It's not about trying again in general. It's about Joe." Sarah blows on her tea and watches the patterns her breath makes on the liquid as she moves her lips around. This conversation has not gone the way she planned. But maybe it's the conversation she needs? "Even if I could get over the guilt..."

"You *have* to get over the guilt," Gabi insists.

"But even if I could," Sarah continues, "I can't help but think if I jump, the bungee cord is going to break and I'm going to sail headfirst into the gorge, never to be seen again."

"Or," Dana says gently, "it could be the single most exhilarating ride of your life."

***

Joe spends his morning in teleconference meetings with the L.A. team, discussing every project on the slate and doing his damnedest not to think about Sarah. He just about manages it. Marty's tentatively in on the New York project, so they start hashing out next steps, which should be absolutely thrilling. And it is, sort of. These are the kinds of opportunities Joe used to dream of, and now he has them, he recognizes the gift they are. Yet, they don't thrill the way they used to. They still excite him momentarily. When he first read that script, he nearly vibrated in anticipation of the possibilities. But like everything, the joy faded a little as the details took shape. Instead of growing more vibrant and real with each step forward, somehow all his projects dim with the daily minutiae and endless headaches of talent dropping out, directors overrunning their budgets, behind-schedule shoots, and misbehaving actors.

It was easier when he was just the actor himself, but when he was on-camera constantly, he discovered he wasn't willing to trade every shred of his privacy and anonymity to feed the fame monster. All he wanted was to act, but nobody wanted him to just act. He had to be a movie star with all the trappings. So, moving behind the camera seemed like the answer. Creative fulfillment without quite as much notoriety. He still gets recognized, of course, but pulling back has finally begun to ease the burden of fame. Slightly. And yet, the headaches persist.

Of course, even the headaches used to be fun, but as he signs off from his last meeting of the morning, he droops into his seat and thinks about the only thing – besides his kids at least – that's brought him real joy in a long time. Sarah. The first time he felt really excited about this project since its earliest inception was when he saw her at the Chihuly party the first night. Sure, he'd faked it well. He is an actor, after all. He knows how to schmooze and charm and dazzle. He knows how to *seem* alive while shuffling along half-zombied out on disillusion and burnout. And he genuinely tried to recapture that spark repeatedly, but something was always missing. Until the moment he laid eyes on her and came to life for real. Every synapse in his body fired off tiny fireworks announcing the start of something wonderful.

Suddenly, he was excited about every new day at work, not just because it was a chance to see her, but because it was a chance to watch her work, problem-solve, and bask in the spotlight she has so clearly earned. Once upon a time, she'd been mired in her own darkness, but he'd seen her light from the start. He'd shown it to her, then thrilled to witness her coming into her own, to find her way back to the accomplished, unstoppable woman she was always meant to be.

She became his inspiration without even trying. And now she's given him the boot in no uncertain terms.

Randy pops his head into the production trailer Joe is using. "Milo problem," he says.

Joe rubs his face. Milo Penn might be the biggest star in the world at the moment, but Joe's not entirely sure he's worth the cost. His paycheck, sure, but looking after the over-inflated, high maintenance manchild is like babysitting a toddler with a gummy bear addiction and Mummy on speed dial. "What now?"

"Something's wrong with his trailer."

"Don't tell me. It's not big enough for his hyperbaric chamber."

"If only."

Joe heaves an exasperated breath. "Give me two minutes."

Randy nods, but pauses before shutting the door. "Listen, come have drinks with us tonight. We're staying in the hotel where it's safe."

"I don't know," Joe says. "Will Sarah be there?" If she's determined to shut him out, then it's time he starts protecting his heart. He needs to make a clean break. Sever the inseverable. Find a way to stop thinking about her because this shit can't go on. And drinking with her probably isn't the best way to do that.

"Would that be a bad thing?" Randy retorts.

"I better not. I'm a little under the weather," Joe finally says.

"She's not coming," Randy replies. "I invited her, but she declined. Sounds like she's got the same bug as you."

Joe opts not to take the bait. "I'll try to stop by."

***

Sarah walks out of her budget meeting utterly depleted. The budget is solid and everyone's relatively happy, but the amount of energy it took for her to smile and cheer on her team for an entire hour straight was something akin to running a marathon at full sprint. She'll be crawling to the finish line on this day, if she even makes it with that hundred-pound sack of sadness on her back. At least she gets to keep her toenails. Clearly, she needs to carbo-load and sleep tonight, though not necessarily in that order.

She closes the door to her office, drops into her chair, and opens her phone to the photos of the troll and Joe. His salt-and-pepper suits him, and the beard is so hot. He'd had a beard the first day she met him, and it had toned him down enough for her to get through her first full day of "knowing Joe," something that seemed unimaginable at the time. She actually *knew* Joseph Robert Parker. It was an impossible dream come true back then. Now, it's unimaginable that she ever didn't know him.

Of course, in a sense, maybe she has always known him. Ever since the day they were born in the same hospital, slept their first night in the same nursery, their lives have been twisting and turning with each other's. New Year's in college. That day in Asheville. The love affair that saved her life. What other impossible moments would they never discover? Too many impossible things to ignore. Too many impossible things to accept.

She studies his beard and wonders what it would be like to kiss bearded Joe. Would it be soft and tickly? Or scratchy and rough? He'd already shaved by the time they kissed the first time. She'd never kissed him with a beard. And now she never would. She's made her decision and she needs to live with it, so staring at his facial hair and dreaming about his lips probably isn't the most helpful course of action. And yet, it's almost the only thing she can do that doesn't weigh her down with impenetrable grief. On the contrary, she realizes with no small consternation that she's practically levitating.

She clicks back to her texts and reviews Randy's invitation. She said no initially. Too much risk of seeing Joe and rehashing what can't be unsaid or undone. Walking away from Joe has already put her heart through a blender. Seeing him again now, in a social setting, trying to play nice like they could ever be normal again, would be like clicking up from 'chop' to 'puree.'

But what if she's wrong? What if Gabi and Dana are right and she's being a fucking idiot? Admittedly, she's dissected this thing a hundred different ways and never come up with anything other than a chopped-up frog. But why does she always need to dissect everything in the first place? Has slicing the things she cares about into a thousand pieces and then wildly overthinking them ever done any actual good? Has anything ever been made better by vivisection? Maybe she should find the courage to try stitching something back together for a change.

***

Joe walks into the bar right as the group of three is relocating from a small, low table to the newly vacated large, U-shaped booth in deference to the growing group that's expected shortly. Joe sits on one end with Randy at the other end and two others who are familiar, but whose names Joe can't pull from the recesses of his mind as he slides in. One of them might be Zelda? In any case, maybe this is what he needs, a night with relative strangers to get the hell out of his head. Let someone else take center stage for the night instead of the interminable tragedy running laps in his brain.

They order drinks and talk about the day, and before long, the first AD Geena turns up and pulls a chair to the outside of the booth. More drinks, more laughter, and it's a welcome relief honestly. Sarah's never far away. She lingers in his thoughts like a floater in his eye, always there, but when he focuses hard enough, or completely loses focus, he can tune her out for a while.

Then Kelsey Cartright shows up, followed within seconds by another unknown, smiling face, but Kelsey swoops into the booth and cozies up to Joe before the newcomer can claim a seat. When no free chairs are immediately available, Kelsey offers the newcomer, whose name is Ted apparently, a spot to her other side. The gesture plays as welcoming at first, until Kelsey pushes her chest followed by the rest of her into Joe and her ulterior motives are suddenly indisputable. Joe shoots Randy a silent "help," and Randy instantly scoots to the very edge of the booth on his side. But the booth is packed and the extra two inches do little to free Joe as Kelsey usurps them on her side. All in the interest of giving Ted enough room, of course.

Joe lifts his arm to the back of the booth to give himself a hint of breathing space, but he almost immediately realizes his mistake as Kelsey giggles and leans in. And while his arm is very definitely on the back of the booth, and not on Kelsey Cartright, the way she bunches her shoulders adorably and wrinkles her nose makes it clear she intends to change that.

She's a beautiful girl certainly. She's shaped the way a starlet should be, with big doe eyes and breasts that arrive several seconds before the rest of her. The problem is she knows it, and she never hesitates to use her apparent assets to her advantage. She's been focused on Joe like the Hubble telescope since their first meeting. He's ignored it until now because she's good box office and not a bad actress. Or at least, she has potential when she grows out of her pouting and preening phase. But tonight, her advances hit different. She's not just an ingenue on the climb, she's everything Sarah isn't. And Joe's too miserable to resist.

Joe takes a deep breath and tries to lean in. If this is where the night has taken him, so be it. At least he's not sitting alone in his room rehashing the disaster of his one true love stomping on his heart like a world-class flamenco dancer. Surely, tap-dancing through an evening with Kelsey Cartright has to be better than that. A little friendly flirtation never hurt anyone and acting has always helped him through the tough times in the past. Maybe it can help him through this. He orders another round for everyone and orders himself to lighten up. And it works.

Until Sarah walks in.

He spots her at the entrance a moment before her eyes land on him. They're hopeful and open and his heart sings. Every blasted, well-faked moment of good cheer and "fuck it, I don't need her" energy he's summoned all night is expelled in an instant as his chest floods with the truth of his feelings, a truth as inescapable as his breath. And now she's here, maybe he doesn't have to escape anything – because she's decided to give him another chance. She must have or she wouldn't be here.

Then her eyes land on Kelsey and Sarah's face sinks. She eyes his arm, ostensibly stretched around Kelsey who is sitting far too close to be easily explained. He snatches his arm back to his body, elbowing Kelsey hard in the process, but it's too late. Sarah has turned to run out the door.

His muscles twitch with the urge to jump up and charge after her, but he's locked in by multiple people on both sides. Short of climbing over the table, there's no quick enough way to catch her, and the way his soaring spirit crash lands in a treacherous thud as he realizes what's happened tells him everything he needs to know. He can't keep playing this game. He can't keep yo-yoing back and forth. The constant to and fro is making him sick.

Despite her appearance tonight, Sarah's made it clear a relationship with Joe is off the table. Hell, she might not even have known he'd be there. Maybe Randy told her the same thing he told Joe, that it would be safe tonight. Maybe she came specifically because she thought the coast would be clear. His desperate leap to hope was entirely a confection of his over-addled brain. Sarah knows her own mind. If she says it can't happen, it can't happen. It will never happen.

The room dims. The cheerful glow of laughter and camaraderie now glares as artificial and ugly as a neon sign in an hourly hotel. He needs to get out of here. He smiles politely through the rest of his drink, then begs his exit, forcing Kelsey and Ted to slide out so he can access his escape route. Kelsey leans into him for a hug before he goes and whispers in his ear. "Want some company?"

The words creep through his system and tempt his basest instincts. He has no interest whatsoever in this woman, who's barely more than a girl, but she could distract him for a night or two. Or the rest of the shoot. And to be fair, he could desperately use a distraction because pain is slowly shutting down every system in his body and he could really use a jumpstart to avoid total system failure. This isn't the kind of loss he's going to just get over. Ever.

But this isn't Joe. He pulls her arms from around his shoulders and nudges her backward. "I think I need some sleep," he says.

"I sleep," she says coyly.

"Kelsey, you're a beautiful woman," he says, and she smiles appreciatively at the encouragement. "But I'm going home alone tonight."

Kelsey shrugs and tips her head to the side. "Next time," she says before giving a little wave and dropping back into the booth.

On his way out, Joe glances at the bar and does a double take that turns his body a full one-eighty – because sitting at the bar is none other than Sarah's current beau Nick. Hope sparks at first when he assumes Sarah must be with Nick, but it's extinguished a half beat later because that's not Sarah. It's a dark-haired woman a few years younger. So, what is Nick doing with another woman in a hotel bar this late at night? This night really couldn't get any worse, but if Nick is screwing around on Sarah, that goes directly into the "need to know" file, so he marches up to Nick with a polite tap on the shoulder. "Hi," he says.

Nick startles, then offers a nervous smile. "Joe, hi. Nice to see you again."

"Want to introduce me to your friend?" Joe turns expectantly to the woman who's more than a little confused, and if he's not mistaken, slightly starstruck.

"Of course," Nick says. "Joe, this is Lisa. She's a city administrator for Portland. We've been working together to put on the city administrators' conference that's in town this week."

Lisa lights up from the reflected glow of meeting an actual movie star. "Mr. Parker, it's so nice to meet you," she says, and Nick wears his dejection on his face.

"It's nice to meet you, Lisa," he says before turning to Nick. "Could I talk to you for a minute?"

Nick politely excuses himself and they retreat to the lobby outside the bar where the bright light throws their conversation into high relief. "It's not what you think," he says.

Joe balks. "So, you're not here on a date with that woman instead of Sarah, who you're supposed to be seeing?"

"Okay, it is what you think," he corrects. "But only kind of. Look, I wish Sarah cared that I was here tonight."

"You don't think Sarah would care that you're at a bar with another woman?" This guy is something else.

"Maybe she would if we were actually seeing each other. But we broke up three months ago."

"You what?" Joe says, his mind reeling as his stomach roils with the alcohol he's consumed.

"I'm sorry, really. But Sarah asked me to pretend to still be together, so I did. As a favor to her. She's a great woman. I wish we were still together. Believe me, I tried. But I guess it wasn't to be." Nick shrugs and waits for Joe to absolve him of his sins, or lack thereof.

Joe's head and stomach both stir uncomfortably as he processes this new information. Sarah lied to him. Pretended to have a boyfriend just to keep him at bay. What other reason could there be? His body and mind are crashing hard. He needs to get to bed and obliterate this day as soon as possible. "I understand," he says. And he does understand, all too well. It doesn't make it sting any less. "Have a good night."

***

Libby taps her pen on her pad as she says, "And this said to you what? That he wasn't truly serious about you?"

"No, not that." Sarah hurls her body against the arm of the couch and slumps her head into her hand. "It was just a sign. You know? Like, he's moving on. Maybe he's forcing himself, but still. When push comes to shove, our moment has passed."

"But you didn't have a moment," Libby observes. "Did you? Or did I miss the moment?"

"The moment happened seven years ago."

"Ah, right," Libby says.

Sarah jumps up and paces. Her mind is too active to let her body rest. She barely slept last night. She muddled through her day at work, avoided Joe when she glimpsed him in the distance during her daily set visit, and now that she's here with Libby, in her designated time to talk about it, her brain is moving too fast to get it all out. "I can't be with Joe. I can't. Not after what I did to Ben."

"So you've said. But let's set that aside for a moment. Let's stipulate as an exercise that Ben isn't a factor."

Sarah bleats in response. "Of course, he's a factor!"

"This is an exercise, remember? So, let's stipulate Ben isn't a factor for the moment. What are you afraid of?"

Sarah continues to pace, searching her mind for an answer that won't sound pathetic. Answers like "too much happiness" ring hollow even to her. It may be true, but she can't bring herself to say it. Finally, she sags into the couch and shrugs, unable to give voice to anything that doesn't make her feel foolish and stunted, even here with her therapist, the one place where she's supposed to face her fears.

When it's clear Sarah has no intention of answering the question, Libby sets her pad down and leans in. "Sarah, I want to offer you a suggestion I'd really like you to try this week. I want you to try to be honest with both Joe and yourself. No matter the consequences."

Sarah shakes her head. "It's too late for that."

"The thing is, I think you're telling yourself a story right now, full of should's and shouldn't's, and I don't think it's a helpful one," Libby says. She speaks slowly as she continues, "Do you really think Joe was with this other woman?"

Sarah shrugs and casts her eyes away before almost imperceptibly muttering, "I don't know. I suppose not."

"And even if he was, would it change what's going on inside you?" Libby waits again on a silent Sarah, then goes on. "So, I want you to try telling the truth for the truth's sake. Don't worry about this other woman and don't even worry about Ben. Have the courage to admit what you really feel and don't worry about the consequences. Good or bad, they'll take care of themselves. But if you keep this bottled up, you're going to make yourself crazy." When Sarah crinkles her face with concern, Libby adds, "In the figurative sense, of course," and smiles.

Chapter Twelve

Then Again, Maybe I Will

By Joe's third night in a row of drinking with crew, he's switched to soda water and soft drinks. His body can't handle the nightly boozefests as well as it once did, but the bliss of escaping his thoughts all evening is too good to pass up. Every day he keeps himself as busy as possible on set, losing himself in the endless daily headaches that typically sap every bit of joy out of the process, but now serve as indispensable tools of distraction. And every night he chats away with whatever mix of strangers and friends rolls into the hotel bar for the evening. If he can keep this up, he might have a shot at surviving the rest of this shoot.

Once he gets finished with the relatively short location shoot and can escape to the much longer remainder on the London soundstage, he will be golden. He can CGI over this whole bloody nightmare like it's a 1962 Space Needle dwarfing all his problems in its towering shadow. He can let all of this drift into the past along with the rest of his Sarah history. But he's still got to get through two more weeks in the very real Seattle of today, a city in which even the fucking crows remind him of her.

He gazes at the crow tattoo on his arm and gets momentarily lost in the thoughts he typically dodges so effectively, until his new show buddy Ted walks in and he pops up to welcome him with a hand-slap greeting. Kelsey follows, and others trickle in as the evening continues apace with more than enough laughter and bitching to erase any other pesky thoughts for the evening.

Except when his pesky thoughts walk into the bar. Randy, who sits at the other end of their table, looks up from his text thread to spot her, then eyes Joe. "Joe," he says with a nudge of his head toward the entrance.

Joe freezes. She's looking right at him and her face is so soft, so sad, and maybe so hopeful, that he instantly melts until his anger and hurt remind him why he's here every night. To escape Sarah. To remove her very essence from his soul, even if he can't remove her ink from his skin quite yet. Not that he could probably do either one when push comes to shove. But he was really hoping to do a passable job of it for the next couple weeks at least. And yet, there she stands.

She walks slowly toward the table and stops directly in front of him, and something about the heft of the moment silences the group. The table chatter tapers to nothing as everyone turns to Sarah. Kelsey is the last to notice, but eventually, she too stops talking and raises her eyes to the woman from Randy's dinner now staring at Joe.

"Hi," Sarah says.

Every head at the table swivels to Joe. "Hi," he replies. Joe considers saying more. Considers inviting her to sit. Considers asking her to leave. But instead, he sits in stunned silence and waits for Sarah to let him know what game they're playing tonight, and whether it's one he ever has a shot at winning or not. If he's not too angry even to play, that is.

Sarah quickly clocks the denizens of the table and gives Randy a small wave before returning her focus to Joe. "Could we talk a minute?"

Joe considers his audience and agrees. As much as part of him wants to withhold even a conversation, let alone his wounded heart in this moment, he doesn't need a bunch of drunken busybodies listening in. So, he stands and aims his head toward the back hallway to the bathrooms, the only place in sight – besides the overly bright and almost certainly heavily surveilled lobby – that's not crowded or too close to others.

When they reach the hallway, he leans back against the wall and crosses his arms. He's a good enough actor with a high enough level of body awareness to know what he's doing. He's blocking her, and though it's something most people would do subconsciously, he means every aggressive, angry, and defensive inch of the gesture. He'll talk, but he won't let her close enough to further scorch his charred remains.

"I came here tonight," she begins before tapering off. She leans back against the opposite wall and folds her own arms, and Joe has to restrain a sardonic smile at the absurdity of it all. Sarah stares down in silence, then back at him. "I came here tonight to tell you the truth."

The truth. Sounds promising. "I'm listening," he says.

"What you and I have… is terrifying." Her face cracks with fear that matches the crack in her voice, and he fights every instinct to grab her, hold her in his arms, and comfort her. But she hasn't said nearly enough to earn that comfort, so he continues to hold himself instead as she goes on. "Last time, we had walls to limit us. This time, it's so… big. I don't know how to process you and me. It's like trying to put the universe in a box. And I think it's making me into a person I don't like very much. A person so afraid to do the wrong thing that I won't do anything at all."

Joe's rage begins to dapple in and out as she speaks, slowly fading as inevitably as the evaporating rain. In his heart, he knew he could never stay mad at her long. But he's still deeply wounded, so he holds himself firm. "Sarah, you lied to me." She almost jumps as her eyes dart from the floor back to Joe at these words. For a moment, he can't tell if she knows what he means or not. How many things has she lied about? But whatever games she's been playing, he's out. "About Nick. You're not dating him."

She screws up her face as if she knows how what she's about to say is going to go down. "I didn't *technically* say I was dating him."

"Technicalities? That's your defense?"

Her pained expression returns. "I'm sorry. I needed a buffer. I needed time to think through everything without leaping straight into 'Open for Business' mode."

"You could have said that."

"I know. But I didn't know how. I've been a jumble of the most insane, chaotic, deeply problematic nerves since the moment you came back into my life. And instead of just being happy to see you again – and I mean, obviously I am so fucking happy it hurts." She pauses here as a tentative, woeful smile slips onto her lips, as if even this fleeting moment of happiness is costing her something. "But I'm also sadder and more afraid than I've been since Ben first died. And I haven't known how to put all these messy pieces together into any kind of picture that makes sense. Like I was aiming for Norman Rockwell and getting Picasso. So I decided not to try."

"And I was out, just like that," Joe says. It's half a question, half a statement, and entirely a challenge to Sarah's stubborn need to control everything.

"I really am sorry," she says.

"Okay...," Joe says. He takes a deep breath and forces himself to drop his arms. He rubs his thighs instead to shake out his resistance before adding, "Well, thank you."

They stare at each other a long minute, the kind of minute that would have led to immediate sex in their prior life together. In the version of Joe and Sarah where they loved each other unreservedly and without fear. The version where being soulmates forever tethered by an invisible string was more than enough to make every moment together right. But that version appears to be gone. Neither of them can ever deny the ways their lives have been interwoven, or the way they saved each other once upon a time, right when they most needed it. But if Sarah is determined to deny the importance of all of that, there's clearly not a damn thing Joe can do about it.

"I should get back," he says.

"There's something else," Sarah finally says, taking a single step forward.

Joe studies her as she parses her words and prepares herself to speak. She's stiff and still, a tree rooted deep in the ground, as if she needs to anchor herself before she continues. As if, maybe the next storm will sweep her into oblivion unless she finds a way to hold on. It could just be Joe's projection, his wishful thinking as he allows his hope to creep back in despite his every effort to protect himself. But whatever Sarah wants to tell him, he will listen, because as long as they're talking, there's hope.

"I was there. In Asheville. At the museum," she says. "With Gabi." Light pours into his chest, but he doesn't move or speak. He needs to hear everything. "I sat in front of that painting for more than an hour. I remember I was wearing this huge, billowing, white shirt," she continues. "Which I remember because we went to dinner right afterward and I spilled marinara sauce on it and it was ruined."

An echo of a conversation long ago rings through them both. They've been here before, discovering the catalog of moments that have always connected them. The madness of a bond thrust upon them by a power much larger and more incomprehensible than they will ever know, fusing them together like two sides of the same coin, so forcefully as to have branded them for life. "It was October," she says.

"Two thousand seventeen," they both say in unison. Joe's mouth hangs open in wonder as he finishes the words, but he can't help himself. The impossibility of Sarah will always leave him awestruck.

"Yeah," she says with a nod. "But before we left, I saw you walking around the corner. I told myself at the time it was impossible, that it couldn't have been you. Why would Joseph Robert Parker be in some random Asheville museum? But in my gut, despite my denial, I knew it was." She nods again, her own wonder at the realization overtaking her. "It was you," she says as a tear forms in her eye.

It's everything he's known in his gut. Nothing about it is a surprise. Yet, hearing the words stirs something so mystical and deep in him. He stares at Sarah in amazement for a long moment. "Sarah, this is..."

She gives him a small smile. "I already know what you're going to say."

"Impossible."

"I know," she agrees.

"We're impossible," he says, and she nods at the indisputably true words.

It's all the confirmation he needs. She whispers his name like a plea, head tilted, eyes watery, and his restraint breaks like a taut leash snapping. Suddenly he's freed and he charges Sarah, presses her back hard against the wall, and melts into her with a desperate kiss. The force of the shove shocks them both, but only fuels the fury of their heated embrace, their lips colliding with violent desperation as the past seven years disappear in an instant.

He grabs her jaw and holds her mouth to his, unwilling to surrender even a single, unshared breath of air as his other hand roams her body rediscovering the fleshy softness that has kept him up at night more times than he'd like to admit. She feels too good and he's waited too long for this. The possibility looms of actual, horny hall sex reminiscent of reckless twentysomethings getting off in the bar bathroom until someone walks by and clears their throat. They pull apart and giggle. They are not twentysomethings and this is not the place. But God, it feels amazing to be this alive.

Joe's composure momentarily returns. He smiles softly at her and takes her hand. "Come on."

He tugs her toward the bar, which they need to pass through to leave. Sarah tugs back. "Everyone will see," she says, terrified.

"Good," he says with a delighted, defiant smile.

He leads her by the hand, out through the hotel bar, waving "goodnight" to his fellow cast and crew as he goes, making damn sure every one of them sees them together. He's proud as hell to be leaving the bar with Sarah at his side, and he has no intention of hiding it ever again.

***

In the elevator up, Joe tamps down his heartbeat to just below sonic boom level. Part of him has been waiting for Sarah to come back to him since the moment he kissed her goodbye and got on the plane that would return him to a life without her. Fortunately, although she had vacated his life, she remained a permanent fixture in the world he now knew – and that had made all the difference. He returned home whole, for the first time, finally knowing what the missing piece all his life had been.

He carried Sarah with him always, which was enough for the time being. He recommitted to his marriage, determined to be more kind and patient, more present and loving. If his marriage failed, which of course it did eventually, no one could ever say it was because he didn't try. They'd simply grown apart, grown in different directions. But they continued to love each other and parted as amicably as possible – which was only possible because Joe returned from Sarah healed enough to meet Melanie where she was with grace and forgiveness. Joe felt no regrets, and that was because of Sarah.

But at his best times and his worst, he'd remained confident that someday, somehow, life would bring Sarah back to him. Just as it had done time and again already. And when it happened, it would be forever. Now, as the elevator dings and the doors glide open, he squeezes her hand tighter and leads her down the hall to his suite.

Once they step inside, he presses her against the wall again, but this time gently. He kisses her slow, easy, and sinks into the sweetness of her mouth. Now that he has her, now that he knows her full, supple, gloriously real body is his, he will not rush it. Every day he's faced with beautiful, skinny, fake women with lifted brows, boobs, and butts. On camera, he pretends he's enamored with women dying from eating disorders. On red carpets, he's expected to pose with women sculpted and taped into dresses smaller than his thigh. But now, he holds Sarah in his arms, and she is real and soft and perfect. She is divinely woman. And she is his.

***

Joe's mouth trails down Sarah's neck and she ascends. Goosebumps erupt everywhere and she finds herself simultaneously floating and deeply grounded in her physical being as his lips catch her earlobe. The part of her floating above, watching this happen with the benevolent distance of an angel, recognizes the super-shot of oxytocin rushing through her system for what it is. Love. Her heart has belonged to Joe since the day she met him. Now her body is his and the profound relief of giving herself so fully to a man who will always cherish her is more than arousing. It's transcendent.

Still, her body pulses with the electricity of his hand as it slides gently up her thigh, softly taking in every inch of her anatomy. He slides her skirt up to touch her bare skin, then squeezes the dimpled flesh of her hip and moans. He whispers into her ear, "You feel so good, Sarah."

His mouth reaches for hers again and as their tongues dance, she slides her hands up and across his pronounced pecs, rediscovering the strong, wide breadth of his chest. He's a little broader now, a little sturdier, but still so muscular. His long, firm, swimmer's frame twitches with pleasure at her every touch and he moans again. A gasp escapes her throat as he glides his hands from her ass to the top of her dress where he tugs her zipper down, down, down. He pulls her dress off her shoulders, then pushes it over her hips and drops it to the floor.

Sarah stands before him in her underwear, vulnerable and shy. With anyone else, she'd be nervous and embarrassed, unsure how they'd react to the rolls of her stomach, the dimples on her bottom and thighs, the sag of her middle-aged breasts – which still hold up in a bra, but how long will the bra remain? But when she's with Joe, all doubt evaporates. Joe's hungry eyes devour her as his hands consume every crevice of her body.

"God, you are so fucking gorgeous," he says. He stands back and simply stares at her for a few seconds, taking in every curve, and she feels utterly perfect exactly as she is in this moment. Nearly naked and entirely beautiful.

She reaches for him and he steps back up to her, allowing her to undo his shirt, revealing his own perfection one button at a time. He watches her and smiles as she pulls his shirt from his pants and slides it off his shoulders. "I need you, Joe," she mutters. "I've always needed you."

"Fuck yes," he says.

Together they walk to the bed and while they don't rush, they also don't waste a single moment on hesitation, doubt, or shyness. They've waited too long, pushed through too many obstacles, to allow anything into this room but each other. He kneels in front of her, slides down her panties, and immediately presses his mouth to her sex. He grinds his mouth into her while his hands slide over her belly, squeezing and tugging as he goes until he reaches her breasts, which he massages so reverently it could almost be devotional. He tugs her bra straps down to lift her breasts free and resumes his worship until Sarah can take no more and collapses onto the bed.

Joe quickly removes his jeans and underwear and joins her there. When he climbs between her legs and peers deeply into her eyes, Sarah swears a choir is singing. Maybe it's a neighboring TV or maybe it's her imagination, but either way, she knows this is as close to a true religious experience as she's likely to have. As their bodies merge, so do their souls.

They lie still and kiss softly. They've found each other at last and their lips tell each other a story they will never forget. It's gentle, wet, delicious. Slowly, they begin to move together, each stroke a restatement of their bond. Joe pushes into her again before looking straight into her eyes. "I love you, Sarah," he says with a gasp.

Sarah holds his gaze and nods through her own gasps. "I love you, too, Joe. So much." With that, their rhythm picks up and they lose themselves entirely in each other. There is no more Sarah or Joe as individuals. There is only *Sarah and Joe*. Perhaps there was always only Sarah and Joe. And it just took them half their lives to figure it out.

Suddenly, Sarah becomes aware of Joe's beard, of the gentle scratch and light tickle she hadn't noticed until this moment, despite her prior musings. It's an oddly pedestrian detail to notice in this otherwise celestial moment. How she can be so utterly rapturous and still so present in her body escapes her understanding in the moment.

But what she does know without a doubt is that this is her person, the man who will always anchor her to earth and raise her to the heavens. This is her Joe. The man who will hold her body, her heart, and her soul in perfect reverence. Forever.

Chapter Thirteen

Sunrise

Joe has officially reached the age where morning wood is generally not a thing anymore. He's achieved enough self-control in his advancing years to keep his penis in check most of the time, only coming to life these days when he summons it. But as he stirs into wakefulness today, the presence of this gloriously perfect woman strewn naked beneath the sheets of his bed is more than enough to return him to his youthful enthusiasm.

He rolls over to spoon her and her sleepy body settles happily into him as she drifts back off. His cock twitches against her, straining for the heat of her again, but he wouldn't disturb his sleeping angel for the world. Instead, he simply nuzzles into her neck, silently inhales the scent of her morning skin, and holds her close.

Half an hour later, she wakes up for real and sings quiet sighs as his hands roam her body. She rolls over and he pulls her on top of him, kissing her deeply. Within minutes, he's inside her and she's rocking softly, their morning breath and knotted hair long forgotten.

Afterward, he holds her tight and says, "Let's play hooky today."

Sarah snuggles into him and kisses his chest. "I can't. I've got a real job."

He catches her mouth with his by way of enticement, then says, "Tell them the producer needs your help with something important."

"Something important, huh?" She giggles. "Unfortunately, I can't just be your girlfriend today. I'm trying to get a promotion, remember?"

"Can you at least get away early?" he asks. "I've got something special planned."

Sarah agrees with a soft smile, then hops up to shower. She rushes to dress so she has time to zip home and change, but before she leaves, they agree to meet on-set at three.

"Oh, and Sarah...." Sarah pauses as she's opening the door and turns back to him. "Bring an overnight bag," he says with a mischievous wink.

***

Sarah snaps her laptop closed, slides it into her bag, and heads for the door. She's running late to check-in on the production before her rendezvous with Joe. She's checking her phone as she rushes toward the door and nearly plows into Pilar on the way out.

"Headed out?" Pilar says.

It's only two o'clock and she worries Pilar will think she's slacking. Pilar doesn't make a habit of coming down to the third floor without a reason, so her presence rings a quiet alarm in Sarah's head. "Just heading over to the set. Did you need something?" She doesn't want to delay her outing with Joe, wherever they're headed, but she can't afford to neglect Pilar with her job prospect lingering. Pilar is on her side, but Sarah can't risk showing up anything less than one-hundred percent at the moment.

"No, I was coming to check how it's going."

"Good, I think." Sarah puts on her most confident smile and reminds herself she really is good at this. "Any feedback from your end?"

"The mayor's office is very happy!" Pilar says with a grin. "Apparently, they've heard from the production team that you've been a godsend. No surprises there."

Sarah's shoulders drop as she relaxes. No bad news then. "I'm glad to hear that."

"In fact," Pilar says as she leans in conspiratorially, "They say you've already saved the production like half a dozen times."

"I don't know about *saved*," Sarah says. "I've helped with a few odds and ends. Where I could."

"Well, whatever you're doing, you're making the city look great and it's not going unnoticed. Keep this up and you'll be a shoo-in."

***

Sarah pushes past the ever-growing crowd of looky-loos behind the ropes and waves at the security guy. She checks around with all the usual suspects, but everything on set is going swimmingly today. No one needs a thing from Sarah. Within fifteen minutes, Joe turns up. He sneaks behind her and wraps his arms around her, pressing his lips to the back of her neck beneath her messy bun. She smiles as she tugs away and faces him, but she takes a step back before he can kiss her lips. "Joe, this is work for me," she says with an indulgent plea.

"This is work for me, too," he says. He pauses and considers their surroundings, then adds, "But I don't want to hide you, Sarah. I'm not ashamed."

"Yeah, but you're a big star and you're running the show. I'm just the local liaison gunning for a job. I can't afford to be dismissed as the boss's girlfriend."

Joe drops his head. "Fair," he says with a sigh. "So, let's get out of here to somewhere no one will see us."

Before they can make their escape, however, Randy calls from the distance as he approaches. "Joe, we've got a Milo." "A Milo," Sarah learns, has become their secret nickname for any of the never-ending, high-maintenance, low stakes problems Milo Penn seems to have. "Milo says his shoulder hurts," Randy explains when he arrives.

"Oh dear," Joe replies with a tone more irritated than sympathetic. "Is he doing something physical today I'm not aware of?"

"Nope, just walking and talking. But he says it hurts so much he can't concentrate."

Joe squeezes his eyes shut a moment. "Was he injured?"

"Nope," Randy replies, shaking his head. "He was completely fine before lunch, and he hasn't done anything more physical than lifting a sandwich today. I'm pretty sure it's psychosomatic, but you know Milo. Once he gets something in his head."

"Yeah," Joe says. "Okay, give me five minutes. I'll talk to him."

At this, Sarah jumps in. "Can I try?"

Joe chuckles in appreciation. Somehow, Sarah has proven herself indispensable time and again on this shoot. And she saved the day more than once on Joe's last film. Now she's got an idea. She's not sure it will work, but it's worth a try. Joe nods and Sarah tells them to stay put a minute.

She makes her way to Milo, who's sitting in his appointed director's chair, scrolling his phone while he waits for the crew to reset. She spots Joe and Randy watching from afar as she greets Milo and chats with him. After a minute, she reaches out to pinch his shoulder. She holds it for thirty seconds, then releases. They chat another minute, she smiles widely at Milo, and then walks back to Joe and Randy.

"So?" Joe says.

"So, I gave him my grandfather's secret nerve pinch, which he learned in Korea, to neutralize pain and told him I knew the top Reiki expert in the city. I promised to get him an appointment by tomorrow afternoon if he could hold out that long."

They watch Milo walking toward set swinging his arms in wide circles and smiling with relief. "Your grandfather's secret nerve pinch?"

"Sounded good, I thought," Sarah says with a smile. "At least, Milo liked it."

Joe and Randy burst into laughter. When Randy can breathe again, he says, "What about the Reiki master?"

"I've got until tomorrow and I know a lot of people in this city. One of them will know a good practitioner, I'm sure." She shrugs. "And if all else fails, there's this thing called the internet."

Joe purses his lips with noticeable self-restraint. "God, I want to kiss you right now!" To which Randy laughs and raises his brows. Joe goes on, "I'm going to get the car before anything else comes up. Meet me by the curb in five minutes."

As soon as Joe goes, Randy sidles up to Sarah and bumps her with his elbow. "Good night last night?" he says with a delighted giggle.

"Shut up," she says as she loops her arm in his and smirks like the cat who swallowed a very fat, extra delicious canary.

***

When Sarah hops into the car, she asks, "Where are we going?"

Joe refuses to say and tells her she'll just have to wait. Instead, he turns on the radio and they begin to sing, their voices in the same perfect harmony they discovered almost from the start. Every note bonds them closer and closer, far past the point of super adhesion, to something approaching singularity. Yet again, there is no Sarah *or* Joe, there is only Sarah *and* Joe as one. Always as one.

Thirty minutes later, Joe winds the car down a steep hill into a tiny cove of huge, deeply private homes on Lake Washington. He hops out, runs over to open the door for Sarah, and grabs her bag from the back. "There's a garage opener inside, but we can park here for now."

Sarah marvels at the spectacular home, which is quite modern, but with enough traditional touches to be timeless. "What is this place? Airbnb?"

"Nah, it's a regular house," he says as he taps in the code and pushes the door open.

"And you get to stay here? Damn, they hooked you up!"

Joe chuckles. "Pays to be a movie star, I guess."

Sarah gawks at the twenty-foot ceilings, then quickly pans the giant, open-plan room and lands on the huge kitchen to her right. It's filled with warm woods that are almost Scandinavian in tone across the bottom cabinets, with bright white countertops matched by the flat panel white cupboards overhead. Open shelving covers one wall, filled with beautiful glassware, pots, and jars of various and sundry items. Everything about it speaks of luxury, but in a simple, homey way that puts Sarah instantly at ease. Despite what must be a gargantuan budget, Sarah can immediately imagine herself cooking in this space.

"Come on in." Joe takes her hand and tugs her inward. "I could have been here all along, but it would have felt too lonely. It was easier to stay with the crew at the hotel," he explains as they walk. "But now…"

He leads her to the living room where she gazes out the huge wall of glass doors and windows to the pool, yard, dock, and finally to the lake that lies beyond it all. She does a slow one-eighty and her eyes fall onto the open stairwell which leads to a landing with an enormous wooden wall with an inlaid mosaic of three magnificent evergreen trees of varying heights. Two birds, crows perhaps, fly away from the trees near the top. Only a master craftsman could have created something so wonderful and so very Seattle.

Joe watches her carefully as she takes in every nook and cranny of the space, smiling in awe again and again, almost like she's in a museum. Yet a museum that's meant to be lived in. Somehow, despite all the elegant artwork and delicately crafted moments, the home's surprisingly warm and comfy. "This place is something else."

"Yeah? You like it?" he says.

"Like it? If I had a few million dollars to spare, I'd get one just like it."

Joe laughs. "Yeah, the designer did a terrific job."

"How do you know they used a designer?"

Joe stutters as he glances around. "Everyone with a house like this uses a designer."

"Well, you would know better than I," Sarah says with a smile as she notices a large sculpture of a crow on a platform in an alcove carved into the wall. It's made from books that have been painted black.

Joe explains it's made from five, large ornithology books, each sprayed black all over the outside, then glued together. Then that giant book block was carved into the crow, leaving black in many places including along the back and back of the wings, while other portions show the carved pages of bird books. "See? If you look closely, there are bits of the birds on the pages."

"It's incredible," she says. She beams in happy delight. "How do you know so much about it?"

He grins and blushes. "I ask a lot of questions." She leans in to kiss him and he holds her face in his hands to prolong the bliss. When he finally releases her, he says. "But wait, there's more! I'm going to grab a few things and then our adventure really begins."

***

They make their way down the long path from the house to the dock, and Sarah gets her first good look at their destination. Tied to the dock is a gleaming, vintage-looking wooden speed boat. The front is styled into a dashing wood pattern in multiple shades of golden browns and tans. It shines brightly in the late afternoon, summertime sun. Like the house, the boat is warm and inviting, but this boat is also deeply cool. It's like something James Bond would drive into a dock in Monte Carlo, then use to make a dramatic, fire-and bullet-laden escape later that evening.

Joe beams at her. "What do you think?"

"Wow!" is all she can muster.

Joe places the picnic basket he somehow already had assembled onto a backseat, then reaches out to give Sarah a hand onto the boat. They settle in and he gives her a life jacket "for good measure." He putters them slowly out to the center of the lake, giving Sarah time to acclimate. They reach the middle, far from either side where any wake would be disruptive. "Ready?"

Sarah grabs a handle, then nods, and Joe immediately opens up, tearing through the water at top speed. The front of the boat bobs thrillingly and the spray hits them in the face as they laugh. Sarah's body seizes with terror, but she's delighted nonetheless as they work their way well down the lake, past the Husky stadium, under the 520 bridge, and into a spot where Mount Rainier stands proud and noble in the distance. Finally, Joe slows the boat and turns off the motor, allowing them simply to float.

He fishes the meat, cheese, grapes, and bread from the picnic basket, followed by plates, napkins, and the picnic set cups. Next he glides out a bottle of wine along with a smartly remembered bottle opener. He's thought of everything. It's perfect.

They eat mostly in silence and enjoy the spectacular beauty of an evening on Lake Washington. It's another glorious, hundred-hour Seattle summer day, so the sunset hasn't even hinted at its approach, but the heat has broken and the mountain view provides all the magic they need. They toast to togetherness, and then to the beautiful Seattle summer, and Sarah stares at Joe, thinking once again she must be the luckiest woman in the world. Twinges of Ben guilt sneak in now and then when she lets down her guard, but Gabi, Dana, and Libby have collectively persuaded her that her job right now is to embrace the present, build for the future, and release the past. So, she pushes away the twinges and takes another sip.

"You were great with Milo today," Joe says after a while.

Sarah holds back a gentle laugh. "Ahh, he just needed something to get him unstuck. Speaking of which, I got a text from a friend who's got a Reiki person who's perfect. And they already said they'd happily clear their day to work on Milo Penn."

"You're a wonder, you are!" Joe tips his head thoughtfully. "You should be a producer."

Sarah yelps out a dismissive, "Ha!" No need to say more.

"No, I mean it. You're good at it. You're a problem solver."

"I know a lot of people. Helps get things done."

"No, it's more than that," he says. "You're smart. You're good with people *and* budgets. You think in solutions. And you understand the movie business. What do you think producers do?"

"Yeah, alright," she says, and she says it with enough gentle derision that he has no choice but to drop it. The evening is too beautiful to waste on a ridiculous flight of fancy.

Joe pours himself another glass, then tops off Sarah's, before looking at her seriously. "This is it, right? You and me," he says. "I mean, we can figure out logistics later. That's just math. But we're happening? We're real?"

Sarah sinks into the cerulean of his eyes and smiles softly. Ben pangs through her in a sad wave and she reaches for her necklace instinctively, giving the wedding ring a single twist, but she pushes on – because that's what she's supposed to do. And what she wants. "Yeah, we're real."

Joe releases a deep breath and his face washes over with a joy so seeped in love as to nearly melt Sarah. He smiles broadly, but his eyes are wet as he leans across to kiss her. "I mean, I suppose we should give it some time. Go slow." He pauses, then adds quickly, "I don't need time. To be clear. But if you do, I completely understand."

Sarah thinks about it only the briefest of moments, caught up in a bullish burst of optimism. "No, I don't need time either."

"So, we're doing this thing?" he asks one final time, desperate for the reassurance only Sarah can provide.

"Yes," she says, suddenly nodding her head with a giddy fury, "we're doing this thing."

For the next couple minutes, they simply hold hands and stare at each other. They marvel at the gift of their good fortune to have finally found their way back to each other. When they remember, they marvel instead at the beauty of their surroundings, at the water, the hillsides dappled with houses, and the mountain in the distance. The sun is finally showing signs of dropping, the sky just hinting at the pinks and oranges to come, though sunset is still a ways away. The long summer day continues to work its magic on them.

Speech returns at last and Joe says, "I shoot my first scene tomorrow."

"Oh?"

"Means it's time to lose the beard."

"Aw," she says, "I was just getting used to the tickle."

Joe runs his hand through his beard. "Wanna shave me?"

Chapter Fourteen

Storm Clouds

SARAH RUNS THE RAZOR under the water, then lifts her hand to Joe's lathered face. "You sure about this?" she says with just a hint of anxiety.

Joe reaches for her hand, still hanging in the air in front of his face, and holds her wrist. His thumb caresses the soft skin where her vein feeds into her palm. "I trust you implicitly."

Sarah raises her brows dramatically at him, but says nothing as she reaches for his face and makes the first stroke. Then another. And another. The razor scrapes lightly over his jaw and the intimacy of the simple act stirs the deepest parts of Joe. This is the woman he will spend the rest of his life with. She is his and he is most assuredly hers, body and soul. She's nearly finished already and it's all gone too fast. He wants to keep her fingertips brushing over his skin forever.

That night they make love, then sleep in each other's arms. On a giant mattress in a bedroom big enough to host a small ball, they dog pile into the smallest imaginable space, not a millimeter between them all night. In the morning, Joe wakes first, kisses his angel's shoulder, then heads for the shower.

As the hot water washes over him, he runs his hand over his newly shaved face. Then he notices how loose and fluid his body feels. How every muscle is utterly relaxed. His tension is gone. The oppressive heaviness of the day ahead, which has always lingered in a corner even on good days, waiting to pounce when he least expected it, is nowhere to be found.

Joe has been living a dream life for so long, but it hasn't been perfect. His job, as glamorous and fulfilling as it appears, and often is, is still a job – filled with the same frustrations, bureaucratic roadblocks, and egotistical assholes as anyone's job. In fact, they probably have a much higher than the national average number of egotistical assholes. Not that he would ever complain when he knows he falls squarely in the "lucky mother-fuckers who others dream about being category." But despite all the good, the burnout is real. The exhaustion is real. The deep, soul-crushing frustration with the bullshit is a daily companion.

Or rather, it was. Because now, he has Sarah. And every irritation is offset by her kiss. Every rage is soothed by her words. Every urge to politely strangle someone is erased by the touch of her hand on his. His Sarah.

When he comes out, Sarah is sitting up on the side of the bed, staring out at the glorious view of Lake Washington. She turns and beams at him as her phone pings. He drinks in her shining face, looking for all the world like the queen she is in this beautiful room made so much more brilliant by her presence, and he knows it's time. "Sarah, I want to tell you something."

"Yes, my love?" she says as she grabs the phone and clicks it open. But before he can speak, her face wrinkles in confusion. "Gabi texted. She says, 'Oh my god, are you alright?' What is *that* about?" Sarah puzzles over it only a flicker before another message comes in. "'I can come over,'" she reads aloud. Joe's as baffled as Sarah and waits while she dials Gabi. "What are you talking about?" she says into the phone.

Joe watches her expression migrate from perplexed to horrified. "What?!" She goes ashen. "Oh my God. Jesus. Oh my fucking God... No, send me the link." Then she repeats herself more emphatically. "No, send me the link!"

By the time she hangs up, Joe is kneeling by her side, waiting to comfort her from whatever this is. "It's in The GabZone," she says. "Someone got pictures, I guess. Of you and me. Now other outlets are picking it up."

"Oh, shit!"

Sarah clicks the link Gabi has sent her and reads aloud. "Chubby Chaser: Joseph Robert Parker Spotted with Mystery Woman." She stops and closes her eyes to blot it out.

Joe slides the phone from her hand and skims the beginning quickly before she regains her composure to continue. Those fuckers. "You don't need read it," he says.

"Yes, I do."

"Sarah."

"Give me the phone, Joe." With a sigh, he hands the phone back and she continues reading aloud. "Does Joseph Robert Parker have a new lady love? The celebrated Hollywood recluse is rarely seen on the town in Tinseltown, but he was spotted this week at a hotel in Seattle with a dangerously curvaceous mystery woman. They were seen together at a swanky hotel bar before leaving hand-in-hand.

"The beloved heartthrob was seen kissing his pleasantly plump paramour's hand as they exited while onlookers wondered who was the delicious blonde with the ample assets, who had so bewitched Parker.

"The sexy leading man/mega producer sported a neatly tucked button-down while his buxom beauty slinked her full figure into a sleek, tight-fitting, navy dress that showed off all her curves. No word yet on the morning after attire.

"We say good for the super fit A-lister and his zaftig sweetheart! Enjoy Seattle, Joe!" She drops the phone, then says sarcastically, "Well, that's nice."

Joe stands and pulls Sarah up for a hug. "Don't worry about a thing. I'll call my people and we'll get it taken care of."

"What are you going to take care of? The story itself or the fact that they referred to my weight eight times in four paragraphs?" Sarah drops back to the bed. "I told you a long time ago I didn't belong in Hollywood. Now we see why."

"Sarah, they're idiots who will say anything to make a buck. It's clickbait. They needed an angle for their story. They chose a shitty one." He takes her by the arms and holds her gaze. "I'm sorry you had to read that. But I will take you anywhere and beam with pride doing it. You are so fucking beautiful and I love you. And I don't give a shit what some stupid fucks on a gossip site have to say about it."

Sarah picks up the phone. "Where did they get these pictures?" she says, scrolling through and pausing on the one where Joe's pressing her hand to his lips. "Was there paparazzi at the hotel?"

"I doubt it. There's not much paparazzi in Seattle, and even if there were, the hotel wouldn't give them access. Plus, they're hard to miss with all their equipment." He leans in to assess the photos. "These look like they were probably taken by a fan and sent in. But I'm going to take care of it." Joe goes for his own phone to start making calls. "Look, I already have a message from my publicist."

Sarah's phone pings one more time and she reads Gabi's text. "She says not to read the comments."

"That's good advice," Joe says as he types a joint message to his attorney and publicist.

Curious, Sarah scrolls a little further and reaches the comments. As Joe taps away, she begins to read them out.

"Jokesonu: She looks like she was probably hot a long time ago. I don't know, maybe on a slow night.

MaxiMama043: She's beautiful. Good for him.

John457: Is she pregnant or just fat?

GarrisonFTW: Isn't he like the biggest star in the world? Where's that hot Hollywood p*ssy?"

Sarah groans with disgust as she tosses the phone across the bed, then plops onto her side and covers her face. Lost in his furious texting, Joe hasn't been listening as well as he should, but the words "Hollywood pussy" bring him back to Sarah. "What are you doing? Baby, I told you, don't read the comments!" When he notices her prone position, he climbs onto the bed and spoons her into a safe cocoon. "I'll handle it. I'm talking to my team, we'll get it taken care of. Sarah, don't let this shake you."

"I'm going to be sick," she says.

He kisses her hair softly and says, "The first time something like this happens, it's awful. Like your world is falling apart. But they're vultures, and vultures always move on to new food sources. We'll get through this, I promise." Sarah groans again and he squeezes her tighter. "But I mean it. Do. Not. Read. The comments. Ever."

***

Sarah sits at her desk listlessly staring at her phone and fiddling with her ring. She should be answering emails or reviewing proposals or something, but all she can do is stare at that horrible story and that god-awful headline. "Chubby Chaser: Joseph Robert Parker Spotted with Mystery Woman." It's so gross.

She cringes again. It's hard not to when people are talking so openly about her body like she's a piece of meat, not a real, whole human being with a mind and soul and her own feelings about her body. She long ago came to terms with her shape and learned to love her curves. She'll never be everyone's cup of tea, and that's fine. The world has all types and somebody to love them all. But she knows how to turn out, knows what makes her look good, and knows exactly how sexy many men find her. This shouldn't bother her so much.

It's the focus. That's the problem. It's not a simple observation of her shape, which might be disconcerting enough in a context where it shouldn't be relevant, but at least that would just be factual. This is no simple recitation of the facts, however. This is a paragraph-by-paragraph, banging drum emphasizing how manifestly fat she is, and by implication, how poorly matched she is for Joe. Sarah's normally got a pretty thick skin, but this level of scrutiny is more than any mere mortal is meant to endure. It's less about the weight, more about the magnifying glass. Sarah definitely didn't sign up for this.

Despite her better judgment, and despite the warnings, she scrolls through the story to the bottom, where those horrific comments sit. She can't help herself. She has to know what they say. A few aren't so bad.

I think she's pretty.

Weight shouldn't matter as long as they're happy.
Glad he's found someone.
Lucky girl.
She's gorgeous!
Wow, wish Joe Parker would look at me like that.

Unfortunately, the nice ones are interspersed among a grotesque litany of nastiness. The things horrible keyboard warriors will say under cover of anonymity turn her stomach. They are repulsive, every shade of disgusting, from leering to insulting to downright filthy.

Man likes a fat ass I get it
This chick's got her own zip code.
Damn Joe Parker knows where the good pushing is
Maybe she's got a good personality?
Joe Parker likes fat girls? Quick, somebody give him my number!

Fatty fetish Joe. Who knew?
I'd slap that ass into shape

Plus, the word "would" appears at least half a dozen times, and it only gets worse from there. So much worse. Joe and Gabi were right. Why did she look? Sarah's head pounds as she finally clicks the story closed and tosses the phone on her desk. This isn't how she imagined it. Plus, what was it Joe said? "The first time this happens…" The first time? As in this could happen again? And again and again? Is this what she has to look forward to now? Being pressed on a glass slide and assessed in microscopic detail by strangers the world over? Is this the cost of being with Joe?

A text pings on her phone and when she looks at the screen, suddenly, everything gets even worse. She hadn't imagined that was possible, but it's a text from Ben's sister Wendy. And she's seen the photos. A quick barrage of fast messages pour in.

Is this you?

This isn't you is it?

I think this is you.

With Joe Parker? Call me.

With any other friend, these messages might foretell excited gossip and an eager, delighted need to know. But Wendy remembers. She ran into Sarah and Joe alone at the park that day seven years ago, and she was suspicious as hell. They'd managed to ride it out with an easy lie about catching up with others in the location scouting party, and eventually it had all been smoothed over and forgotten after Sarah ended up helping on the film. But Wendy's Spidey senses were on high alert that day, and Sarah has no doubt whatsoever that they've been piqued again now. Suddenly, her past sins are back to kick her ass yet again.

Sarah drops her face to her hands for a mournful moment and twists her wedding ring frantically on the chain, first one way, then back the other. After a minute of nearly strangling herself with the tightened chain again and again, she forces herself to type back, *Not sure what you mean, but I'm swamped today. I'll give you a call later.* With a little luck, that will put Wendy off the scent for now at least. With a lot of luck, maybe she'll drop it entirely. If this thing with Joe is really going to happen, then eventually, she will have to tell Wendy and the rest of Ben's family, but with more time, she can come up with a way to ease them into it. Maybe gloss over the less savory bits. But she needs time. This is all too much too fast.

A knock at her door jars Sarah from her misery. Pilar carries in the darkness as she drops into one of Sarah's guest chairs. Sarah attempts a smile. "Two visits in two days! To what do I owe this honor?"

Pilar's face is serious. "I saw the story. I'm sorry. It's awful."

Sarah droops a little more. "Ugh! It really is."

"How are you doing?" Pilar asks.

Sarah considers her answer. She could say a hundred things because she's cycled through them all in the last couple hours, but she settles on the easiest one. "Like a heifer offered for auction and found wanting."

"Well, that's descriptive," Pilar says. "You know that article's bullshit, right? You're talented, brilliant, and I hope it's okay to say in this moment, beautiful." Maybe it's not technically the right HR thing to say at work, but Pilar is a friend, too, and Sarah appreciates the encouragement. "Everyone here loves and respects you. I know, I've been asking around for... other reasons."

Ah, yes, the other reasons. The job. Sarah hasn't even had a chance to consider there might be the professional ramifications of this shitstorm. She leans forward and presses her arms firmly into the desk to steady her body, if not her nerves.

"Actually, about those other reasons," Pilar says. "I think you should know, from a job candidate perspective, this isn't great."

The words hit like a freight train. It hadn't even crossed her mind that any of this could impact her candidacy. As Pilar speaks, Sarah feels her brain sinking into tunnel vision.

"I mean, you have my sympathy," Pilar continues. "And hey, Joe Parker? You have my envy, too. I want to talk about *that* another time. But remember the part about making the city look good? This isn't what I meant."

"I understand."

"Do you? Because, look, I don't want to tell you not to fool around with Joe Parker. It's none of my business, and who wouldn't want to fool around with Joe Parker? But the mayor's office is pitching a fit. They don't like it when their people become objects of mockery."

Sarah sinks into herself. "Oh God! How did they even find it?"

"They're monitoring any news alerts about the film and its stars right now. Fortunately, your name's not out there publicly yet, which is a good thing. But there's serious potential for it to explode." Pilar hesitates a moment, giving Sarah a chance to put on her game face for what is clearly coming. "There are also some people, not everyone, but a certain contingent who don't like the idea of you sleeping with a visiting celebrity. They think it looks trashy."

"Oh, good grief!" Sarah says. "Why do I doubt they'd say that about a man?"

"Well, you can't do anything about that now. That cow is out of the barn and she's not coming back. So, focus on what you can control. I don't know if this thing you've got going on is serious or not, but if your name does get out, you might have some hard choices to make."

Sarah and Joe haven't had even one single conversation about what a future life could be and already she's being asked to choose between the love of her life and everything toward which she's worked for years. This is every nightmare she's ever had all rolled into one. But she hasn't magically stopped wanting her job just because she wants Joe. Her irrational fear of happiness is looking more rational all the time.

***

"I hear you," Joe says into the phone. "Yeah, I get it. But I'm not sure she will." The grim reality of what's happened with the GabZone piece is slapping Joe in the face like a gauntlet glove. He has been challenged and he's more than ready to fight, but this fight might put Sarah herself in the line of danger, which is a fucking terrible choice to make. "Okay, but I'm not signing off without talking to her... yeah, will do."

When Joe hangs up, he clicks to the screenshots of the story he got from his PR team so he wouldn't reward them with any extra clicks. He's been around long enough to know clicks are the name of the game and he will never reward those bastards with his own if he can help it. His team knows this as well as he does and had the screenshots ready for him before he'd had a chance to check his phone. One click from the team is all they'll ever get. But Sarah has clicked it, probably repeatedly if her anxiety has been acting up the way he suspects it has. It wrecks him to think of how Sarah has probably been stewing in this shit show all day. And it's his fault. He should have been more careful, walked out of the bar more discreetly, if only he hadn't been so in love and beside himself with absolute blind optimism that all the obstacles were at last behind them. All he wanted was the girl.

A production assistant taps on his trailer door with a ten-minute warning. His break is nearly up and he'll be back on set soon. Thank goodness. He needs to get back out of his head. Every time they call cut, his brain jumps immediately back to Sarah. He's been a pendulum all day swinging from super professional, cinematic, elder statesman to wildly unhinged, hyper-emotional, and dangerously angry schoolboy. He's a fucking mess.

Every time he thinks about it, he wants to rip the photographer's face off. But really, it's the whole disgusting system that rewards invasions of privacy, blasts personal joys, celebrates embarrassments, gloats over downfalls. Even in this case, when the piece was ostensibly just a run-of-the-mill, "friendly" gossip piece in theory, they'd managed to lace it with so much hateful toxicity and implied shame as to make it practically a hit piece in its execution. Which is why his team's suggested solution is a good one. Take the sting out of their tail, and tale, by proudly claiming Sarah and loudly proclaiming his love. He'd have to tell the kids first, of course – Avery would be thrilled – but he'd do it without hesitation. However, thrusting Sarah into that kind of spotlight comes with its own complications.

Joe spots Sarah arriving on set, but leaves her to her rounds. She needs to check in with everyone without his distractions. Plus, the story has probably made its way to every cast and crew member twice over by now. No one but his closest friends would dare say anything to Joe, and they probably won't say anything to Sarah, but the last thing she needs right now is to give everyone a reenactment in living color. From now on, discretion must be their watchword. If only he'd thought of that sooner.

When she finishes, he's already back on set between takes. As they finish resetting the shot, she texts Joe from way across set. He quickly makes plans to meet her for dinner at the house in a couple hours, then hands off his phone to Randy. Reality will have to wait.

***

Sarah lifts the chopsticks to her mouth and nabs one last piece of sesame chicken to give herself strength. Then she tackles the question they've both been dodging for the past forty-five minutes. "Okay, I'm suitably fortified now. Let's talk about it."

Joe's eyes flit up from his plate, then back down. "You're not going to like it," he says.

"That's a safe bet," she says. "But it can't be worse than that article, so whatchu got?"

"Well, legally, we don't have a foot to stand on, unfortunately. There's no law against paparazzi photos, which is what these constitute no matter who took them." Sarah watches Joe contemplate his next words. "Technically, there are some issues around image rights we could try to pursue, but no one does that for pap shots. It just makes the story blow up bigger than it already is, and it's a tough battle because they can argue it's newsworthy, which means they can invoke the First Amendment."

None of this is a surprise. Sarah didn't know the specifics, but she's seen enough pap photos splattered across social media and web browser click bait stories to know it's not easily stopped. It would be like trying to stop a speeding train by standing on the tracks. Yet, hope dies last. "So, what? I'm supposed to ignore it and hope it goes away eventually?"

Joe lifts his head and gives her his best hangdog eyes. "I don't think it's going away."

A nasty, gurgling bubble pops up around the sesame chicken in her stomach at Joe's words. "I mean, it has to eventually. Right?" Joe stares at her, but momentarily says nothing. "Right?" she repeats.

"The thing with stories like this," Joe says after taking a deep breath, "is they're rooted in a mystery. The mystery is what makes them fun. For the readers, that is. The mystery makes them click. They won't stop until they find out who you are."

"They won't stop?" Sarah casts her eyes out to the perfect, sunshiny view of Lake Washington, then back to Joe. She knew all of this was too good to be true. It was never going to last, but she did think it would outlast the week at least. "Only a couple days in and already the death knell is tolling." She shrugs her shoulders and laughs bitterly. "Well, we had a good run."

Hurt darkens Joe's face into a tight grimace. "Baby, don't even talk like that. What are you saying? You don't mean that, do you?"

Of course, she doesn't. But is this shit really her new life, daily vivisection in the court of public opinion? How can that be her only choice? "No. Not really…" She should give him more reassurance. But all she can think about is the scroll of those vicious comments she made the catastrophically stupid mistake of burning into her brain.

Joe takes Sarah's hand. "There is something my publicist has suggested, and I think it's a good idea. But you're going to hate it."

Sarah recognizes the hand move for what it is, an attempt to calm her before he goes on. An attempt to tether her before she runs. "Fine. What is it?"

"We do our own story." Joe stops to let Sarah process, then rushes the rest before she has time to object. "Drop a short PR piece in a friendly celeb outlet, then it gets picked up via others. 'Meet Joe Parker's New Love' kind of thing. We write it ourselves – or rather, our PR people do with our review and approval – short and sweet, just enough details to remove the mystery. Name, age, what you do, a sanitized version of how we met. No more than half a dozen paragraphs." Joe stops

"You've got to be kidding me."

"Then the day it hits, we post a launch photo of us on my Instagram," he says. "And that puts an end to all the curiosity and mystery."

"And my name is everywhere!"

"But people would move on then. And would that be so bad? To have the world know you're with me?" He's looking at her with such hope.

"That's not the point, and you know it."

"It could even be a blessing in disguise."

"A blessing?" Sarah pushes away from the table and walks over to the windows, her fingertips instinctively tracing the circle of the ring at her neck. The lake glimmers and the beautiful wooden boat now tied to the dock rocks ever so slightly. It was all so simple just last night when they were out on the water. The picnic. The wine. The two of them floating happily and not another person in the entire world. Like it was when they first met. Before Joe became a freaking megastar. Those were the days.

It's so different now. Not her feelings, of course. The real stuff never alters. But the trappings are so much more complicated these days. Pilar explicitly warned her about the risks of her name coming out. How it would endanger her chances at a job she's been busting her ass to get, a job she genuinely wants. And now Joe wants her to willingly step into the light and announce herself to the world. How would that go down with the city folks?

"I know it's a lot to process," he says. "And I know you didn't ask for the spotlight."

"I certainly didn't," she grumbles. She lifts a finger to the window and slowly trails a boat passing in the distance.

"Baby, if you don't want to do it, we'll find another way. Somehow."

Sarah appreciates the sentiment, but she can hear the truth in his voice. He doesn't see another way, and he lives in this world. He pays a whole team of professionals a lot of money to figure these things out for him and this is what they came up with. "Can I have a day or two to think about it?" she says with a sigh.

"Of course," Joe says. He comes to wrap his arms around her from behind. "Take as much time as you need," he adds. "In the meantime, we'll stay in and keep a low profile, yeah?"

"Yeah," she agrees with a nod, the first gentle wave of calm beginning to quiet the gurgles in her gut. They sway gently and Sarah allows the softness of the moment to soothe her. It will all be okay. Somehow. It has to be. Even if she doesn't have a clue how at the moment. They'll figure it out together.

"Actually, this is good timing," Joe says. "Because I was planning to make dinner tomorrow night anyway."

"Oh?"

"Yeah, my daughter Avery is coming into town for a grad school interview and I want you to meet her."

Chapter Fifteen

Avery

Avery emerges onto the large plaza from a steep climb up from the parking garage. She's lightly winded, but mostly with excitement. This is her third and final grad school interview for the time being. There are other program possibilities, but with a Stanford degree in her back pocket, she's hopeful one of her top choices will pan out. She rounds the corner from the garage exit and spots a large fountain down the stairs and along the walk a little, and in the far distance, what she thinks must be Mount Rainier. The fountain and the mountain together make for a stunning view.

She checks the GPS on her phone and determines she needs to walk the other way, so she makes her way past a grand building her phone tells her is Suzzallo Library. The quad she crosses to get to the Art Building is covered in huge, lush shade trees and loads of green grass, surrounded on all sides by beautiful, old, historical buildings. Students lounge under trees and throw frisbees, and she can't help but imagine her life here.

She's missed being in school. Since she graduated college, she's worked first as an assistant at an art gallery, and then as a welcome host at the Hammer Museum. She liked the work more at the gallery, but the benefits more at the Hammer. Not that she really has to worry about benefits since her dad is always there for anything she needs, but she's determined to make something of herself on her own terms. She's grateful for the safety net, to be sure, but resolved not to use it except in case of emergencies. So, she sticks it out at a boring day job for the benes. Like every other twenty-five-year-old basically.

Of course, neither job has compared to her time at school. She loved being on campus and engaged in academic discussions and intellectual rigor. Much to her dismay, she's finally realized she might actually want a life in academia. The idea initially horrified her sunny, SoCal girl instincts. They were supposed to be pretty, shallow, and entirely self-involved – and to choose careers that capitalized on those so-called assets. Realizing that wasn't her path, that maybe none of it was her path, except the pretty part, was a rude awakening. But eventually she came to terms with her annoying intellectual bent and started applying for master's programs. A PhD would likely follow, but one step at a time.

Now, she steps into the beautiful Art Building, follows the directions she copied into a note for convenience, and lands at the door to the Dean's office. Here goes nothing. She steps in with purpose. If there's one thing she's learned from her actor father, it's how to play a part. If she wants to kill it in the interview and be selected for UW's Art History program, then she needs to walk in like she belongs. She needs to own the role. "Hi, I'm Avery Parker. I have an appointment with Dean Carver."

"Oh, Avery," the student behind the desk says with a mild panic. "Hold on." The girl dashes away from the desk and returns a moment later with a middle-aged man who is definitely not Dean

Katherine Carver, unless she's had some dramatic work done re-cently.

"Avery, hello, I'm Bryce Peterson," he says. "I guess you didn't get our messages." He goes on to explain they've been trying to reach her, but their number for her must be wrong because it hasn't been connecting. "We did email you a couple of times, but I guess you didn't see them. Unfortunately, Dean Carver won't be able to meet with you today."

Suddenly, Avery's confidence feels as hollow as her stomach after skipping lunch today. This isn't supposed to happen. "Why not?"

"She's had an accident, I'm afraid. She tripped over a tree root and broke her leg, believe it or not. She's out for the day, maybe longer, depending on how it goes."

"That's terrible! Please give her my best." She pauses, unsure where to go next. "So, what does this mean for me?"

"Well, I'm happy to talk with you, if you'd like, and we can still provide a tour, but we'll need to reschedule the formal interview. I'm so sorry. We can do the interview via Zoom, of course. You won't have to make another trip."

Avery came a long way for this and knows how important it is to meet with the person in charge. Now she's going to be reduced to a Zoom chat? She knows lots of people who interview via Zoom, but it's always best to show up face to face if you can. Her father taught her that. Make an impression. Stick in their minds. Her dad always said he much preferred auditioning in person to auditioning on tape, back when he still had to audition, because the personal connection makes such a difference. Even the handshake matters, he'd always say. "No, it's okay," she says with a disappointed sigh. "I can come back."

***

Sarah climbs the steps to her bedroom and pushes the door open. She stares at the plain back of the poster, at the wire drooping across the frame, waiting to be returned to its hook and hung over her bed once again. She lifts the frame at last and turns it around before setting it back on the floor. There they are, the painted versions of Sarah and Joe. That's impossible, of course, like everything with Joe. Inevitable and impossible, all rolled into one.

Joe has always accepted their connection so much more easily than Sarah. But then again, of course he did, because he did it in the right order. He met her and fell in love, the way normal people do. Admittedly, it was more instantaneous than average, what with the soulmating and all, but it was the normal way of things.

But for Sarah, it had never been normal. She'd fallen in love with Joe the instant she saw him over twenty-five years earlier on her television screen. She hadn't called it love, naturally. She couldn't allow herself to "love" some complete stranger on TV. But her eyes glued to him every second he was onscreen like he might step off the screen and sweep her into his arms if she didn't watch him like a hawk. Like he was both a gift from the heavens and a deeply existential threat at the same time. And in the end, isn't that what he is? But accepting that the very thing she'd dreamt about for decades had come true was disconcerting. People assume life is perfect when dreams come true, but sometimes it's just disruptive, confusing, and downright uncomfortable. Because how do you accept something so purely good and healing has walked into your life without passing go – and without consequences?

Now she sees it isn't without consequence at all. She and Joe have always been purely good, and he certainly healed her, but the consequences are rearing their horrid heads like an angry hydra at the moment. They're snapping at her from every side and there's no obvious escape. If she runs from this, tries to keep a low profile, she'll be hunted by an increasingly hungry pack of wild entertainment reporters and photographers. But if she comes out, she becomes public fodder and alienates the powers-that-be who will select the next Seattle Arts Czar, a person who will most assuredly not be her. Both options suck.

She shifts her gaze from the man in the painting who is undeniably Joe to her own painted avatar. She's so peaceful, so hopeful, so at ease with the wind blowing her shift and the night sky falling heavy around her. No fear as she gazes up at the shooting star that unites them both. That version of Sarah has clearly never read a nasty GabZone story about her body. Lucky girl. She's probably not a widow with an elephant-sized guilty conscience either.

Sarah thinks through the options again. She tries to imagine every permutation, seeking an equation that equals a happy ending, but she just can't do the math. She gazes across the room to the picture of Ben still sitting on her bedside table. She should move it at least back to the mantel downstairs, now that she's sleeping with another man, but she hasn't yet spent a night at home, so she hasn't gotten as far as the ceremonial re-removal of the dead husband's photo. "What do I do, Ben?" When he says nothing, she adds, "Maybe I leapt into this too quickly." Ben peers back at her with stoic silence. "You're no help," she sighs.

She spots the clock and bristles. It's time to go. She's still entirely undecided about which terrible option to choose, but she's got a dinner to attend. She's going to meet Joe's daughter Avery. No pressure there.

***

Avery pulls up to the house and nods approvingly. This is the sort of house her dad should get for himself. Maybe a little bigger. Maybe on the ocean instead of a lake, but still, this is the right idea. Not that there's really anything wrong with his current rental, but even setting aside the fact that her megastar father is *renting* a house, the house is so decidedly middle class. It's a pleasant house for a successful, growing family, not a Hollywood superstar bachelor pad. It's time for Dad to step up his game, to embrace the success he's achieved, to get unstuck. Hopefully his stay in Seattle will inspire him.

Her father mentioned introducing her to a friend of his, so she prepares herself for an evening of industry talk. It's not her industry, but she's grown up around it and certainly knows how to talk the talk for an evening. Still, she hopes to get at least a few minutes alone with her dad because she needs the scoop on that GabZone story Nathan sent her. If her dad has finally found someone of interest, she needs the details. But for now, she throws an "on" smile onto her face and knocks.

The door pops open a moment later and her father greets her with a giant grin and a bearhug. "There she is!" He tugs on her arm and beckons her in. "I want you to meet Sarah," he says as he gestures toward a heavy-set, blonde woman wearing a tentative smile. Avery's jaw drops. *Holy shit, is that the woman from the article?*

Sarah steps forward and offers her hand. "Hi, Avery. It's very nice to meet you. I've heard a lot about you," she says.

"Well, I'm always grateful for my fan club of one," Avery says with jovial elbow at her dad. She needs to play this cool. No mentioning the article now. She'll just chill and watch how things unfold. He offers her wine and announces that dinner should be ready in about twenty minutes before they settle into the living room. "Nice digs, Dad," she says. "How'd you land this joint?"

Joe chuckles. "Long story. I'll tell you another time." He drops to the sofa next to Sarah and sits a hair too close, though Sarah quickly shuffles in the opposite direction. But the way he goggles at Sarah as she moves away sends Avery's glee system into high alert. Has her father finally found someone he likes? This evening has just gotten so interesting.

"So, Sarah, what is it you do on the film?" Avery asks, suddenly fascinated indeed by this dinner guest.

"Oh, I don't work on the film," Sarah replies.

"Yes, you do," Joe corrects.

"Well, sort of, I guess. For now. But actually, I'm the director of the Seattle Film Commission by day."

"So… you're local?" This puts an entirely different spin on things. Seattle isn't exactly convenient, but it wouldn't be impossible. It's not like her dad can't afford to go back and forth. And it takes longer to drive to San Diego in rush hour than to fly to Seattle. So, what the hell! If this is what she thinks it is and her dad is *finally* giving someone a chance, she's all in. "And how did you meet?"

"Oh, um…"

Before Sarah can answer, Joe jumps in. "We met a long time ago actually. Sarah helped on 'Jazzman's Blues,'" he says as he brushes her arm with his hand. Sarah blushes and smiles, but doesn't add to Joe's comment.

Joe goes on to say something else, but Avery misses it entirely. She's still stuck on that arm brush. And on the fact that they met seven years ago while he was working on "Jazzman's Blues." And then he came home changed. Did this woman have something to do with that?

Maybe she's jumping to conclusions. A lot of people worked on "Jazzman's Blues," and a number of them are bound to still be here in Seattle. There was no reason to think Joe's change had been due to a specific person. Yet, how many Seattle connections did Joe maintain after leaving? Why is this woman, of all people, suddenly in his life – unless there was some deeper connection? "So, did you two stay in touch all this time?" Avery asks with as much sunshine as possible.

"No," Sarah says quickly. "Not at all. We just reconnected the last couple weeks. Because of the film."

Okay, so they weren't in touch all along. That's good. And yet she's here. Sarah's made her way into Dad's inner sanctum after just a couple weeks. Her father who wouldn't even go on a single date with Val, despite Avery's pleas. And Sarah's not even in the business, so this isn't a work thing, whether she's working on the film or not. She's a fast mover to go from work acquaintance to dinner with the daughter in under two weeks.

Unless she had a headstart.

The oven dings and they relocate to the table while her father pulls everything out. Sarah jumps in to help him and she knows exactly where to find the plates, silverware, and napkins. He's only been in town a couple weeks, yet she's already been here enough to know where the silverware is. Joe flashes Sarah an almost imperceptible, yet knowing smile and suddenly Avery knows something, too. Her father had an affair with this woman. With every light touch and careful glance exchanged, it's so obvious he might as well be wearing a neon sign flashing "I slept with this woman and I'm doing it again!"

So, this is the reason Joe came home different. This is the woman who turned him into a broken Picasso of a man. Sure, his career soared, but he divorced her mother and never managed to commit to another woman in all this time. He's barely even dated. Hell, he couldn't even commit to a house. Like Avery told Nate, their father has been permanently stuck. And this woman is to blame.

Now he's setting the table with her like they've spent a lifetime together, like she's *his person*. This woman who slept with her married father and destroyed her family. Maybe they haven't carried on through the years. Nothing about his demeanor or behavior ever suggested he was having a long-distance romance all this time, but clearly she jumped at the chance for another roll in the hay when movie star Joe Parker came back into town. Avery could almost admire her gumption – if she didn't now hate her.

Avery smiles politely throughout dinner and makes conversation like she's not entirely infuriated and disgusted. She tells them about the misfire at UW and her plans to return next week for an actual interview, and she listens with a reasonable facsimile of an appreciative smile as Sarah talks about her work and the job she's going for. She watches her father beam at Sarah all evening and seethes at the realization that this woman has manipulated him into a bowlful of lovesick jelly. The woman who split up her parents. Maybe not directly, but Avery saw the writing on the wall as soon as her dad came home so different. Something big had changed and she could tell even then that it was only a matter of time before it would materially impact her own life, even if she didn't know how at first. The divorce that broke her father, and broke her own heart, may have taken three more years, but she could absolutely trace its seeds to Joe's first movie in Seattle. And now, to Sarah.

After dinner, Joe pulls out the fixings for individual strawberry shortcakes. He's made the strawberry syrup, but announces that he wanted to keep it simple. "I figured we could assemble them ourselves." Sarah coos with enthusiasm for the endeavor until Joe emerges from the fridge and announces he's forgotten the Rea-di-whip. "You know what? There's a little corner shop at the top of the hill. The guy has already gotten used to me. I'll run up there and get some. Ave, want to come with?"

This is her chance. "I'll stay here with Sarah, get to know her some more," she says with a smile before turning that smile sweetly on Sarah. After Joe leaves, her smile turns into a laser beam. She only has fifteen minutes, tops. "So, you go way back with my dad, huh?"

Sarah shifts uncomfortably. She turns and lifts her leg onto the sofa as if in protection. "Yeah, you could say that. But it's been nice reconnecting since he came back." Sarah clearly doesn't want to give anything away, but she can't think Avery is stupid. She's holding her cards close.

"Right, well, it's obvious he really likes you," Avery says. Sarah smiles and floods red, but studies a painting on the wall to avoid the subject. "Here's the thing…," she says, but then she stops completely to watch Sarah's reaction. She traces the twitch of Sarah's mouth and the tension creeping into her shoulders. Good. She's paying attention. Avery goes on, "I love my father with all my heart. And I love my mother."

The words make Sarah sit up extra straight. She smiles as broadly as she can as she says, "Of course, you do, Avery! Your dad is great and you're great, so I'm sure your mom is as well. She would have had to be to raise such a smart, beautiful daughter."

Avery winces out a pinched smile. Flattery will get Sarah nowhere in this conversation. "I remember when he came back from Seattle last time, you know. I remember it clear as day, because he was so different."

"Oh?" Sarah says hesitantly.

"Now I think I know why. You and he had an affair, didn't you?"

Finally, Sarah turns her head slowly toward Avery and holds her gaze. "Avery…"

"Didn't you?" Avery repeats.

"You should talk to your father."

"I'm talking to you."

"There's a lot you don't understand."

"I understand enough." Avery troubles her cheek with her tongue as she plots her next words. Is she really going to do this? Her conscience niggles her only a little, but it's enough to give her at least a moment of pause. She would never want to sabotage her own father's happiness. But that's not what she's doing here. He's stuck. And he's been stuck for seven years. Ever since *this woman* came into his life, apparently. Obviously, she's the problem, which means if she's gone for once and for all, he'll finally be free to move on and be truly happy. Besides which, she can hardly be expected to root for her father with the very woman who split up her parents. "And here's what you need to understand. You need to leave my father alone."

"It's not that simple."

"Of course, it is. You've had your little fun. You can tell all your friends you had a fling with a movie star and write it in your little diary or whatever. But it ends now."

Avery watches Sarah turn a fiery red that speaks more of anger than embarrassment. "I don't think I can do that."

"You leave," Avery says, "or I leave." It's a brutal ultimatum, but she's not going to let this woman, of all women, take her mother's place.

"What?"

"I'm not going to stand by and watch my father partner up with the woman who broke up his marriage to my mother."

Sarah shakes her head in protest. "I did not do that."

"You leave or I leave," Avery says again. "My father loves me and I know it will hurt him, but I will *not* see him if he's with you."

"That'll kill him," Sarah says.

"Well, then you have a choice to make," Avery says. "I hope you choose well." She stands and gets her bag from the chair at the island. It's safer to be gone when her dad gets back.

Sarah follows, growing more desperate with each step. "Avery, please, you can't do this to him."

"The ball is in your court, Sarah. What do *you* want to do to him?"

"Please."

"I think I'll try to get the late flight back to L.A. Please tell my dad bye for me. And that I love him." Avery reaches for Sarah's limp hand and shakes it like a floppy noodle. She considers one last shot before she goes, but she's done enough. "I'll text him tomorrow." With a deeply sarcastic smile, she turns and walks out the door.

Chapter Sixteen

Impossible Choices

Joe walks into a strangely quiet house. He'd hoped Sarah and Avery would be chattering away like old friends, so sure was he that they'd get along like a cozy campfire brimming with warmth and easy laughs. But the stone silence alerts him to another possibility, that the campfire he left grew into a four-alarm dumpster fire. He walks into an empty living room with no sign of either woman. "Hellooo," he calls. "I got the whipped cream." He scans out back, and seeing no sign of them, heads for the stairs. "Sarah?"

She emerges at the top of the stairs with her weekender bag over her shoulder. "Hey," she says as she descends.

"What happened? Where's Avery?"

"She said she wanted to catch a late flight back to L.A." Sarah reaches the bottom of the stairs and tries to push past Joe, but he catches her and kisses her. She gives in to the softness of the moment, but she's definitely holding back.

"It's only been fifteen minutes," Joe says as Sarah sets her bag on the island. "Couldn't she have waited?"

"She probably had to hurry to catch her flight," Sarah says with not much conviction. "She said she'd call you later. And she said she loves you," she adds dully.

Joe slides up to her and snakes his arms around her waist. He stoops to her ear and says, "I'm glad you got to meet. What did you think?"

Sarah pulls away and crosses the room to get her purse. "She's obviously very smart." She pauses to dig through her purse for her phone, then adds, "And a skilled communicator."

"Takes after her dad," Joe says with pride. Yet, something is very off about all this. Coming home, he was sailing high on his two favorite women in the world finally meeting. Now, barely two minutes later, he's discovered that one has already dashed – and the other is zipping up her weekender? "Hey, what's going on? You're not leaving, are you?"

Sarah avoids his eyes as she answers. "I should go home tonight. I've barely been home in days. My plants are going to forget what I look like."

"Your plants don't have eyes," he says as he pulls her to him. "Come on, what's going on?"

"Nothing," she says, still avoiding his gaze. "I just have laundry to do. And blind plants to water." She laughs, then tugs free to collect the empty wine glasses from the coffee table.

"You know you can use this house as your own," he says, clocking her response as he speaks. "Go home, do what you need to do, then come back. Let yourself in."

"Don't you have to check in on set later? Night shoot tonight, right?"

"I was hoping to cuddle up to you when I got back." Joe watches Sarah darting around nervously and is reminded of the old Sarah. The Sarah who was terrified of what was between them, terrified to let Joe in and accept the inevitability of what they were to each other.

That Sarah fought the truth of them tooth and nail, unable to accept that a power far larger than either of them had a plan for them. But once she'd accepted it, she'd been so soft, so beautifully present and unafraid. He thought they were there again, and this time for good. But watching Sarah frantically wash the wine glasses now, it's plain something has shifted. It can only be that damn GabZone story.

Sarah rinses the glasses and sets them next to the sink on a tea towel. He watches her back straighten and she appears to nod at nothing at all. Then she turns to face him and says with a falsely bright smile, "Tomorrow."

"You're not worried about that story, are you? Because we'll figure it out." He's actually not sure there is any solution short of exposure that will make the rabid celebrity gossip machine forget about them once they get a bone in their mouth. But he would extinguish the sun and sink the world into permanent darkness if it would make this woman happy. So, yeah, he'll figure it out. "No matter what you decide about going public."

"It's not that...," she says before trailing off, her eyes drifting to the mid-distance.

"No? Then what? Baby, did something happen with Avery?"

Her face tightens, but she manages a solemn smile. "No, of course it's the article. I just need a little more time to think about what to do."

"About the story?" he prompts. Something more rustles over his senses, but he can't find a path to dig it out if she won't at least stay and talk to him.

"About the story," she replies definitively. She grabs her bags, places a hand on his cheek, and plants a gentle kiss on his lips.

Somehow, it feels more like a kiss-off. "I'll talk to you tomorrow," she says as she closes the door behind her.

***

Sarah scoots further under the umbrella to avoid the blinding mid-day sun as Gabi returns from restroom. "Did you know they have a sculpture of Rosa Parks in the bathroom?"

"In the bathroom?" Sarah echoes incredulously.

"I think I want to move in," Gabi says as she shuffles her seat back in.

"At least you'd eat well." Sarah eyes the park across the street where a small group of kids strum guitars haphazardly and hum out a tune together. "And have a soundtrack."

"Alright, enough about my dream life. Let's get back to your dream life," Gabi says. She takes a bite of her sandwich and says through her stuffed mouth, "You can't give in to her."

"Can't I?"

"We don't negotiate with terrorists."

"She's not a terrorist," Sarah says. She stirs her soup listlessly, then tears off a piece of her roll instead. "She's a young woman who loves her father."

Gabi jumps in quickly at this. "*You* love her father."

"Yeah. Enough to not come between him and his daughter." And that's the crux of it, isn't it? That's always been the deciding factor. The first time around, the thing that had convinced Sarah to break it off with Joe was his kids. He loved them too much to hurt them, but he couldn't bring himself to walk away from Sarah, so she had to do it for him. She also knew that Ben had changed, seen the error of his ways and was ready to rebuild with her. She'd gone back to Ben and found true happiness with him. For a plethora of reasons, it was the right thing to do for Sarah and Joe to walk away from each other and return to their lives. But it had started with Joe's kids. "There's nothing more important to Joe than his kids."

"You sure about that?"

Gabi waits patiently for Sarah to reply. Is she sure? How can she be sure? She knows what Joe means to her. The way their lives have intertwined for nearly fifty years is surely the work of the gods. And now that she has this second chance with him, she wants to believe nothing is more important.

But Sarah doesn't have kids. She never stayed up late when they had fevers or rushed to the hospital when they broke bones or ran around shuffling them to games and concerts. She's never worried about paying for college or stayed up late when they missed a curfew. She's never lived the life of a parent and passed through all those countless milestones that cement those little people in a parent's heart like the jewels in a crown that bestow it all its beauty and value. Without the jewels, it's just a metal hat. She's seen the way Joe lights up when he talks about his kids. She knows how much he sacrificed in the lean, early years of his career to keep them safe and fed. His kids are what have made Joe's life beautiful, made his metal hat shine. "Of course," she says.

"So, tell him what's going on. Maybe he can talk to her." Gabi always makes sensible things sound so absolutely, positively sensible. But this isn't a question of sense. This is a question of the heart, and Joe's heart would break if he lost his daughter.

"And put him in the middle? What kind of position does that leave him in?"

"In a position to make an informed decision."

She makes a decent point, but Sarah's not in the mood for reason. Because her gut is saying run. Get out of this thing before everyone is ripped to shreds and all that's left is the bloody debris of a once perfect thing. Get out while it's still perfect. "He should never have to make that decision," she says.

"No, but you're not the one making him choose."

"Not if I don't tell him, I'm not."

"Jesus, you're a piece of work, you know that?" Gabi says. "Can we break up?"

"Sorry, the thirty-year return policy just expired. I'm afraid you're stuck with me." Sarah watches most of the teens packing up their guitars. They slap hands and wave as they wander away, leaving one lonely girl sitting on the low, cement bench, staring into space. "Anyway, I'm not sure I'm cut out for this life. A life with Joe. In the spotlight where he lives. Maybe Joe and I were only ever supposed to be what we are. Ships that pass in the night now and then."

Gabi rolls her eyes and kicks Sarah under the table. "You don't believe that."

"Ow!" Sarah whines as she kneels down to rub her leg dramatically. Why can't this all be easier? As much as she loves Joe, she's still pushing through all her Ben stuff as well. He still lingers in her mind all the time, and she's had to keep making an affirmative choice to believe that what's before her is really hers to have and to hold, despite her guilt. Meanwhile, she still hasn't even had the guts to get back to Ben's sister about those photos yet. So yeah, still on the struggle bus. And now this. "I don't really know what I believe anymore."

***

Joe stares at the highly engaged face of Terry Blanchard and draws a total blank. Terry is standing there in costume, every ounce the 1960s civic leader Edward E. Carlson with a fake receding hairline, black framed glasses, and a spiffy blue suit waiting for an update on the construction of his signature tower, the so-called "Space Needle" that will draw people from all over to the World's Fair a year later. Joe knows he's supposed to say something about the excavation of the site, but whatever it is, it's completely gone.

"Cut!" yells Beltran.

"Reset!" shouts Geena.

Betran comes up to Joe and Terry and leans in. "Joe, buddy, you okay?"

It's been like this all day. Joe's been forgetting his lines, slipping out of character as his mind wandered to Sarah and this whole mess with GabZone. He can't get his head on straight. But this is his job. And he's good at it. Usually. "Sorry, guys," Joe says, shaking his head. "I didn't get a lot of sleep last night. I'll get it. Let's go again."

"You sure?" Beltran says. "We could take a short break. Give you a chance to review your lines if you need to. Get your head in the game."

"Yeah, no problem," Terry says as he pats Joe on the arm. Terry's always been a gem of a human being.

"No, no," Joe says, "I'm okay. Let's get this thing done."

They finish resetting, call action, and Joe and Terry go again. This time, Joe stays in it almost to the very end when he begins his next line, then stops short and simply says, "Fuck."

"Cut!" yells Beltran again.

Joe contemplates Terry and all the crew whose valuable time he is absolutely wasting with this ridiculous lack of professionalism. He needs to pull it together. "You know, maybe I could use a short break. Could we take ten?"

"Take ten," Beltran says quietly.

"Take ten, everybody!" Geena echoes with a shout into the megaphone.

Ten minutes isn't enough time to retreat to his trailer which is parked quite far away, so he settles for his chair and Randy is at the ready with his phone. He also hands Joe a copy of the sides in case he wants a refresher on his lines, and a La Croix with a straw. Joe loses not a second in dialing his publicist Casey. He's been texting with Casey on and off all day, but it's so damn hard getting info in tiny text size snippets. "Hey, what's the latest?" he says as soon as Casey answers.

Casey blows out a puff of air before saying, "You're not going to like it."

"Now tell me something I don't know."

"It's officially gone viral," Casey says. "Yesterday, it was just a handful of Instagram and Twitter accounts, but today, it's exploded. It's popping up in a bunch of TikToks now as well, and even on Facebook."

"Jesus, when it gets as far as Facebook..."

"You and your lady love have crossed the Rubicon, my friend."

Poor Sarah. She didn't ask for any of this. She never signed up for fame, let alone the brutal scrutiny of celebrity gossip rags. Of course, neither did Joe, but he accepts it as part of the business, part of the cost of being Joseph Robert Parker. He always knew he'd trade a certain amount of anonymity for the gift of doing the work he loves, and he's enjoyed the benefits from it for a long time, even if he's had to endure the costs along the way. But it was his choice. He agreed to that bargain. Sarah didn't.

Casey goes on. "We've had about a dozen calls for comment so far. I don't think they're going to stop anytime soon. Obviously, we haven't said anything yet."

"And we won't," Joe says pointedly.

"Of course. But it would be best if we could move forward with the launch sooner rather than later. Any word from Sarah on that?"

"Still working on it."

"Well," Casey says, "the sooner the better. Because the hungrier they get, the nastier they'll get. Better to feed the wolves on our own terms."

When Joe hangs up, his ten minutes are nearly up. He skims his lines and they look exactly like the lines he learned last night. He knows his lines. It's not his memory that's failing, it's his concentration. He's got to get his shit together, and that starts with protecting Sarah. He needs to find a way to remind her that this is all worth it, despite this awful interlude. Something spectacular. He waves Randy over. "Listen, I want to do something special for Sarah."

Chapter Seventeen

Tulips

Sarah turns the key and pushes open the door, fully prepared for an empty house. Joe will still be shooting and she needs the time anyway to prepare herself for the conversation. Maybe she'll sit outside and enjoy the view of the lake. A beautiful, quiet place to think.

But when she walks in, a big, empty house isn't what she finds. Instead, she's greeted by an entire floor flooded with tulips. Tall vases, short vases, planters on stands, giant bouquets blooming from bowls that disappear under the weight of their flowers. An explosion of color tinting every corner of the living room, dining room, and kitchen. There must be hundreds of flowers, thousands even. Pinks, purples, yellows, reds, oranges, whites, and every combination imaginable. It's not tulip season in Skagit County, so Joe must have bought out the Netherlands. There can't be a tulip left in all of the Northern Hemisphere.

"Do you like it?" Joe asks from the doorway behind Sarah.

"I wasn't expecting you home yet," Sarah says without turning.

Joe approaches her from behind and wraps his arms around her waist. "I had a tough day today. I couldn't remember my lines to save my life."

Sarah turns her face back, her cheek brushing against his chest. "I'm sorry," she says, unsure what more to say.

"But then I thought of your face when you walked in and were welcomed by all this and it focused me like a laser beam. Because I wanted to be here to see it."

Sarah turns in his arms to face him. "They're beautiful, Joe. I don't even know what to say."

"They pale next to you."

"No. They don't." She gawks across the room again, finding flowers in every corner. "I can't believe you did this."

"I debated between roses and tulips, but tulips felt right."

"I've always loved tulips," she says.

"Why did I know that?" he says with a chuckle before pulling her to the couch and down onto his lap. "I know that article has been getting you down."

Sarah sighs. If only the article was all that was bothering her. "It hasn't been easy," she admits.

"So, let's not worry about it tonight, okay? Let's just be us. Sarah and Joe. Joe and Sarah." He cups her face and snakes his other hand through her hair to the back of her neck. "You and me and nobody else. At least for tonight." He tugs her so gently and her lips pull towards him as if by magnetic force as their mouths connect and their tongues mingle with a sweetness that washes away all the worries of the day. "Like we used to be."

Once upon a time, they hid from the world in a hotel room where they made their "just us" agreement. No one else could know. And no one else was allowed in. It was their respite from the world, their sacred place to be solely with and for each other. And it was perfect.

Now, they're free to be together in theory, yet the outside world remains an enemy. Somehow, they're still hiding, still only safe in each other's arms, only safe as long as they can keep the world at bay. And everything Sarah has longed for and imagined with Joe feels just as impossible as it ever did.

Yet, here in his arms, they're also as inevitable as they ever were. This isn't how she thought this evening would go, but for one night, they do as Joe suggests. They eat pizza, they sing showtunes and Brandi Carlile, they skinny dip in their extremely private pool, and they make love. They shut everything out but each other.

***

The next morning, Sarah wakes to the sound of the shower. Joe is quietly humming and it's the sweetest song. His voice is so happy, so content, that it breaks her heart. Joe has lugged several of the tulip arrangements up to the room under cover of the night, all so that Sarah can wake to such beauty as befits a queen. And she's never felt like anything less with Joe. And yet... and yet.

This is the right decision. She hates it and she'll regret it forever, but she would regret coming between Joe and his daughter, too. And she would regret betraying Ben by choosing Joe. She had just about managed to convince herself that she'd finished mourning Ben, but this whole thing has made it clear that she's not ready to move on. Certainly not with Joe. Certainly not when choosing Joe would tear apart his family and savage Sarah with guilt.

Sarah curls into a ball and nurses the sinking boulder in her gut. She knows she should be steeling herself, but this is the hardest thing she'll ever do and she doesn't want to make herself okay about it. Her heart is broken and she won't feign nonchalance. This should hurt. It should slice into her like a modern-day crown of thorns. It's only right.

She pulls herself out of bed and dresses quickly. When Joe comes out, she needs to be ready. She rushes around and gathers all her things into her bag. Her toothbrush and face creams are still in the bathroom, with Joe, but everything else makes its way into her bag until the only trace of Sarah that remains is Sarah herself. And even she is only a trace of Sarah.

The water shuts off. Sarah sits on the side of the bed facing the bathroom, her bag next to her. She waits, imagining Joe stepping from the shower, his beautiful body still so muscular, though a touch softer than it once was, a hint wider than it used to be. The body that has shown her such pleasure and enfolded her in absolute safety. The body that always reacts to her touch and magnetizes to her presence. The body that he would willingly give to her forever, yet she will never hold again.

Joe steps out of the bathroom, a towel wrapped around his waist and a grin beaming his joy in her direction, until he sees her. His smile fades instantly as his head tilts. "Sarah?"

It's written all over that perfect, chiseled face. He knows what she's going to say. "Joe… I need to go."

"What do you mean, go?"

"This was always just a fantasy. This house? Our make-believe domestic life? This was never sustainable and we both know it."

"I know no such thing," Joe says as he quickly tugs on a pair of sweats.

Sarah can't blame him for not wanting to have this conversation in the nude, so she waits for him to put on a tee-shirt, despite her growing agitation to get the hell out of this room. "Our lives are too different," she says as he tugs his shirt downward. "You'll never live in my world and I can't live in yours."

"Let's talk about this," Joe says. "We can figure it out. Lots of people in the industry are married to non-industry people. They make it work. We can find a way."

Sarah wonders if those people also have angry daughters who have secretly threatened to cut their parents out of their lives. "It's not that simple."

"Fuck simple. Nothing about us has ever been simple. We are by far the most complicated thing in my entire life. But Sarah, I want every one of your complications."

This is it. This is the moment when she has to say it like she means it. She has to convince Joe that it's really over. "I don't want it."

Joe drops to his knees in front of her. "I know you don't mean that."

Sarah softens, her resolve flickering for the length of a heartbeat, just enough to let the words slip out. "No, I don't mean it. I do want it. But I can't have it."

She stands, takes her bag, and pushes past Joe to the door. He remains on his knees and his head drops as he says, "Sarah, I love you." His voice cracks with hopelessness as the words come out, and Sarah's heart cracks with it.

"I love you, too," she says as she pauses to study this version of Joe one last time. To soak him into her bones before she casts him out of her life. "But it's not enough." Then she is gone.

Chapter Eighteen

Last Chance

The boat is still moored on the private dock of the house. Joe sits in the back seat, his feet up across cushions, gently floating. He stares out at the lake through his sunglasses that tamp down the bright sunlight to an almost bearable shade. Beneath him, the gentle slosh of water around the pilings and boat as the wake from a passing jet ski finally reaches shore and the boat rocks soothingly. He hasn't moved in hours.

It had started to make sense again with Sarah. The joy was back. After "Jazzman's Blues" proved itself a very palpable hit, the whole world had opened up for him. Suddenly, every script was being sent to him and every director wanted to work with him. All it took was one big movie – well, one movie plus twenty years slogging through the business – to go from vaguely recognizable minor leaguer to universally beloved household name. All thanks to the movie that Sarah helped him make. And for a while, it was fantastic. It had been a dream come true to finally have the work he'd always longed for. That had eased the pain of the inevitable end of his marriage a couple years later, softened the edges of a new life sans partner or even kids as Nathan followed Avery to college. The success kept him afloat. More than that, it kept him sailing high for a long, long time.

Then, one day, he felt his face twitching over a tiny thing. Some small problem that was easily solved, so minor he can't even remember what it was anymore. But he remembers that twitch. That twitch made its way through his body as various other production problems popped up. He was losing patience for the small things, and he gradually realized that the joy was fading. Not because the work was less gratifying. To the contrary, the work had been better than ever before. But because he didn't have anyone to share it with. Without sharing his joys, they floundered and diminished, while the headaches grew, pounded, and weighed him down. He pushed on, of course, because that's what you do. But he needed someone with whom to share the joys, to bring him back – and there was only one person for that.

From the corner of his eye, he sees a body approaching. He doesn't look, but his peripheral awareness slowly shapes the figure into Randy. Randy reaches the dock and says, "Going boating?" Joe doesn't answer. He simply stares at the water. "They were looking for you on set."

Joe heaves a frustrated breath. "I finished my shoot."

"Yeah," Randy agrees. "But you're still a producer."

"I'm allowed a day off," Joe says.

"Of course you are," Randy agrees quickly. When Joe says nothing, Randy holds up a glass. "Made you a smoothie."

Joe ignores the smoothie, but finally turns to Randy. "Have you heard from her?'

Randy shakes his head. "No. I tried calling her, but she hasn't called back. Or texted," he says. "I think she's ducking me."

"You're not the one she's ducking," Joe says before finally standing to take the smoothie.

He invites Randy onto the boat. Randy looks askance at the scenario, as if he's evaluating the pros and cons of descending into a floating meeting space. He hands Joe his own smoothie so he has his hands free, then grabs a pole and shakily steps down. Once safely onboard, he takes his smoothie back and installs himself in the captain's seat while Joe settles back into his lounging position across the back. "You doing okay, bud?"

"Define 'okay'," Joe says before taking a drink of his smoothie. They sit in silence and rock for a minute, and Joe imagines a world where this perfect moment sipping smoothies on a beautiful, wooden boat on a glorious summer day doesn't shred his guts into chaos and carnage. But without Sarah, that world doesn't exist.

It was different before she came back. When they'd separated the first time, they'd known it was right. It was for the best. They healed each other, then they went back to their lives to live more fully and joyfully, knowing that a little piece of each of them would always be with the other. The ending had been right and good. Noble even. Sure, it had gradually faded into the half-life he was living, but it was a life he knew how to live. He still had his work and his kids. His work was laudable, if not joyful, and his kids were everything to him. It was enough.

But this? They found each other again. They were both available. And, of course, they still loved each other. Their hearts still sang together. Their bodies still melded together. Their souls still merged. They would always love each other. That part wasn't even remotely in question. And still, she walked away. She just said "no" and left. And now, she won't even talk to him. And he's expected to go on like before. Like it never happened. Like the angels didn't show him paradise before snatching it away and hurling him back to Earth, which has now transformed into hell in comparison. Funny how perspective can shift a perfectly good life, great by most standards, into intolerable darkness and torment in the blink of an eye. He knows he lives a blessed life. But none of it means anything without Sarah.

"She won't talk to me. I've tried and tried, but nothing," he says. "It's like it never even happened. Sometimes I think I imagined the whole thing."

"Oh, it happened. I saw it," Randy says. "You two might as well have walked through town ringing a Hannah Waddingham bell, you were so obvious."

Even Randy's cheeky "Game of Thrones" references aren't enough to pull Joe out of this slump. "What am I supposed to do? Shrug and let her go? She seems pretty fucking determined."

"Have you told her about...?" Randy trails off, but nudges his head backwards towards the house. Joe shakes his head, but says nothing. "Well, maybe before you give up entirely, you should do that."

***

Sarah rereads the email inviting her to interview for the Arts Czar job. This is her moment. All her work for years, first as Director of Operations, then as Executive Director of the Film Commission. And now, if she can pull this off, she'll be in charge of all Seattle Arts. It's a heady prospect. She needs to be on her A-game, not moping about something that was never meant to be.

She puts a smile on her face and types her response, making sure her confident, jovial façade translates to the message. Inside, she may be slowly decomposing into a stinky mulch heap, but outside, she's determined to be as bright and cheerful as an English garden. She proofreads, then reads again for good measure, and finally hits Send. She's one step closer to realizing her dream. This is good. This is what she wanted.

All that stuff with Joe was just a distraction. A wonderful distraction, to be sure. A beautiful interlude, much as it was the last time. Joe is an amazing man. Hell, who is she kidding? He's pretty much perfect. But that life could never be real. The love will last forever, but that doesn't mean they actually work in the real world. Their lives are too different and the glare of Joe's spotlight burns too hot for Sarah. She had only the slightest taste of it and it scorched her to the core. She's lucky she got out before someone who recognized her sold her name to the highest bidder.

And then there's Avery. The one thing she knows about Joe, more than literally anything else, is that his kids mean the world to him. She would never dream of making him choose between her and his kids. That would be cruel. Besides, if she won, the guilt would eat away at her. And if she lost, the pain of Joe's rejection would be so much worse than anything she can self-impose. Walking away is the only option that makes sense for so many reasons. But why does her soul have to ache like it's gone through the woodchipper?

Her phone pings with a message from Joe. She glimpses his name and sighs, then picks it up carefully and opens the phone to read it in full. *Can you come to the house tonight? There's something I need to tell you.*

Sarah mulls over her response, then types, *I don't think it's a good idea.*

It's important, comes Joe's immediate response. *Then if you want to go, I'll let you go. Please?*

***

Sarah sighs up at the spectacular house one last time. It's a dream house, the kind of place she never even imagined setting foot in, let alone treating like home for a few days. It's been a beautiful place to live out the fantasy. But every fantasy must eventually end. She knocks on the door.

Joe pulls it open and welcomes her in. "You do still have a key," he says.

"I didn't feel right using it," she says as she slides it off her keyring. She holds it up to show him, then places it on the counter. "I was going to give it to Randy, but now I don't have to."

Joe moves toward the kitchen in a gesture of optimism. "Do you want something to drink?"

"I can't stay long," she replies, shutting him down.

"Will you at least sit?"

Sarah nods and walks across the room to the living room where she plants herself in the very stiff, but surprisingly comfortable chair she'd enjoyed reading in on several occasions. It's a molded mid-century modern curve, but in the perfect shape for sitting straight up, with bright orange and chrome armrests framing either side. Like Sarah, the chair has firm boundaries. "So, what did you need to tell me?"

Joe paces a little, apparently working up the courage to speak. "I don't suppose you'd be willing to tell me what's going on. Why you left so suddenly?"

Sarah's heart races at the question. She worked so hard to prepare for this conversation, thought she was ready for whatever he had to say and then to walk away exactly as planned. No matter what happened, she was ready to handle it and carry herself out with her head held high. But she wasn't ready to account for her own actions, which in retrospect was a pretty monumental mistake. "I'm sorry, I don't want to talk about it. I can't."

"Why not?" he says. "You've always been able to talk to me before."

Sarah scratches her head, then smooths her hair, giving herself a moment to think. But no words come. If the words exist to explain what's happening without exposing the rift with Joe's daughter, Sarah hasn't discovered them yet. "I'm sorry, Joe, I can't do this."

She moves as if to stand, but Joe drops quickly to the couch next to her and pleads. "Wait! Please." And the strain of desperation freezes her to her seat. He sighs and says, "Okay, here's the thing... Did you happen to notice what that boat out there is called?"

"The boat?"

"The wooden boat. That we took out the other day. Did you happen to notice its name?"

Sarah peers through the giant wall of glass to the boat in the distance. Like last time, the boat is facing the house and she can't see the name, not that she'd be able to read it from here anyway. "No, I didn't."

Joe nods his head mutely, then raises his eyes to her. "Would you do me a favor and walk out there and look?"

"Can't you just tell me?" Sarah asks. While she knows it's a reasonable question, if he's asking her to go look, she also knows what his answer is probably going to be.

"It would mean a lot to me if you'd go look."

Sarah nods and heads for the door. She slides open the glider, walks past the pool and into the yard. As she walks, her mind dances through a million possibilities about why this exercise could be necessary. It seems crazy, but nothing this important to Joe is ever crazy. She assumes it will somehow be some big, dramatic reveal, that's meant to change her mind. But why would a boat name do that? She steps onto the dock, walks to the end, and takes a deep breath before turning to take in the boat. *Sarah's Smile*. It's called *Sarah's Smile*.

She should have walked more slowly, given herself more time to calculate the possibilities. If she'd thought long enough, she would have gotten to something like this. She could have prepared herself, readied her brain and steadied her heart. But the thirty-second walk had barely been enough to imagine the outline of this moment, let alone to color it in. And now, she's staring at a boat that appears to be named after her. Shit.

She walks slowly back up to the house where Joe's waiting in the doorway. "Is that me on that boat?" she says. She already knows the answer, of course, but feels the need to confirm for good measure, and more importantly, to buy herself processing time.

"Yeah," Joe says as he steps back into the house.

Sarah follows him in and waits, unsure what to do next.

"This is my house, Sarah," Joe says.

"What?"

He gestures to the glass French doors off to the left side of the house. "You never went into the office here, did you?"

"Well, I didn't want to pry in someone else's house."

"Let's go in," he says before leading her to the doors and pulling them open.

A pit in Sarah's gut grows. She doesn't want to walk into that room. Everything in her nervous system screams *Run!* Still, she steps through the doors behind him. In front of her is a beautiful vintage desk and chair, and behind her, a large wall of rustic shelves, covered in photos of his kids. He walks over to his desk and turns around the only two frames on his desk. One is a photo of the two of them, a selfie they took the very first day they met at Kerry Park, with the whole span of the Seattle skyline behind them. The other is a photo she doesn't recognize, but she can tell it's the two of them again. This one is from the back, holding hands on a beach, which could only be from their getaway to that Airbnb, though she has no idea where the photo came from.

"This is the only room I personalized," Joe explains. "When I first bought this place, right after my divorce, I thought I'd live here full-time when I wasn't on shoots. You'd made me fall in love with Seattle, you see, and I thought I could be happy here."

"So, you live here?"

"No, I don't. It turns out, without you, it felt empty. And it hurt more than I expected. Too much to stay here." He pauses, lost in thought about the years this house sat empty. "I thought I bought the house for me, but once I tried to stay here alone, I knew it needed you to make it a home. Without you, it was just my 'maybe someday' home."

Sarah's mind reels at what Joe appears to be telling her. "I don't understand," she mutters, though the revolting, terrifying churn in her stomach warns that she actually understands more than she'd like to admit.

"Yes, you do. You've always understood," Joe says, calling her on her bullshit. He leans back on the desk and laughs a little sadly. "You're it for me, kid. You're my North Star. My fixed point. You're the air in my lungs and the blood in my veins. You have been from the start and nothing – not even you – can change that. And I know you know that." He pauses, either to process his own emotions, or maybe simply for dramatic effect, then adds, "So, yeah, you do understand. What I don't understand is why you're resisting this so hard."

"Joe..."

"Sarah, you and I were always meant to be. You know that."

"It's not that simple," she says as she fights like hell to stay strong. But her resolve is fading.

"Here, I'll make it simple." He leads her to one of the two guest chairs in front of the desk. As she sits, he grabs the other and scoots it right in front of hers before sitting and leaning in. He takes her hand again and forces her to hold his gaze. "Do you love me?"

"You know the answer."

"I need you to say it."

"Yes, Joe, I love you," she says. As if that could magically erase everything else.

"And do you like this house?"

Sarah gapes up to the abnormally high ceilings, around at all the impeccable finishes, then out to the pool, the boat, the lake.

Everything about this place is perfect. She couldn't have dreamed a more perfect setting. "Yes, I like this house… I love it."

"I would never have intentionally bought a house for you without consulting you. I didn't know that's what I was doing, I swear. I was just looking for a place I could be happy. But I know now, this isn't my house. This was never my house. This is *our* house. Without you, it's an empty shell. But if you don't like it, we can get another house."

"It's not about the house."

Joe nods at her, then leans in and whispers, "We could make a home here. Away from Hollywood. Away from the spotlight. Just you and me. Just us. Like it used to be."

The words waft over Sarah like a summer breeze, gentle and warm. So soothing, so full of promise and sweetness in the air. *We could make a home here. Just you and me. Like it used to be.* Maybe they could do it. Maybe Fate wasn't screwing with them at all, but giving them a real chance this time.

"I will retire for you," Joe says. As if she could ever want that for him. "I will be Greta Fucking Garbo for you. Just say yes!"

She smiles softly, surrendering to the tenderness in his eyes. The kindest, most beautiful man she's ever known. She opens her mouth, preparing to give him the yes he wants, and she pauses only a flicker as she sweeps the room again to process the words forming in her throat. To make sure they're the right words to meet the moment, words that will usher in a future she's never dared dream of.

But as her eyes traverse the space, they land on a family picture of Joe, Nathan, and Avery. Then she jumps to another, and another. The whole wall is full of Joe and his kids. Then she lands on a photo of Joe with Avery at her graduation, standing tall and proud, beaming with sunshine, hope, and so much obvious love for her dad that it pours out of them both. Suddenly, Avery's words are echoing in her ear. *You leave or I leave.*

Sarah blows out a slow, measured breath, then pushes her chair slowly backward and stands up. "I'm sorry, Joe. This isn't the life I want." The lie batters her heart like a punching bag, but she ignores the inner devastation and focuses on calmly walking out.

Joe jumps up to follow her as she exits the office and heads for the door. "This is it, Sarah. I bought a house. I named a boat after you. I'm grand gestured out. I can't keep holding onto a dream if you're not willing to grab for it, too."

"I understand," she says, and she's pretty sure her voice only shakes a little as she says it.

"You're the only one for me, you know. There's no one else," Joe says as she reaches the door. Her hand on the doorknob, she waits as he says his peace. "There never will be anyone else. This isn't Mad Libs. You can't just fill in the blank labeled 'soulmate' with any proper name."

Sarah stares at the ground, stiff and unmoving, afraid that any movement will give her true feelings away. "No, you can't," she concedes.

"I don't know what's going on, but I know you. I know how you think. If you don't want this for some crazy reason, that's your prerogative, but don't kid yourself that you're walking away as some noble sacrifice." Joe's slowly running out of steam, and thank goodness, because he's tipping too close to the truth. If he says much more, Sarah may break, and that's the one thing she absolutely cannot do. "Like you're doing me a favor or something, when the truth is you're breaking my heart." His voice cracks at the end and he stops at last, depleted.

Sarah pulls the door open, eyes to the ground and says quietly, "I'll always love you, Joe." Then she closes the door and drives away.

PART TWO

DESTINY

People get the wrong idea about Destiny. They always assume that She's only interested in the major players who change the world. Martin Luther. Catherine the Great. Queen Elizabeth. Marie Curie. However, most people don't get to change the world. That doesn't mean they don't get destinies. They're just of the smaller variety.

Destined to go to this college where you'll discover history and become a professor. Destined to stop for beer on the way to a friend's house and just miss the accident that would have killed you. Or skip the beer and have the accident... Or meet the person who will change your life forever, even if the relationship is destined to be short-lived.

But once in a while, if you're really fortunate, Destiny offers up a lasting peace. A real, true love for the ages. If only you're smart enough to grab it.

Chapter Nineteen

The Theater (Age 23)

THE TAXI PULLED UP and Joe shuffled his bag toward the trunk as the driver popped it open. As a broke actor, he hadn't indulged in many cab rides since he got to New York, and yet, he still felt a tinge of nostalgia as he climbed into the backseat. Living in a city with taxicabs always circling, always ready to shuttle you wherever you wanted to go, was an essential Big Apple experience. Like pizza slices and 24-hour delis. Even if cabs were a luxury he could seldom afford, he was going to miss them.

Los Angeles would bring many new, exciting opportunities. He knew that. Two weeks ago, a young man with thinning blonde hair and a blinding smile came backstage and introduced himself as Clark Kincaid, an up-and-coming agent at a boutique talent agency Joe had never heard of. Then again, he was a New York theater actor. What did he know about Hollywood agents? But when Clark offered Joe representation on the spot based on the strength of his Seymour in "Little Shop of Horrors," he knew enough to say yes. He would have been stupid not to. And now he had a chance to audition for a huge Hollywood movie and the only downside was he had to miss the last week of performances of "Little Shop."

At the theater, he hopped out and rolled through the stage door like the conquering hero. He had just enough time to say goodbye to everyone and wish his understudy luck before heading to the airport. He timed his arrival well, so he found almost the whole cast onstage stretching, doing vocalizations, and shaking out their nerves to warm up. He made his rounds hugging folks and promising to stay in touch. He riffed a quick thirty-second, in-joke ditty with the Greek chorus ladies before doling out goodbyes, then gave his "Audrey" an extra hug and jokingly wished her well kissing the new guy taking over for him.

He climbed the steep stairs to the dressing room that was still his last night and found Anthony, his replacement, sitting at his mirror putting on makeup and repeating his lines to himself. He tapped twice on the door and walked in. "You got this, dude."

Anthony turned to him with a grin. "Hey, look who it is! The big movie star!"

"Not yet, man. Not yet," Joe said.

"Ahh, just a matter of time," Anthony said with a pat on Joe's arm.

"Maybe," Joe said with a thoughtful, angst-ridden shrug. "But how much time is anyone's guess. Anyway, I wanted to stop in and tell you to break a leg. You're gonna do great."

"Thanks, man," Anthony said with a grateful bow. "Hey, you, too. Go knock 'em dead in Hollywood."

Mindful of his own time and Anthony's need to prepare, Joe stood. "Okay, I'll get out of your hair. Make me proud," he said as they slapped hands then shook before Joe headed for the door.

"Send us a postcard," Anthony shouted as Joe made his way to the stairs.

Joe said goodbye to a few more crew members as he descended and waved across the stage one last time. He paused one more brief moment to take it all in. His theater life was over, at least for now. He had a starring role in an Off-Broadway musical, which was pretty fucking close to making it in New York, and he'd only been here a year. And now he was walking away from the greatest success of his life to date to march blindly into the complete unknown. What an absolutely asinine risk to take. What was he thinking?

The notion flickers that this may be the worst idea of his entire life. Leaving a successful, burgeoning career where he was beginning to make a name for himself to go be one of a million nobodies with nothing but a pretty face and a resume that's almost entirely academic in nature was a recipe for obscurity if ever there were one.

He should have at least stayed for this Sunday matinee. Would one more day have killed him? He suddenly had the strongest instinct that he should stay and do this show. Why didn't he stay one more day? They were dark on Monday. That would have made so much sense. He fleetingly pondered whether he could still go on today. He could go find the director and stage manager, announce his plans, run up and get into costume. The urge to go onstage today yanked him like a magnet toward the stage. Just one more show. *This show.*

But no, that was ridiculous. The role was Anthony's now. The dye was cast and it was time to go. On the way out, he stopped to shake hands with Tom. "Heard you coming and got you a cab. Go be a star," the old security guy said. "Make us proud."

"Thanks, Tom," Joe said as he walked out the stage door. He turned back to Tom to wave one last time, and in the process, he inadvertently bumped someone passing on the street outside. He stumbled with his luggage and got it caught on the doorjamb as he turned, causing the bag to pull away from his hand. But instead of immediately reaching for his toppling suitcase, his instincts told him to turn as he felt his body pulled backwards like an invisible tether had lassoed him.

He spun quickly and saw the person he'd bumped. A curvy, blonde vision of a woman walking in the street with an older woman at her side. The blonde glanced back over her shoulder at him and for a fleeting second, they locked eyes. She was positively aglow in the sunlight. She slowed her pace and turned her body just a little, as if deciding between walking on and walking back toward Joe. And all he could do was stare.

"I'll get this," someone said over his shoulder. The voice jarred Joe who didn't want to move from his spot, lest the girl disappear, but the motion behind him demanded his attention, so he turned to discover the cabbie rolling his bag to the car. And when he spun back to the girl, she was running to catch up with her companion. Damn! Yet another reason he shouldn't be leaving New York. The cabbie slammed the trunk closed and headed for his own door. "Ready?"

Joe was not at all convinced he was ready for any of this – he'd much rather chase that girl – but it was time to go. He watched the girl disappear into the theater foyer, sighed, then climbed into the cab and rode away.

***

As her mother stepped into the Will Call line to pick up their tickets, Sarah stepped back out the front door to find that guy. That incredibly tall, unbelievably hot dude. At least, she *thought* he was hot. She'd seen him so briefly that the vision was already fading in her head, yet her instincts screamed "YES!" when she saw him. She was even a little light-headed and her body buzzed, though surely that couldn't have anything to do with him. Still, a little peek couldn't hurt.

She watched a cab door close right where he'd been a moment earlier, so she waited until the car started to move and drove by. The light at the corner had gone green so she only got another very quick glance as the car accelerated past her, but her whole body vibrated as he passed. She should have stopped walking when she had the chance. She should have gone back. She should have listened to her instincts.

"Got 'em," her mother said over her shoulder. "Ready?"

Sarah turned and smiled at her mom, attempting to shake off the sense that she'd just missed something extraordinary. "Sure," she said and they headed for the end of the long entry line. As they worked through the line toward the entrance, Sarah read aloud the review her friend had sent her about the show. It talked up the charismatic performance of the guy playing Seymour, who her friend had also told her was amazing. This show was the finale of her mother-daughter trip to the Big Apple, their first adventure together since her parents divorced, and she was sure it would also be the highlight based on everything she'd heard.

When they walked into the theater, Sarah clutched the program she'd been handed like a precious keepsake, something she would always cherish. But when they settled into their seats, she flipped it open and found a small slip of paper announcing that the role of Seymour would be played by someone else today. Not the guy in the review who she'd been so excited to see. The news fell like a hammer and Sarah felt unaccountably bereft. Why should it matter whether she saw some guy she's never even heard of in this play?

"Oh well," her mother said. "I'm sure the understudy will be good, too."

"Yeah," Sarah agreed at half volume, but she found herself flipping to the cast photos page anyway to get a look at the guy she wasn't going to see. And wait... was that him? The guy in the cab? It couldn't be, could it? He was so young and handsome, with dark hair, bright blue eyes, and something about him that simply echoed through Sarah. Why wasn't he going to be onstage today? She was gutted, despite her mother's reassurances.

When the show began, Sarah forcefully shoved aside her expectations so that her disappointment wouldn't sully the whole thing. And Seymour was very good. The whole cast was excellent. Everything they say about the best of the best landing in NYC was clearly true. Any of these people could be stars, and probably would be one day. She applauded loudly at the end, cheered for everyone, including Seymour, and shuffled out of the theater happy. And yet.

"Well, that was wonderful!" her mom said as they exited.

"It was really good," Sarah agreed.

They made their way toward the subway and her mother hooked her arm in Sarah's. "Told you. We didn't miss that other guy at all."

"Nope," Sarah said. "We didn't." Except, she did. She really, really did. She had no idea why, but she couldn't shake it. She dug through her bag for the program to look again, but couldn't find it. She must have accidentally left it behind. And she didn't even remember his name. "I do still wish I'd gotten to see him though."

"You're really upset, aren't you?" her mom said.

Sarah laughed at the absurdity. He was just a guy in a play. What was the big deal? She was being an idiot, clearly. "Oh, it doesn't matter," she said, brushing off her own melancholy.

"You know what, my dear?" Her mom stopped and pulled her daughter into a hug. "If it's meant to be, you'll get another chance. He'll be in another play, or who knows, maybe you'll run into him in the street sometime!" Her mom stopped to let out a delighted guffaw at the notion. "Fate has a way."

Sarah's heart zigged joyfully at the recognition, grateful that her mother knew her so well, even as it zagged at her entirely irrational longing. She rolled her eyes in a showy dismissal and laughed. "Yes, Fate is very likely to bring me back to some random actor dude I've never even seen act. I think Fate or Destiny or whatever has better things to do with its time."

"Trust me, you never know what Destiny has in store," her mother said. "Just pay attention. And when the moment comes, be sure to buy a ticket."

Chapter Twenty

The Awful Aftermath

"And you haven't talked to him at all since then?" Libby says from the perch of her high, leather chair.

"No," Sarah says plainly. "That was it."

Libby speaks slowly, carefully. "And... how are you feeling about that?"

"Good," Sarah says quickly, as if she trying to convince both of them. "Yeah, good," she says again more slowly.

"Well, good. I'm glad you're feeling positive about it." Libby speaks in her usual, even, yet upbeat way, but the way she pauses rankles Sarah. There's more coming.

"Absolutely!" Sarahs in a showy, and entirely unnecessary show of emphasis.

"I wonder," Libby pauses thoughtfully, then continues, "if we could talk a little about your approach to that conversation."

"My approach?"

"It sounds like you left with what you wanted, which was an end to the relationship, and you tell me that you're in a good place with that decision. So, let's call that a positive. Now, do you think you left Joe feeling good about that conversation?"

The question slams Sarah in the face. "I mean, no one ever feels good being broken up with. But he'll understand one day."

"Will he?" Libby says. "Did you explain your reasons?"

A pang of guilt ripples through Sarah's conscience. "He knew about the article, how awful that was for me."

"Yes, and did he also know about the ultimatum that his daughter gave you?"

Libby's getting annoying these days. What's done is done. It can't be changed. Sarah's torn Joe's heart into a million pieces. She knows that. And if he does ever manage to knit those pieces back together, he won't be letting her anywhere near it to try it again. What does it matter what she did or didn't tell him? She sighs and answers Libby. "I couldn't tell him that."

"Was that fair to him?"

Sarah shakes her head in exasperation. "Telling him wouldn't have been fair to him."

"Sarah, listen, I'm not asking you these questions just to put you on the spot. I'd like you to interrogate your reasons a little bit and think about why you made the decision you did."

"I saved Joe from having to make that decision." She broke his heart to save him from an even worse break. And it was the hardest thing she's ever done in her life. Far harder than walking away the first time because back then, she'd been sure it was the right thing to do. This time, it was the only thing to do, but that doesn't mean it was right.

"Yes, you did. And in the process, you also robbed him of his agency," Libby says calmly.

Sarah's back goes tight, yanking her upright with indignation. "I was protecting him."

"Yes, you were, one hundred percent. One thousand percent. I know you were." Libby pauses and waits for Sarah to relax back into her seat, ready for more. "I also think you were protecting yourself."

Her energy waning, Sarah's no longer able to make eye contact with Libby, but she casts a listless glance her direction and asks, "How so?" before dropping her gaze back to the tissue box on the coffee table.

Libby studies Sarah, then offers her insight gently. "You told me yourself you were afraid of being too happy. And I know that the article was terrible. And I know that your experience with his daughter was painful and revealed very real issues to address." Libby stops talking and allows her words to sink in. It's clear she's got more to say, but she's giving her comments room to breathe. "But I suspect those are both issues you could have worked through with Joe. A man you love and who, by your clear accounts, loves you dearly. Instead, you chose to run."

Sarah yanks a tissue from the box, not because she's crying, but because she needs somewhere to exorcise her sudden kinetic energy. She crumples it again and again, then presses it flat, and finally begins to shred it.

"Sarah?" Sarah continues to shred, so Libby asks, "How do you think Ben fits into all of this?"

At this, Sarah stops cold and her hand flies to her necklace. "Oh my God! I completely forgot Wednesday night!"

***

Joe steps out of the production tent and into the sunshine. He peers up as the Monorail passes overhead and he watches it disappear under the curve of the MOPOP arch before gliding into the station. He drifts back to his first morning in Seattle when Sarah took him first to the Pike Place Market, then onto the Monorail to this very spot. Seattle Center welcomed him to town, but more than that, it was the scene of the crime. The place where he fell in love. Sure, technically, he fell the instant he saw her on that corner. Felt that connection from all the way across the street. And yes, he knew he was fighting it already at Pike Place Market, and when they got caught in the rain walking to the Monorail. But it was here, over falafel, standing by a fountain, walking a labyrinth, and singing like buffoons at MOPOP – here is where his impossible, inevitable love was cemented. It's the reason he wanted to make this movie about building Seattle Center for the World's Fair. His tribute to the place that made him. And the day that day changed his life.

But now, the whole project has become an eagle pecking his liver out on the daily.

Randy bleeps him on the walkie, "Don't move." Joe scouts around and catches Randy in the distance heading toward him. Randy should be running this thing. He's so smart and on top of things. And he's still having fun with it, which is more than Joe can say these days. Joe should talk to him again about coming back to producing. He senses Randy is ready at last, after being burned last time. "We've got a little Milo," Randy says as he reaches Joe.

Another Milo problem? How anyone so generally good natured, young, and healthy can be so wildly high-maintenance is quite beyond comprehension. "A little Milo? Or a big one?" Joe asks.

"Little," Randy says with a shrug. "I'd say little this time."

Joe rubs his face and squints at the sun. "Can you deal with it?"

Randy eyeballs his surroundings as if maybe Joe is talking to someone else. "Um, sure, yeah. I can handle it."

"Good man," Joe says with a grateful smile. "Listen, I think I'm going to head back to L.A. This part of the shoot's almost done and miraculously, Beltran's still on time and on budget. I'll meet up with everyone in London next week."

Randy gives Joe a sad wince. "Sure, no problem. I'll make the arrangements."

"I need a couple days to get my head together." Joe pauses to weigh his next words. "And I might take a longer break when the shoot's done."

"Of course," Randy says as he pats Joe's arms. "So, it's a no go, huh?"

"It is very definitely a no go," Joe says. "Walk with me."

They meander down the steps and Joe marvels at the colorful, pinkish-purplish-orangish pattern reflected on the ground, sparkling down from the mirrored surface of the MOPOP building. *Color and light,* he thinks. That's what Sondheim wrote about in his masterpiece "Sunday in the Park with George." Sondheim would have loved this gorgeous, magical display of color and light. Or Georges Seurat would have. They've merged in his head after so many years. And then it dawns on him, musicals are another thing he had in common with Sarah. Another thing that's soured now she's gone.

"You don't think there's still a chance?" Randy asks.

"She made it pretty clear. Something is holding her back. I don't think I can get past it."

They reach the spot where they're shooting a simple walk-and-talk across the plaza, right across the labyrinth Joe once walked with Sarah. Joe is again stunned by how quickly this once joyful, passion project has evolved into a painful, daily crawl down a war-torn memory lane. The sooner he gets out of here, the better.

Kelsey beelines for them, Diet Coke with a straw in her hand. "Joe, how are you doing? I haven't seen you in days."

There's a reason for that. Joe glances at Randy, then replies as politely as his churning soul will allow. "Oh, you know, just taking care of business."

Randy jumps at this opportunity to extricate himself from a conversation with Kelsey. "I'm going to go get you booked. Tomorrow morning?"

"Thanks, Randy. And hey, when we get back, let's book some time to talk," he says before returning to Kelsey. He offers his most *producorial* smile. "Everything going okay today?"

"Absolutely!" she beams. "Milo's being Milo, of course. But you know me, always happy, always ready to give it my all." At this, she bounces a little, and somehow, despite being fully buttoned up in a suit, she finds a way to flash her cleavage. She really is an artist at whatever this is. They should have a craft award for this. She'd nab it every time. "Seattle's been amazing. This is my first time here."

"Yeah, it's a great town," Joe agrees.

"And I can't wait to get to London. Maybe we could take in the sights while we're there."

Not this again. How many times does she have to be told no? But she's a starlet on the rise, and clearly, her ambitions know no bounds. Joe shakes his head gently. "Kelsey, I'm very flattered." She crinkles her nose at this and bounces again. "But I'm not in the space to consider... *taking in the sights* right now."

Kelsey's light dims a little, but she thrusts her chin forward and says, "Is it that woman?"

"You've met her several times. Her name is Sarah. And yes, she's very special to me." Kelsey is the very last person Joe wants to discuss his personal life with, but he is utterly unashamed of Sarah and he's not about to let Kelsey's "that woman" jibe go unaddressed.

"So, even after that GabZone story, you're still stuck on her? I thought you would have seen the light when you saw those photos."

Joe flashes back to the photos. He and Sarah were walking out of the hotel bar where he'd been having drinks with the gang. And who else was there that night? A few random strangers and a table full of friends. Randy, Terry, Ted, Geena... and Kelsey Cartright. Kelsey had alternated flirting with Joe and scrolling her phone all evening. Her phone never left the table or her hand. She had it at the ready at all times, which means she would have had her camera ready as well. And yeah, now that he thinks about it, the angle was right.

"Kelsey, did you take those photos?" He watches her carefully as she flashes her teeth in an embarrassed chuckle and looks away, suddenly very interested in the pair of strangers entering the museum in the distance. "I think you did. And then you sent them to GabZone, didn't you? Why?" Even as he asks, he realizes he knows the reason. Pure, petty jealousy. But it will still be interesting to hear what she says.

Kelsey balks at him and blurts out, "You don't belong with a woman like that. I thought if you saw the photos, saw yourself there in glorious color with her, you'd see it."

Joe isn't inclined to easy anger or name-calling. It's simply not in his nature. Yet, when he hears these words, and stands in front of the woman who effectively tore Sarah away from him through such a callous, cruel, and unnecessary act, only one thing comes to mind, and he doesn't have the wherewithal to hold it back. "You diabolical bitch!"

"Come on," she says with her sexiest purr. She lowers her chin so she can sparkle up at him with her kitten eyes. "Read the comments. Everyone can see it."

"The comments? You think a bunch of random, nasty, pathetic keyboard warriors on some gossip site can change the way I feel?"

"That woman—," she stops herself and corrects course. "Sarah is very..."

"Sarah is the love of my life."

"Sure, she's pretty enough in a homespun, middle America kind of way. But you're Joseph Robert Parker. You need someone who can shine as bright as you do. Blind the world with the combined wattage."

"You?" Joe asks incredulously.

"Joe, you and I could be a real power couple."

"Kelsey, you and I will never even be friends. And if you keep going like this, we might just be enemies. Care to put your Hollywood clout up against mine?"

At this, Kelsey backs off. She might be the hot thing of the moment, but she's basically had one good year. Joe's been in the business over twenty-five years and is sitting on top of the freaking world at this point. She may not know how many It Girls burn out within five years, but she has enough sense of her own fragility to shift into self-preservation mode. "I'm sorry," she says in a chastened mewl. "I didn't realize she meant that much to you."

Joe is still bristling. "And it would have been okay if she didn't?"

"No, I suppose not." Kelsey studies her feet. "I probably should have thought more about the consequences of what I was doing."

A blast comes from a nearby bullhorn. "Places, everyone. We're back in two."

"Saved by the bullhorn," Joe says.

"Yeah," she says, casting a quick smile and flash of eye contact before her gaze returns to the ground and she darts away.

***

Shut everything else out. Sarah sits solemnly on a bench in the lobby and breathes deeply. Nothing else matters for the moment. Not Joe. Not Ben. Not her forgotten appointment with the email. Certainly not Avery or some dumb article that will fade with time now that she's walked away.

Right now, all that matters is this interview. Another deep breath. This is her future. This job is her next step. This is the life she has chosen. For the next hour, she must force herself to forget everything else. It will all be there when she's done, after all. She heads for the elevators and hits the Up button.

***

The panel around the table are all smiles and nods as they take notes and sip their coffees. Pilar is there, and so is Nick, along with five others. She knows all but one of them, but of course, this is an internal hire, so any other candidates will probably know them, too. Sarah's not sure who her competition is, so all she can do is focus on herself. Do her very best, then go home and scream into the void to vacate her anxiety. At least Pilar and Nick are on her side.

The mayor's Chief of Staff leads the committee and he's the next to speak. "Finally, Sarah, we do have a tricky question. We want to address the elephant in the room, so to speak, but we have consulted with HR because we don't want to go awry of any legal limitations."

"Okay," Sarah says tentatively.

"I'm going to ask this question carefully, and I'd suggest you answer it carefully as well."

"Okay," Sarah says again, a quiet terror growing in her rumbling guy.

"You were in the news recently, and it got some attention across our offices. Obviously, we would never ask or dictate anything about how someone spends their free time or conducts their personal life." The Chief of Staff pauses here to read his notes again before continuing. "However, we do ask the person in this position to sign a contract, which includes a kind of morals clause that says the individual will conduct themselves in a manner befitting city leadership and will not engage in any activity that may reflect poorly on the city. Do you have any concerns about signing such a contract?"

Sarah recognizes the real question behind what they're saying. Are you going to embarrass us with more pap photos? And the answer to that one is a categorical *no*. "I understand your question," she says, "and I can promise you, there will be no more... incidents. That part of my life is over."

***

Sarah curls in her chair and gazes up at Ben's photo on the mantelpiece. That lovely, warm face. That good man. And she just forgot about him.

Okay, she didn't exactly forget about him. She thought of him at some point every day. He remained in her heart, of course. She would always carry him with her. But she forgot her Wednesday night appointment to not open his link, and she's racked with guilt about it. Admittedly, it's about the stupidest reason anyone's ever concocted to self-flagellate. Failing to ritually open an email and *not* click it at an appointed hour on an appointed day. The ritual itself is absurd. She's known that almost since the start. But the routine, the commitment to showing up, even if she couldn't take action, was her weekly proof that she hadn't let him go. That she was still the good wife who deserved him, despite her past transgressions.

She had to show up every week to stare at that email and she had to stay away from Joe. That's what she promised herself she'd do for Ben. Two things. And in the end, she failed miserably at both. Yet Libby called that progress. She considered the fact that Sarah broke the pattern of fixating on the past in favor of enjoying the present to be a marked success. She called it hopeful. Maybe Sarah would agree if she'd done it on purpose, but she hadn't done it on purpose. She'd just gotten distracted by living and forgot to set her alarm. Of all the gall. Still, Libby might have a point.

It's been a complicated few weeks, to be sure, but she has grown. She can feel it. Her heart has opened more. Her attachment to an idea of a perfect Ben has faded. Her baggage, while not eradicated, does feel lighter. Like someone shedding books and clothes along a journey as she finishes with them. She may have walked away from Joe for the last time, but he did help her realize something vital. Widowhood doesn't have to equal martyrdom.

"What do you think, Ben? Is it time?" Ben looks back at her, smiling in approval. "Okay," she says quietly.

She calls Gabi, and when Gabi answers, she says, "Can you guys come over tomorrow?"

Chapter Twenty-One

Moving On

Joe hangs up from his call with Naomi and the London team and spins in his chair. The framed museum poster of "Destiny" hangs above his desk. He stares at the curvy, blonde woman in white who is undeniably Sarah. Will always be Sarah. Will apparently be the only Sarah he'll ever have.

He grabs his phone and dials Clark, who picks up on the first ring. "How's my favorite client?" Clark chimes across the line.

"Not as good as you," Joe replies. "I saw the pics of your new Porsche."

"A little something to bring me joy in my declining years," Clark says with a laugh.

"Well, good. It will keep you warm while I'm away."

"Going somewhere?"

Joe sighs. "I need a break, man."

"No problem. After this shoot, take a couple months. What, two, three months?"

Joe smiles to himself at Clark's optimism. Three months isn't going to do it. With the way he's feeling, he's not entirely sure he'll ever be back. But if he is, it's definitely going to take more than ninety days. Clark is not going to like this. "Try a year, buddy."

"What? Joe, come on. Plan a couple months and see how you feel. Get yourself a hut on a beach somewhere, drink some coconut water. You'll be back in no time."

If only it were that easy. If only tropical drinks and a couple months watching the tide roll in and out were enough to fix what ails him. Sure, it would be nice, might help a little, but you can't put a band-aid on your scarred soul and call it healed. The reality is that the tectonic plates of his life are shifting and he needs to find a new land mass on which to settle. He was an actor first, and back in the early days when he was pure ambition and naïve optimism, that was enough. But he'd met Melanie almost immediately after arriving in Hollywood, and within a year, they were settling down with Avery on the way. For over two decades thereafter, he'd proudly worn three hats: actor, husband, and father. And even when his marriage ended, he had actor and father to carry him.

Yet, he can't keep living for his kids much longer. Nathan's already spending a lot more time with his girlfriend. It's only a matter of time before he moves out on his own, or in with her, or at least with friends. The next phase is inevitable, a rite of passage that Joe can see approaching like a speeding semi barreling down the road toward him. And good for him. Launching his kids successfully into the world is a sign that he's done his job well. He wouldn't have it any other way. But that doesn't mean it doesn't hurt.

Meanwhile, Avery will be moving away again for graduate school before he knows it. As far as that goes, he hasn't even spoken to Avery since Seattle. It's only been a few days, but in their family, that's a long time. Something is off there. He'll have to look into that.

Clark's voice stirs him from his musings. "Hello, you there?"

"Sorry," Joe says. "But I think it's going to take a lot more than coconut water."

"Joe, pal, did I mention I've got a Porsche to pay for? You can't take a year off."

Joe laughs at Clark's implication, but he knows better than to take the bait. "I've got three movies out in the next year, and your twenty percent of my backend—"

"Backend?" Clark interrupts. "Don't you know you've got the best agent in the biz. You've got frontend, too, my friend."

"Even better. I think you'll be just fine."

"Dammit, dude. Fine," Clark says with mock disgust. "Do what you need to do."

What does he need to do? He really doesn't know, which is precisely why he needs the time to figure it out. All he does know for sure is that he needs to find some way to bring the joy back. He hadn't realized until now quite how important it was to him to have someone to share his journey with, to share his joys and challenges, defeats and triumphs. And even though he and Melanie had drifted apart over the years, she'd still been his sounding board and a hand to hold at events. They were an imperfect couple, and their priorities weren't exactly in alignment, but she'd always stood by him both literally and metaphorically in navigating the business, even if she did lean on him a little too hard sometimes. By the time they'd split, his kids were old enough for him to share at least some of the journey with them. But now he sees clearly that time is ending soon, and Joe will be left alone.

Of course, the obvious answer in his heart is Sarah, but she's having none of it. And since she's the only woman for him, it's time to start figuring out what his next act, a solo act as it were, might look like. And for that, he needs time and space.

"You're a good man, Clark," Joe says.

"You know I'm just giving you a hard time, right?" Clark says. "I've got your back, whatever you need."

"You always have," Joe says gratefully before wrapping up the call. Well, at least he's got Clark. That's something.

Joe looks around the room. Maybe it's finally time to move on, literally as well as figuratively. Find a place to put down roots again before he's too old and gray to grow anymore. He'll be fifty next year, and here he still sits, stuck in the same holding pattern he's been in since the divorce. Sure, he was waiting, but there's no point in waiting anymore. He leaves his office and walks a tour of all the well-worn corners and paths of this house that he's called home for four years. It's a good house. He's never really felt any need to move. Why find a new place in Los Angeles when his future was in Seattle? Except now, his future appears to have relocated.

Downstairs, he crosses paths with Nathan who's just come home from work. Nathan pulls out a soda, leans on the counter, and cracks it open. "Hey, Nate," he says. "I've got a question for you. How would you feel about moving?"

Nathan chugs his soda, then crushes the can. "If you're ready to go, let's go. I'm with you."

Joe smiles. Good kid.

***

That night, Avery comes for family dinner with Joe and Nathan, their first since Joe got back from the shoot, and Joe greets her with care. She seems fine, but he senses a distance he can't quite place. She talks about her upcoming return to Seattle and about all the interesting University of Washington factoids she's been learning. She's getting excited.

"So, you like Seattle?" Joe asks.

"Yeah, I mean, I didn't get to see much of it last time. I wasn't there long enough, but I plan to check it out when I go back."

"I wasn't sure since you left so quickly," Joe says, digging for something he doesn't fully understand.

"Yeah," Avery says slowly. "I probably shouldn't have rushed off. I guess I figured since I'd be coming back, you know."

The room falls silent. Avery apparently has no more to say and Joe is thinking carefully, unsure why he wants to tap this vein. "And what did you think of Sarah?" he says. Why is he asking this question? It's over with Sarah, there's no point in bringing her up, but some invisible force drives him forward. His suspicions need an answer.

Avery flashes a quick smile, then takes a bite of her chicken. "She seemed nice," she says as she chews.

"Who's Sarah?" Nathan asks.

"A friend of mine in Seattle. Avery got to meet her while she was there." He looks sharply at Avery, monitoring her reaction.

Nathan regards Avery as well. "You didn't tell me."

"It was just dinner," she says with an indignant shrug. "I didn't think it merited a recitation."

"You usually tell me everything," Nathan says.

"Maybe we're too close, Nate." Avery grabs her glass and downs her water.

Joe watches all this with an interest that niggles at him. There's something about the way Avery disappeared that night, and the way she's acting now, that's plinking a painful string in his gut. If Sarah's gone, there's no reason to pursue this, so why can't he stop? "You liked her then?"

"I mean, I only had one dinner with her. But she was very pleasant."

"Pleasant? Pleasant is the word you use to describe an afternoon visit with your great aunt Ruby, whom you hate." Avery says nothing, and instead stares at her plate and picks food from her teeth with her tongue. Joe shouldn't do what he's about to do. He's opening a door that can't be closed, but he says it anyway. "Avery, did you say something to Sarah when I left you two alone?"

Avery stops picking her teeth and lifts her eyes to Joe. Her face is frozen in a severe mask of tension that's half angry and half defensive. "I don't think you want to have this conversation right here. In front of Nate."

Then what he's thinking is true. Somehow, she knows. He's avoided this moment for years. He never wanted to hurt his children. He would never hurt his children intentionally. But they're grown ups now, and he's tired of hiding his truth. Maybe it's time to speak it. Even if there's no hope for the future, maybe confessing his past will free him. He puts down his fork and beholds them both seriously. "Nathan, there's something I should tell you. Something I think your sister has already figured out."

"Dad, you don't have to do this," Avery says.

"I want to. It's time. I need you both to know." Joe waits until Nathan finishes chewing and sets his own fork down, ready to listen. "When your mother and I married, we were very much in love. And when we had both of you, we loved you so much. More than words can say. But sometimes it happens, and it happened with us, that it changed over the years. We lost each other. We became partners in raising you, but our marriage was effectively over."

"Dad, we already know all this," Nathan says. Avery turns to her brother, then looks away, preparing herself for what comes next.

"When I was in Seattle seven years ago making 'Jazzman's Blues,' I met Sarah. And we fell in love."

Joe watches Avery's face tighten into a fist as Nathan says, "What are you saying? You cheated on Mom?"

"Yes," Joe says. "I'm not proud of that part. But your mother knows."

"Mom knows?" says Nathan.

"We talked it all out years ago. She's a good woman and a good friend. At least, we became good friends after we accepted the truth and split. But we stayed together a lot longer than we probably should have because we wanted you two to feel safe and loved. I don't know if that was the right thing to do or not, but you both turned out pretty great, so I think in your case, maybe it was."

Avery gawks at Joe in shock at the announcement that her mother has known for years. "Mom really knows?"

Joe nods. "We agreed not to tell you because we knew it would hurt too much. But you're adults now and I don't want to lie about Sarah anymore. Because I love her. I've always loved her."

"Wait," Nathan says, "did Mom cheat on you, too?"

"Nate, buddy, I know this hurts. Everything seems really black and white when you're young, but as you age, you learn that everything's not so easy. Life gets complicated and full of hard choices."

"Did she?" Nate asks again.

"I'm not going to go there, bud. What's past is past. We've both made peace with each other and I hope you can, too."

Nate drops back in his seat and grabs his beer. Avery sticks her hand out as he takes a swig. He hands it over and she guzzles the rest before getting up, going to the fridge, and returning with a fresh beer for each of them. Avery glares at Joe in an angry silence while Nathan summons a melodramatic wail. "My whole life is a lie."

"Well, that's very dramatic," Joe says with a gentle gibe. "But it's not true. Our life as a family was real. Our love for you both was real. Is real. Even our love for each other was real. Your mom and I loved each other, but we didn't work as a couple."

"So, why are you telling us now?" Nathan says.

Joe watches Avery carefully as he speaks. "Because I think your sister thinks Sarah is to blame for ending your mother's and my marriage, and that couldn't be further from the truth. Your mother and I split because we didn't work as partners anymore. It's that simple. Sarah had nothing to do with it. In fact, she's the one who ended our relationship back then because she knew how much you two meant to me and she didn't want to hurt you."

Avery avoids eye contact, but picks up her fork again and begins corralling her food around her plate. She shapes her potatoes into a question mark on her plate, then finally speaks. "So, what, you two are back together now?" she asks in her most petulant child's voice.

"No, actually. Sarah ended it for some reason I'll never understand." Joe pauses to take in his kids. Nathan's leaning back with his arms crossed over his chest, but he's looking at Joe sympathetically. And the compassion in his expression tells Joe that he's going to be okay. But Avery is still staring at her potatoes. "And I'm going to have to learn to live with that," he adds. "But the truth is, she completely broke my heart."

***

It's not Wednesday night. It's not 7:40. And Sarah is not alone.

Instead, it's 6:45 on a Saturday night and Sarah is finishing dinner with her two best friends. Dana's finishing a story about her favorite clients. "The condo was great for them while they only had one kid, especially since they have the other condo right downstairs for an office and guest space. But now that they have their second on the way, they are upsizing like you wouldn't believe. Four bedrooms, giant yard, fancy kitchen, the works."

Gabi jumps in with a sudden memory. "Actually, you would have met her, Sarah! Remember Clarey? The woman who let us use her roof for our wedding?"

"Oh, yeah!" Sarah claps her hands in delight. What a joy to be back with her friends just talking about simple things like work and weddings. Despite the rough waters immediately ahead, she will always stay afloat with her wonderful friends.

"I actually sold them both their original condos," Dana announces proudly. "I love repeat customers!" Dana pours more wine and adds, "And, if I find them a house, we can use the bonus to go to Mexico and lie on the beach for a week."

"Or go hiking and ziplining in Costa Rica," Gabi corrects.

They finish their dinners, carry their plates to the kitchen, and then gather as planned on the sofa. Sarah picks up her laptop and sits in the middle of the couch, while Gabi and Dana take up their posts on each side of her. They both lean in and hug her tightly. "Are you ready?" Gabi says.

Sarah nods and flips open the laptop. She navigates to her email and wastes no time in finding Ben's message. She clicks it open and freezes. There's the link. It's not Wednesday. It's not 7:40. She's not alone. She's breaking the pattern. She can do this.

"You can do this," Gabi says as if she's read Sarah's mind.

"We've got you," Dana says, and they both squeeze a little tighter.

Sarah takes a deep breath, mouses over the link and... *Click*.

Suddenly, the screen jumps to something that's loading. A video. A video is loading, loading, and then there he is. Ben. He's sitting up in the hospital-style bed they'd had installed in the living room for the last few weeks of his life. He's pale and tired, but he's smiling and there's warmth enough there to make up for the bloom missing from his cheeks.

"There he is!" Gabi says affectionately.

"Oh my God," Sarah whispers as her friends hold her tight.

"I miss that guy," Gabi says.

"He was a good guy," Dana agrees.

"Yeah," is all that Sarah can say as she stares at his frozen face, preparing to hear him speak again. She hasn't heard his voice in ages. This moment glows too rare and precious. "Maybe I should wait to watch this another time. This is already good progress. I don't want to go too fast."

"No, no, no, no," Gabi says gently. "Come on, girl. It's time."

Dana nods. "It's time."

Yes, that's why they're here, because it's time. Because even if she's had to walk away from Joe, she can't walk away from the progress she made because of him. She may have been comfortable on the two steps forward, one step back plan for the last couple years, but it's time to switch it up. No more steps back. It's time to move forward. Sarah reaches up to the two arms wrapped around her and squeezes them both gratefully, then she slowly lowers her hand and clicks play. Ben smiles and begins to speak.

Hey, hon.

He pauses a long time, searching for a way to begin.

I'm making this video because there's something I need to tell you. And I've been trying to say it for a long time now and I keep failing. Who knows? Maybe I still will before I go, but I feel like time is getting short and I need to say it. So, here goes...

I'm truly, deeply sorry for the way I let you down after Synergy closed. I know that losing your job, your sense of purpose, and the business you helped build was absolutely devastating and I bailed on you at the worst possible moment. I am so sorry for that and I'm so grateful that you came back to me, despite how I let you down. And I know we've worked through all this. I'm not trying to relitigate all that, but there is a part of it that we never discussed...

Sarah, when I go – when you're ready – there is nothing I want more than for you to move on and be so happy. I want your life to be full of love. It's what you deserve. I know that someone else helped you rediscover that gorgeous, glorious, brilliant light that you always were... and I think we both know who it was. I won't lie to you. It hurt. Of course, it did.

But he brought you back to me, for which I'm forever grateful... I'm so honored that you chose me. Thank you.

Sarah, I want you to know, for the record, that I forgive you. And not only that, but I want you to always be so incandescently happy as we were together. Even more, if you can manage it. You deserve to light up the sky with your joy... So, if that's with... him, you have my total and complete blessing. Don't hold back. Give yourself freely. Love boldly...

Ultimately, whether it's him or someone else, I just beg you to choose happiness. Stop punishing yourself for the past. I love you. I will always love you. Choose happiness. Be brave, my love.

At the end, Ben places his hand over his heart, smiles sadly, then leans forward to click off the camera.

Sarah is a sobbing mess, a puddle of a human being, as Dana gently pulls the laptop from her lap and places it on the table. Gabi rocks her gently and Dana runs for the tissues. "I am a terrible human being," she wails through her tears.

"You weren't listening at all, were you?" Dana says as she shoves a tissue into Sarah's hand.

"I miss him so much."

"I know," Gabi says.

"I didn't deserve him," she says as she leans into Gabi and blows her nose.

"He's not a saint, you kumquat!" Gabi says as she pats Sarah's shoulder. "He was a good man who loved you. And so is Joe. And you deserve them both."

Sarah hears the words the same way she heard Ben's, through the ruckus of noisily crumbling stories she's told herself over the years. She's convinced herself that true, deep happiness – the kind that endures even though the inevitable bumps, cuts, and nasty bruises of real life – was something she'd never have again. Because every time she found it, she lost it. In the end, it hadn't endured, which could only mean that kind of happiness wasn't for her. And hadn't she just proven it? By walking away from Joe who made her absolutely – as Ben had said – incandescently happy. Happiness was the thing that scared her the most, so she pushed it away, convinced it wasn't hers to have, that she didn't deserve it after her mistakes, that it was a gift for others to embrace, while she accepted a peaceful, easy life of contentment with no real highs, but no real lows either. "I want to believe that, but every time—"

"Now stop it!" Gabi says. She is taking no more shit. "Stop making excuses or I'm going lose patience. Yes, sometimes life sucks and Lord knows you've had your share. So, maybe it's your turn for the good again. But you have to embrace it before it passes you by."

Sarah pivots from Gabi's stern face to Dana's serene, but somber expression. "Yeah, that," Dana says.

And maybe they're right because here is Ben right in front of her telling her that she deserves it. Not only that, but giving his blessing for Sarah to go back to Joe. The man she carried with her like a brand on her heart. "Oh, God, I've really blown it, haven't I?"

"Obviously," Gabi says.

"But I can't have Joe. I blew that into the stratosphere. It's gone."

"Why am I one-hundred percent sure that's complete hooey?" Gabi says.

"Hooey?" Sarah says with crumbled brow.

"Her new word," Dana says with a laugh.

Sarah's heart swells with hope, but her head reels through all the possibilities. She wants Joe. She's always wanted Joe. But the way she's already been excoriated in the press is only a tiny taste of the life she'd have with him. For all the good, she's not sure she can take that. "What about that article? You know it's just the tip of the paparazzi-berg. Am I supposed to submit myself to public whipping in perpetuity for having the audacity to be fat and in love?"

"Stand up to them," Gabi says defiantly.

"Fuck yeah!" Dana agrees.

Gabi pumps her chest in a comical show of strength. "Show them who you are. Show them you deserve to take up space. And you deserve Joe."

Dana quickly agrees. "And then shut them out forever and let them wallow in their own filth."

The way her two best friends declare the path forward makes it sound almost noble. Like something she can do and stand proud. Fuck them. This is her life, and their nasty opinions don't mean a thing. Yes, she might actually be able to do this. Maybe.

But it doesn't solve the other problem.

Chapter Twenty-Two

The Truth Will Out

The advantage of going to any museum on a Tuesday is it's basically empty. Nobody goes to a museum on a Tuesday, which is why it's always the best day to go. Closed Mondays, empty Tuesdays. As an art historian, and very amateur artist, this is one of Avery's favorite insider tips to give others, and she's delighted to be able to use it herself for once. After acing her UW interview on Monday afternoon and spending a beautiful evening wandering the Elliott Bay waterfront, she's allocated her entire Tuesday morning to the Seattle Art Museum.

She arrives shortly after it opens, and as expected, she practically has the place to herself. Still, she knows the crowds will grow, even on a Tuesday, so she decides to prioritize the special exhibit first thing while there's no waiting. Timed entries are for chumps, and Avery is no chump. She heads straight for the exhibit, "Rejecting Modernism: Paint, Light, and a Time That Never Was."

Immediately, she's captivated by the selections they've included in the show. It's a wonderful assortment of pieces, from the mundane to the sublime, but each is luminous and fanciful. One portrait features a girl in the woods where the tree branches and flowering vines drape down behind her to form makeshift wings like those of an angel. A delightful cityscape looks very modern at its base, then somehow each of the office buildings molds into the top of a fairy castle or spritely elven home by the time it reaches the multicolored sky. In another gallery, she giggles at a landscape full of whimsical, 2-D animated-looking characters pushing very realistic cars and trains off the sides of the canvas to leave the bucolic scenery at the middle undisturbed. The curators have really assembled a beautiful exhibit.

When she walks into the third gallery, she immediately spots the giant, wide landscape that dominates the far wall. She'd know it anywhere. Two figures, a man and a woman, stand on opposite shores of a lake under the night sky. The large lake is tree-lined in the distance while the two figures in the foreground gaze up at the same shooting star. She immediately recognizes the image as her father's poster, which has hung behind his desk for years. How funny that it should be here, in this exhibit, in Seattle.

She pulls out her phone, snaps a photo, and texts her dad on the spot. *Look what I found. Did you happen to see this while you were here?*

He doesn't immediately answer, so she makes her way over to the painting to study it up close. It occurs to her that she never really looked closely at his poster. Despite her love of art, she'd never really given it much thought. It was just "that poster over Dad's desk." But now, as she approaches it in person, she marvels at the vital luminescence of the last glimmer of sunset at the tree line. She delights in the way the night sky twinkles with the magic of that shooting star. She admires the stillness and quiet pulse of the night as depicted.

Then she studies the man, and for the first time, she sees the impossible. The tall, striking figure with his leg jutting forward looks exactly like her father. She glimpses at the placard to find out when it was painted. Maybe the painter used her father as a model? But no, it was painted decades before he was even born. The likeness is uncanny. As if God took the image as a template and stamped it on her father before he came out of the womb. How could she never have looked more closely at that poster? No wonder her father had wanted a copy for himself.

When at last she can pull her eyes from her father's doppelganger, she turns to the woman on the opposite shore. Her wavy, blonde hair blows gently in the wind, along with her luminous white shift. She is soft and curvy like the old Masters loved to paint, a thick goddess of a woman who would have projected wealth and good fortune in their time. In the 20th century, when this was painted, her generous curves would speak more of comfort and sensuality, of a kind soft desirability that would call to both the heart and the body of a man. Avery evaluates the brushstrokes that create the woman's blowing gown and hair. She's beautifully rendered.

Finally, she brings her focus to the woman's face and her jaw drops. The room spins and Avery's eyes slide in and out of focus trying to make sense of what's before her. The woman in the painting is Sarah. She doesn't just resemble Sarah. She is Sarah. But how can this be?

Her phone dings with a message and she pulls it out. Her father has replied with an unusually terse, one-word response. *Yes.*

When he first saw the painting in North Carolina all those years ago, her dad had connected with it immediately. That's what he said when he brought it home. He'd framed it and hung it on the wall and never took it down, even as he migrated from their one-time family home to his short-lived bachelor apartment to the rental house where he now lives. And now he's confirmed he saw it again in Seattle. Where he reconnected with Sarah. Who's somehow in the painting as well.

The impossible truth spins through Avery's head like a whirligig. Has she made a terrible mistake?

***

Sarah has only just gotten home from work when Randy's text pops in.

Wanted to let you know I'm going to give a go to producing again, he writes. *Joe asked me to be an associate on the Scorsese film. How can I say no to that, right?*

Sarah releases a little yelp of joy for Randy. They discussed it a few times while he was in town and she knows it's what he really wants. She texts back her congratulations with a celebratory gif and heads toward her bedroom to change. Another text pops in a minute later. *By the way, Joe mentioned he thought you'd make a great producer too.*

Joe has always had an amazing imagination, she taps back before pulling off her top.

Randy replies quickly. *Joe has vision, you mean.* Sarah rolls her eyes as she pulls off her bra and sighs in relief before sliding on a tee-shirt. *I agree with him actually,* Randy adds.

Maybe in another life. Sarah hits Send, then drops her phone to change into her shorts, but the conversation nags at her. Not the silly producer bit, but the Joe of it all. Texting about Joe like he's just another guy. Like her heart hasn't been relegated to a subterranean hellscape of torment because of the way she hurt him. As if he could ever really be just Joe, some mutual acquaintance. She drops on her bed and types out another message. *How is he by the way?*

I was wondering when you'd ask, Randy says after a moment. *He's depressed.* A pause, then Randy adds, *Angry. Sad.*

Sarah winces at the answer, winces at the truth that she's done this to him and there's no going back. *You couldn't say fine?* she types.

Call them like I see them, he says. *Btw, give me your address. I'm sending something your way.*

***

Fifteen minutes after she sends her address to Randy, her doorbell rings. She doesn't remember ordering anything, but delivery men are the only people who ever ring her doorbell uninvited, so she pads to the door while pulling her hair into a ponytail. But when she opens the door, it's not a package waiting for her. It's Avery.

Immediately she drops her hands protectively across her chest. "Avery. What are you doing here?" Avery looks her up and down, and Sarah immediately regrets her holey tee-shirt and cut-offs. And no bra. Oh, Jesus, why isn't she wearing a bra?

"Can I come in?" Avery says.

Her arms still crossed over her woefully unsupported boobs, Sarah backs her door open and nods. Avery marches past her and straight into the living room like she's about to renovate or something. Like demo begins in 3-2-1. She's all purpose and zero fucking around.

Sarah's back tightens with every step, preparing for a showdown she's not ready for, and honestly doesn't even deserve. She's given this woman everything. She's broken her own heart and Joe's to keep Avery happy. Not once, but twice when you come down to it. And if Avery has the gall to come here now and give her another bollocking, as if she hasn't done enough, they truly are going to have words.

"Look...," Avery says, but before she can say more, Sarah decides it's time to fight back.

"No, you look," Sarah says. "I did what you asked. I walked away from the man I loved to keep you happy. I gave you what you wanted and I walked away. But I'm through playing nice. It nearly killed me to leave – you have no fucking idea – and the only reason I did it is because I knew it would *kill your father* to lose you. So, you already won. There's nothing more to say. And if you came here to make me your punching bag again, then you can turn around and walk back out the door right now."

"He's miserable."

"No shit!" Sarah spits the words out angrily. Sarah's never this angry, doesn't even allow herself to feel things like this very often, let alone to give them voice. But the instrument of her demise has just strutted into her living room like she owns the place and it's rapidly filling Sarah with hitherto unknown levels of rage. "It's what you wanted for him though, right? For me to leave him alone?"

Avery stares out the window to the large lawn in front of the house and Sarah finds herself wishing it weren't the off-week for the yard guys. Her shaggy lawn will no doubt be another thing Avery can add to her Disapproval List denoting all the reasons why Sarah isn't fit to be with her father.

Avery takes a deep breath and blurts out, "My father once told me that what he wanted was not in my power to obtain. I'm hoping he's wrong."

Maybe she's figuring out how to continue her thought, but Avery pauses dramatically, as if Sarah should magically understand. Sarah stares blankly. "I don't know what that means."

"Sarah, I was wrong. I'm sorry."

Sarah takes an inadvertent step backwards, as if her body needs to back-up with her brain to hear that again. The words rattle around in her head, but they don't make any sense. She's angry and hurt. She wants to blame Avery for ruining her happiness. The fact that she largely ruined it herself is beside the point in the moment. Avery still gets at least some of the blame. But did she just apologize? "You were... what?" she says, still attempting to settle her thoughts into a straight line.

"My dad loves you. And I was hurt... deeply hurt, that he'd cheated on my mom." Avery pauses, gathers her thoughts anew, then goes on. "So, I blamed you. But I know now, this is a lot bigger, more complicated, than I understood. It still hurts, I'm not gonna lie. But I know now, you're my dad's person."

"I'm your dad's..."

"You're my dad's person, yeah," Avery says.

Sarah drops into an armchair in shock, her mouth gaping. She should close it, but she can't make herself do it. She clutches the arms of the chair and holds tight as if she's starting an unstoppable ride whether she's ready or not. "I don't know what to say," she mutters.

"Anyway, I wanted to tell you I'm sorry."

Sarah attempts to settle back into her body, as if she's returned from the ride already, rather than just rolling out. "Well, thank you."

Avery shrugs. "I thought I was over it, you know. The divorce. But this stirred up some new stuff. I guess I have some more work to do."

Sarah smiles sadly. It's been close to thirty years since her own parents divorced, and she still remembers how it devoured her life for the better part of a decade. The lingering scar of her own pain was a big part of why she sent Joe back to his kids. "My parents got divorced when I was in college, too. I felt ridiculous for being so upset, like such a child, like it should be easier because I was a grown-up. But the truth was, it fucked me up pretty good."

Avery looks at her blankly, an echo of recognition washing over her stunned face. "Yeah," she says with a nod.

"Yeah," Sarah says with a firm nod in return.

They allow a quiet moment to linger, the barest hint of a bond forming. Not yet friends, perhaps, but no longer enemies. "Also, I thought you should know, he's selling the house."

Sarah shrinks in horror. "What?"

"Yeah. I didn't even know it was his until this past weekend," Avery says. "But I guess he finds it too painful to keep it now, so he's selling. It's already on the market, in fact."

"He's selling the house?" Sarah repeats like a long-delayed, distant echo. She drops her head in grief, and in the process, notices her boobs again. She clutches her arms back across her chest and shakes her head. "Well, I don't know what to say about that either."

Avery shrugs. "I don't either really. I just thought you should know." Avery turns for the still open front door. "Anyway, I'll leave you to it."

Sarah trudges like a slow-moving zombie behind Avery following her to the door as she rattles through her thoughts. The house. That beautiful home. That life with Joe she briefly tasted, savored like the sweetest dream, before she was forced to spit it out. Now it will be gone forever, and with it the life she and Joe could have shared if only she'd had the courage.

"I really am sorry, Sarah," Avery says as she reaches the door. Sarah smiles as much as she can in her grief and nods. Avery turns slowly back to her with a clamped down smile of her own, as if she's considering whether to say something more. Finally, she laughs and her face cracks into a bigger grin. "And also, I think you should know, I always take off my bra within thirty seconds of walking in the door."

At this, Sarah barks out a sudden laugh that almost frightens her. Avery has officially let her off the hook, and there's nothing to bond two women quite like the sheer joy of taking off a bra. Avery puts her arms out and Sarah opens her own arms at last for possibly the least expected hug of all time.

***

Sarah pauses only long enough to put her bra back on and make a stop at the mantel. She looks a long moment at Ben's picture, then unhooks the chain with her wedding ring behind her neck. She removes it, clicks it closed, then drops the chain around the photo before setting the ring on the mantel next to the frame. "I'm going to leave this with you for now. Okay, hon?" She presses her fingers to his face one last time. "Thank you, honey."

Then she's out the door. In the car, she voice texts Gabi, then Dana, but neither responds, so she runs up to their door praying they're home. She beats on the doorbell like she's playing a tune until at last the front door flings open. Gabi and Dana giggle as they stand face-to-face inside the same hula hoop. It's ridiculous, but a conversation for another time. "I'm not even going to ask," Sarah says.

"We're going on a cruise!" Gabi announces. "Eight port days for excursions!"

"And six sea days to relax!" Dana sings, obviously pleased with the compromise.

Sarah admires her two goofy besties encircled in a plastic hoop, giggling, and shakes her head in amused dismay. "That's wonderful!" she says. "Now I need your help."

***

Sarah waits for the mountain of a man in 32C to move before she slides into 32B and does her best to compress herself into a middle seat sized person. This flight isn't going to be any fun for either of them by the looks of things, but no pain, no gain. She only prays there's a gain at the other end. This has to work.

Three hours, two bags of pretzels, and a Diet Coke later, she disembarks the plane and turns her phone back on. A message immediately pops in from Pilar.

Just came out of the final selection meeting. I couldn't possibly tell you how it went, but let's just say, you're going to get a call very soon, and when you do, PICK IT UP!!! The message is followed by a laughing smiley and a gif of a child in a tutu doing a happy dance.

She immediately texts Pilar back with a series of laughing and crying emojis along with a few prayer hands to let Pilar know how much she appreciates the support, but her heart's not in it. This might be the most important text she's ever gotten. And right now, she couldn't care less.

Chapter Twenty-Three

Grand Gesture

Sarah gazes out at the house as the Uber pulls up. It's a nice house, sweet and suburban. Well-maintained, good size. Not even as big and luxurious as her own home in Bellevue, the same one she once shared with Ben. Certainly not a movie star's home. But it's a lovely, middle-class family home. Sarah asks the driver to confirm the address, which he does, and she nods her okay. She climbs out with her overnight bag on her shoulder.

It's a leap of faith to step out of the car. To let her transportation simply drive away, leaving her abandoned here on Joe's doorstep where she may not be welcome. But this whole trip is a leap of faith, like her relationship with Joe has always been. So, she may as well close her eyes and jump – one last time.

She waits until the car pulls away, mindful not to expose Joe's location. These are the kinds of things she'll need to start thinking of. At least, she hopes she will. But as she prepares to walk up to the door, her fear locks her legs in place. This is insanity. She's flown all the way to Los Angeles on a fool's errand that's sure to end disastrously. What is she even doing here? She should open her app and call another car immediately. Yet, as she opens her phone, she swipes past her open tabs and spots Ben's video, still open on an inactive tab. She watched it fives times over the first night she saw it with her friends, then opened it on her phone for easy access. But now, she just needs to glimpse Ben's face to remember his message. *Be brave.*

She walks slowly up to the door, takes a deep breath, and knocks. To her shock, a young man holding a bowl of cereal answers the door instead of Joe. Of course, Joe said his son lived with him, but somehow she's only prepared herself for Joe. She created a whole scene in her head of exactly how this would all play out and there was definitely not a young Joe doppelganger sitting at the kitchen counter eating cereal in her mind.

"Hi, can I help you?" Nathan says. He's tall and handsome in a boyish way and he resembles his father far too much to ever be in any doubt of his parentage.

"Hi, Nathan," she says. "I'm a friend of your dad's. Is he here by any chance?"

Nathan peers past Sarah to the street and driveway, looking for a car. Sarah realizes how incongruous this must seem since everyone in L.A. has a car. Yet, here she stands sans car or even a good explanation for the boy. "Sure, come on in," he says with a nudge of his head. He closes the door behind her and points her to the front room. "You're Sarah, aren't you?" he says through a bite of cereal. "Sorry, I've got to eat it before it goes soggy," he adds.

"You've heard of me?" she says as fear ripples through her.

"Yeah, I've heard of you," he says. "I'll get my dad."

He leaves her alone and climbs the stairs, taking them two at a time. That's youth for you. Sarah paces, unsure if she should sit, if it's even okay to sit, but she's too scared to stop moving and take anything in. This is Joe's home, the place where he cooks and eats, plays video games with his son, swims his laps, and rests his head at night. His home. And there's something so deeply moving about being in his space that she's afraid to absorb it into her soul, then be expelled. She dares not let any more Joe into her heart unless she gets to keep him all forever. It's basic self-preservation.

After a minute of pacing, which may as well be a year, Joe pads down the steps in his bare feet. As usual, she feels him coming even before his jeans appear on the landing. He still vibrates through her like the very first time, and it's the best-worst feeling she's ever experienced. Best because it always, only means Joe. Worst because this could be the last time she experiences it.

She's squeezing her phone in her hand nervously, and when it rings, she recognizes the number immediately as a Seattle city number. This is it, her moment of glory. This is the job she's been fighting for, but it pales in comparison to this moment. She silences the ringer and shoves it quickly in her pocket. When Joe reaches the bottom of the stairs, he peers at her blankly and simply says her name.

"Hi," she says. And it's been their longstanding rhythm. The softness of their simple hi's that have always knit them together and belied the complexity of the invisible currents weaving their worlds into one. She offers the greeting like bird call, awaiting the response that says her mate is here. She waits.

He looks at her a long, painful few seconds, then finally says it. "Hi."

Well, it's a start.

***

Joe struggles to find words for Sarah. He should be overjoyed to have her standing here in his house, the home where he's the most himself and the most at ease in all the world – surpassed only by his moments with Sarah. To have the person who most brings him joy in the place that most brings him peace would once have been the realization of a perfect dream, but not now. He doesn't have the wherewithal to hope anymore.

His instinct is to get this over with and rush her out of the house before his heart swells out of his chest again. The pain of shoving it back in is too great to endure more than once. But his politesse overtakes him and he offers Sarah a drink. She declines just as politely and they stand there like strangers waiting for a train.

Sarah clears her throat noisily, then finally begins to speak. "I came here today because I wanted to tell you something. Only, now I'm here, I'm not sure where to start."

Joe considers this, then makes his own offering to the conversation gods. "Okay, then I'll start. I put the Seattle house on the market a couple days ago. And I got an offer this morning." Sarah studies him without moving. He's not even entirely sure she's breathing, but he pushes on. "I'm going to take the offer."

"You are?"

"I can't keep holding onto a dream that's never going to happen," he says.

Sarah clears her throat again. "You know, maybe I will take a glass of water after all."

Joe silently walks into the kitchen and Sarah follows. He pulls out a glass, fills it from the fridge door, and hands it to Sarah. She drinks half the glass in one long, slow draft.

When she sets the water down, Joe starts his engine anew. He's angry and hurt, and since she's here, Sarah should damn well hear what he has to say. "We could have everything, you and I. And you know it. But for some reason, you refuse. And you're allowed to do that. You really are. I don't understand it, but it's your choice. You're allowed to walk away from the single most magical thing either of us has ever or will ever experience, however fucking crazy you might be to do so." He stops to take a breath and see if Sarah will say anything in response, but she remains stone silent, so he goes on. "But I don't have to keep waiting for you. I can't. I'm allowed to walk away, too."

"Is that what you want? To walk away?" Her face is sad, but measured. She's not giving anything away.

"I need to trade in the dream for something real," he says. "I can't keep hoping for something that's never going to happen. I'm an optimist, not a fantasist."

"So, we were just a fantasy?"

"Sarah, you are the most real thing in my life, always have been." Joe says this without hesitation. Because as much as he wants to protect his heart, he can never truly hide himself from Sarah, no matter the cost. "I don't know what you want me to say. But waiting for you is like this interminable torture. You're like Godot, and I can't do it anymore. I can't live inside a Beckett play."

"Gosh, existential tragicomedy is kind of my sweet spot."

"Don't do that," Joe snaps.

"Don't do what?"

"Don't be all smart and funny and theater savvy. I'm really angry at you," he says through tightened jaw. "I don't need you being charming and clever, right now."

"It's a defense mechanism. I'll stop." Sarah takes another long sip of her water, nearly draining it. She holds it up wordlessly to Joe who heaves an irritated huff of breath before taking the glass to refill. When he hands it back to her, Sarah takes another sip before speaking again. "I really am sorry," she says.

"Okay, great. Thanks for that. Thanks for making the trip," Joe says. He walks toward the hallway to the front of the house. "I have a lot of scripts to read. Have a safe flight home."

Sarah takes one more drink of water, followed by a deep gulp of air, then says, "Okay, here's the thing I came here to say. You said you're taking the offer on the Seattle house?"

"Yes. It just came through this morning, but yes. I'm planning to accept it."

"Great. Okay," Sarah says. "I just need you to know…" She pauses and gulps down her whole glass of water yet again, then continues. "I just need you to know that I'm the one who made the offer."

Joe's brain short circuits at this. "What?"

"Yeah," she says. "It's my offer."

"You're going to buy the house?"

"Looks like it."

Joe ponders this new information like he's Sherlock Holmes pondering the clues, looking for sense in the madness. Except Holmes would have already cracked the case and Joe's still stuck on the first clue. Nothing about this makes sense. "Why would you do that?" he says.

Sarah looks at him softly, like she's the Mona Lisa about to spill her secrets at last, and Joe braces himself for whatever bonkers thing is going to come out of her next. There's no way she'll ever be able to make sense of this craziness, but it might be amusing to watch her try. Still, when Sarah opens her mouth, it's not an explanation that pours out. "Actually, could I use your restroom?"

"The restroom?" he says, still running a beat behind.

"All that water," she says with a shrug.

Joe points her toward the half bath down the hall, then throws himself into an armchair in frustration. He never thought he'd even see Sarah again. Now, not only is she here, but she's announced she's buying his house. Well, not *his* house, really. *The* house maybe. But really, in his heart, it had always been *their* house, even though he hadn't had the guts to admit it to himself until Sarah came to stay. Suddenly, he knew it had always been their house, and if she didn't want it, then the house had no value for him anymore. The dream was dead. Except, apparently she does want the house. It's just Joe she doesn't want.

Sarah walks back in and takes a seat on the couch adjacent to Joe. She drops back against the cushions and flops in dejection. Joe studies her thoughtfully, then asks, "Can you even afford that house?"

Sarah reflects, then counts on her fingers as she says, "Well, between selling my house – it's a pretty nice house – and Ben's insurance money, which I haven't touched, and what savings I have, plus the promotion I hope I'm about to get... No, not at all." She drops her hand and laughs. "But I managed to convince the bank, so that's good enough for now."

"I don't get it," Joe says. "Why would you buy the house I'm selling?"

Sarah doesn't look at him as she speaks. Instead, she focuses on the dark fireplace in front of her as if she's watching an invisible flame that's captivated her. "Because I needed you to know."

"Know what?"

Sarah turns to Joe, her face serious and flushed with the heat of the moment. "That I'm all in this time. I'm not pulling out. I'm not walking away." She pauses as if her words already weigh too much to continue carrying them, but she bolsters herself and goes on. "And even if you give up on me, I'll be damned if I'm going to let you sell our house to some random strangers. Because despite me being really, colossally stupid about almost everything, I'm not ready to give up on us. Not if there's even one ounce of hope you'll take me back."

"Our house?" Joe says in disbelief.

"Isn't that what is?" A plaintive strain scrapes in her voice, begging for a forgiveness he wants desperately to give, but he holds it back. The hurt has been a crater in his chest, a giant, gaping hole of sadness and regret, and Sarah's the meteor that crashed into him and scarred that crater deep into his crust. He's not ready to give her anything.

When Sarah sees this, she pulls off the couch and drops to her knees in front of him. "Last time I saw you, you told me you were grand gestured out. And fair enough. Time and again, you've made the first move, proven yourself while I ran like an idiot." She reaches for his hands and continues. "But Joe, I love you more than words can say. More than Fate and Destiny could have woven in a thousand lifetimes. So, if this is all I can offer you, then God dammit, I'm gonna do it. I'm all in. It's my turn to get on my knees and it's your turn to choose. Your turn to be in control. You are my forever, Joe. And this is officially my grand gesture."

Joe stares into Sarah's beautiful, deep eyes as tears pool in them. Her every hope and fear is written in the blush of her cheeks and the creases around her eyes. She's terrified and hopeful at the same time and the energy blast of her emotions overwhelms him. How can he think straight when her radiance and vulnerability swirl around her in the most hypnotic dance he's ever seen? He pulls his hands away and stands. He walks over to the glass doors and stares out at the pool, finding comfort and clarity in the bright sunlight washing over him. He pulls the door open and breathes in the fresh air his body needs to produce his next words. "Sarah, I'm going to take your offer," he says as he stares at the gently flickering blue of the almost still pool.

"Oh," Sarah says as she climbs to her feet. "Okay." Her face sinks and her shoulders slump as she turns to leave, but she stops herself and turns back to face Joe. "I want you to know, I've figured it out, why I pushed you away again and again. I was scared, which you already know. I don't know why, I guess I was just made that way. But it wasn't really what you think."

Joe keeps his body, and his heart, angled outside, away from Sarah, but he turns his head to study her. "What do you mean?"

"I mean, it was never really about the article... or Avery..."

"Avery?" Joe says.

Sarah ignores him and goes on. "Or even Ben. I mean, it was about all of those things in a very real way. But they were also convenient distractions from the thing that's haunted me since the moment I met you."

"Which was?"

"Meeting the person who makes every molecule of your body and soul sing is terrifying," she says. "When you meet someone who knits your soul together with a single look, you suddenly become very aware of how frayed and unraveled your life without that person was. Not that I wasn't happy with Ben. I was. He was a good man, and I loved him. But there was still always a part of me that felt incomplete, like a pile of scraps too small and misshapen to fit perfectly into any pattern. And when you're used to feeling like frayed and unraveled remnants, when loose ends and messy edges are your comfort zone, suddenly finding wholeness is wildly uncomfortable."

"Uncomfortable?" Joe repeats.

"It's like this constant agitation that says, 'Don't get too comfortable. Don't enjoy this too much. It's going to end and you'll end up an even messier, tangled, irretrievable knot of a human being than when you started.'"

"I see," Joe says. And he does see exactly how wounded and confused Sarah is, how she's struggled through every barrier to reach his door and deliver her vulnerability as a meal he could feast on if he chose. But she trusts him enough to know he won't do that. He never would, and at least she knows that much.

"And the ironic thing is by pushing you away, I made myself into that knot all by my lonesome. I made myself into a big, gnarled, nasty, hopeless knot of humanity because I guess I thought that was better than you doing it to me. Pretty stupid, huh?"

Joe turns his body toward Sarah at last and nods. "Pretty stupid," he agrees.

"Anyway, I just had to get that out of my system. I truly am sorry, but I understand your decision. I'll go." She heads for the hallway, but Joe's voice stops her.

"Sarah." Joe watches her turn slowly, her shoulders slumped, dragging her sadness like a heavy cape behind her. Her eyes watery, she rigidly holds herself in wait, avoiding the downpour of emotions she clearly doesn't want to reveal. He smiles softly. "When I said I was taking your offer, I meant *your* offer. Of you, you ninny."

Her tears pool rapidly in her eyes. The first of them bubbles to its peak and falls down her cheek. "Me?"

"Obviously. In what world would I ever walk away from you?"

"Me?" she says again, still trying to make the word make sense.

"If you're in, I'm in, baby," Joe flashes his radiant grin at her. "You're my forever."

Sarah nods slowly. "I'm in. I swear on my life, I'm all the way in."

The dam finally broken, Joe rushes to Sarah and pulls her in for a long, soft, wet kiss that's somehow both horny and sweet. "I'm so far in I could drown in you and die happy," he mutters between kisses.

"Hey, don't even kid about that, please," she says.

And as he pulls her tightly into his arms and makes plans to hold her forever, he whispers, "Trust me. I'm never, ever leaving you. It's you and me until the end."

Chapter Twenty-Four

The Wedding

On their shared fiftieth birthday, Sarah and Joe marry.

It's a simple affair held in the backyard of their Seattle house. The weather should be terrible in March, and they planned to hold the festivities inside the huge house, but somehow the weather gods intervene to deliver a perfect summer day three months early. So, at the last minute, they decide to move everything outside.

Only their closest friends and family attend. They are already joined in their hearts, but making it official in front of those they love is the greatest way they can think of to celebrate their joy. Gabi stands at Sarah's side as her Maid of Honor for the second time, just as Sarah once stood next to Gabi for her own marriage to Dana. Dana proudly stands next to Gabi, and next to her, Avery beams with joy as she watches her father marry the love of his life. Nathan shines equally brightly as Joe's Best Man while next to him Clark – who's so much more than Joe's agent after twenty-seven years working together – grins until his jaw hurts for his oldest friend. Randy fills out the tuxedo'd trio while his own husband Carlos looks on from the second row.

Despite the distance and the challenges of traveling at their age, both Sarah's and Joe's parents fly out for the ceremony, and they bond instantly in the way only old people with nothing to lose can. Sarah's mother and father, long divorced and remarried, reminisce about a beautiful life they shared a lifetime ago, and all of the parents sink into a peaceable ease with each other. Their shared love of Sarah and Joe is enough to unite them in laughter and hope for a future that will long outlive any of them.

Wendy and Alec, Sarah's in-laws from her first marriage, flush with joy to see her happy once again. Her two nieces serve as flower girls, despite the fact that at seventeen, Lexi is absolutely too old for such things, even if fourteen-year-old Emma can almost squeak by. But they walk down the aisle hand-in-hand and giggle like the little girls they once were as they toss flower petals gently at the small group as if they were children once again.

Melanie is invited, of course, but in the end, she declines the invitation. She does, however, send them a huge floral bouquet with a note wishing them great joy, along with a listing for a four-bedroom, gated house in the Hollywood Hills.

The ring bearer is the newest addition to their family, a four-legged daughter named Daisy. The pitbull is by far the most affectionate and giddy of all the guests and runs joyfully from guest to guest throughout the day seeking pets and delicious buffet droppings wherever she can find them. However, at go-time, she's a perfectly behaved good girl with the prettiest pink bow she proudly shows off as Pilar, who eventually forgave Sarah for not taking the job, walks her down the aisle to deliver the ring. Gabi takes her leash and Daisy immediately drops to lie next to Sarah's feet where she happily pants and gazes up at Sarah and Joe.

Joe takes in the vista of his beautiful girl and bestest doggie, the sweet pittie they once dreamed about together, and he offers a silent prayer of thanks for the best life imaginable. The job is nice. The fame, fortune, and endless opportunity are incredible gifts. But this moment means more than any of it. This is why he was put on this earth. For this woman standing across from him, taking his breath away yet again.

Sarah gazes into the deepest blue she's ever seen, Joe's nearly electric eyes, and she bubbles with gratitude for the ineffable, unimaginable, extraordinary forces that have brought them to this moment. Fifty years ago, they were born side by side in the same hospital at the same moment. They spent their first night sleeping side by side, and their lives have been intertwined ever since. Now, they will spend every night for the rest of their lives side by side. Because somewhere, powers far beyond Sarah and Joe decided they needed each other and attached an eternal tether to each of their toes to make sure they'd always find their way back to one another.

The last two guests at the wedding congratulate each other happily. They attend unseen from a height beyond the heavens, but They watch every minute and delight in the knowledge that once again, Their interventions have worked as intended, even if these two took a few tries to finally get it right. Fate laughs, Destiny smiles, and then They leave Sarah and Joe to their happily ever after.

Obituary

Film legend Joseph Robert Parker died peacefully in his sleep on March 20th, which in an extraordinary twist of fate was his 100th birthday. Even more remarkable, he was joined by his wife, Sarah Abbott-Parker, who shared his birthday and also died in the night. They had just celebrated their joint birthday and fiftieth wedding anniversary with friends and family earlier that evening.

Although the medical examiner's report has not yet been released, the couple is thought to have died of natural causes attributable to old age. Authorities have indicated there are no signs of foul play and they are not treating the deaths as suspicious.

Parker's long career began with school plays, followed by a degree from the Music Theater program at Carnegie Mellon University. He went on to perform in several Off-Broadway plays before Hollywood called and he was lured to Tinseltown to make his first feature film, an HBO Film entitled "In the Half Dark." It was while auditioning for this film that he met his first wife, Melanie Fletcher, with whom he had two children, daughter Avery and son Nathan, prior to their divorce after twenty years of marriage.

The early years of his career were characterized by a bounty of ups and downs, with highlights including leads on a variety of short-lived television shows including most notably "Doc Hope," as well as the cult favorite "River's Run."

His biggest break came when he wrote and starred in the indie movie "Jazzman's Blues." The film was a notable box office success and garnered international acclaim, including three Academy Award nominations for the film, the script, and Parker himself as Best Actor.

Following the success of this film, Parker's fortunes changed. He went on to star in dozens of films including Academy Award winners "Fortune's Fold," for which he also won the Best Actor statue, and "The Missing Timeline."

Parker himself won a total of six Oscars. Two were for Best Actor in the aforementioned "Fortune's Fold" as well as the beloved love story "Destiny Apart," for which he also won an Oscar for Best Screenplay.

Parker won three Best Picture Oscars, along with his co-producer wife, for "Fortune's Fold," the dark, political comedy "Miscreants," and "The Peckham Front," widely considered a modern masterpiece.

Astonishingly, Parker largely stepped away from acting after ten years at the peak of his career. He continued to act occasionally and to enjoy cameos in some of his films, but he found greater satisfaction in his later career as a producer.

It was in this capacity that Abbott-Parker joined him when they formed their own production company, Second Chance Productions. Shortly thereafter, Parker and the widowed Sarah Abbott, whose first husband passed away several years prior, married on their shared fiftieth birthday.

Their company produced over thirty films and dozens of television series. They were known for impeccable taste and their shows garnered over 40 Emmy Awards and 25 Golden Globes over the years.

Parker and Abbott-Parker shared a singular connection and passionate dedication to their craft. They continued to work well into their eighties before largely retiring from the industry. In an interview with The Atlantic, Parker once said, "I have the best job in the world with the most amazing woman in the world as my partner. I won't stop until she tells me it's time."

By all accounts, Parker and Abbott-Parker shared a relationship like no other. In a 2035 Vanity Fair profile of the power couple, Parker's daughter, Avery Parker, explained, "After my parents' divorce, I was protective of my father, and I didn't understand his relationship with Sarah at first. It was hard to understand the parameters of a bond so unusual... But now, after all this time, I can see they were meant to be. They're true soulmates, no doubt about it."

When not on set, the couple lived in Seattle where they enjoyed a quiet life far from the glitz and glamor of Hollywood. They were avid boaters who counted tailgating University of Washington football games from their boat on Lake Washington among their favorite pastimes. In later years, Parker took up golf while Abbott-Parker filled her time with gardening. Parker also swam almost daily until he was 98 years old.

After their death, the couple was found by their grand-daughter Sylvie Parker who shared her family's home with the pair for the last two years. They lived in a separate suite on the lower level of the home.

The younger Parker indicated in a statement, "My grandparents shared a lifelong love like nothing else I've seen. They brought love, joy, and companionship to each other and to everyone they knew until the very end. While our family will miss them all the days of our lives, it is both a comfort and no surprise they left this world together. The died in each other's arms, just as it should be."

In perhaps the strangest twist of all, Parker's c-pap machine and Abbott-Parker's smart watch indicated they both died at precisely 11:38 PM. While it's certainly possible the clock on either one or both devices could have been inaccurate, it appears the longtime loves died not only on the same night, but at the same precise moment. While most obituaries we write verge on dry at worst, and emotionally evocative at best, it's hard to deny this particular story is unlike any we've written about in the past century.

While searching our archives of past articles for this obituary, we uncovered one final, remarkable twist. We discovered a report of exactly 100 years ago about two babies born in Pittsburgh Memorial Hospital on the same night. It was a short snippet of a story about the babies, who happened to be delivered on the same date, March 20th, at the same time, 11:38 PM, in rooms right next to each other. A fun, human interest piece that only merited a couple paragraphs.

However, this story caught our attention not just because of the date, nor even the simultaneity of the time. Rather, because of the names of the two babies: Joseph Robert Parker and Sarah Elizabeth Abbott.

Yes, after further investigation, we were able to confirm that Parker and Abbott-Parker were indeed those very babies once upon a time.

Although we do not often editorialize in our obituaries, we confess to being struck by this astonishing discovery, which has left everyone both on our editorial board and in our newsroom nothing less than awestruck. A story none of us will soon forget, more memorable than even the very best of their films.

You could almost call it magic.